THE HARVEST

BY: N.W. HARRIS

Clean Teen Publishing

THE HARVEST

ISBN: 978-1-63422-072-9
Cover Design by: Marya Heiman
Typography by: Courtney Nuckels
Editing by: Cynthia Shepp

For more information about our content disclosure, please utilize the QR code above with your smart phone or visit us at www.CleanTeenPublishing.com.

For Amanda, Emily, and Logan

PROLOGUE

Six thousand years ago, on the fertile plains between the Tigris and Euphrates Rivers, the first civilization erupted from nothing. Until this time, humans led a hunter-gatherer existence. Primitive people of the Stone Age who'd done little more than etch images of their prey on the walls of the caves where they dwelt suddenly created massive cities and settled into an organized, agrarian lifestyle. In an impossibly short period of time, they created government, religion, medicine, mathematics, writing—and began keeping records, creating literature, and studying the stars.

How?

Why?

In Mesopotamia and elsewhere, these cave-men-turned-intellects built massive pyramid-shaped structures to honor their gods, crediting these beings from the stars for creating them and teaching them how to evolve beyond their primal existence. Sumerian writings make it clear the Anunnaki came from the sky. They enslaved humans, but also forced their evolution and advancement.

Today, many people still believe the Anunnaki created humans by adding their DNA to that of the Neanderthals to make the perfect slave. They use this theory to explain the abrupt evolution of Homo sapiens and the unlikely extinction of the hardy Neanderthals.

Archeologists have discovered similar stories from other ancient civilizations—the Hopi, the Mayans, the Aztecs, and the Egyptians. Creatures from the heavens are described in many religions, as is a great flood that destroyed most of humanity. For believers in the ancient alien theory, another disturbing similarity can be found in the prophetic writings of ancient and modern religions. They speak of the end of days.

They say humans will bow to these creatures from the heavens once again.

The gods will return.

CHAPTER ONE

Shane's legs didn't react to his command, shock permeating his entire body.

"Easy there," the attractive brunette woman said, extending her hand.

"I'm fine," he whispered.

He cleared his throat and straightened his six-foot frame in front of her. Pain radiating from the gashes left by Steve's knife muted the excitement and relief of being rescued.

"Why didn't y'all come earlier?" he asked, trying not to wince.

"We had to take shelter, or we would have been killed like the rest," she replied, her voice calm and reassuring.

He wanted to collapse back onto the couch, to surrender all responsibility for himself and everyone else to this woman.

Some adults were alive!

They'd come to take the burden of watching out for all these people from him. For an instant, he felt like a kid again and almost wanted to break down, to tell her how the insects and animals had taken his and his friends' families, and how they'd been forced to fight other teenagers. How they had to kill. She would ease the caustic remorse, would say there was nothing else he could've done, and everything was going to be all right. They could take care of him and the others—feed them, shelter them, and patch up their wounds. There'd be no reason to worry anymore, and he wouldn't have to be in charge. He could focus his attention on Kelly, on rekindling that sparkle of joy that used to illuminate her eyes.

Taking a shallow breath, he checked the upheaval of emotion. Self-contempt followed in its wake. There was something suspicious about her showing up out of the blue like this. Why was he willing to trust this stranger—just because she was older than he was?

After surviving the worst hell imaginable and keeping so many kids alive since the world essentially came to an end, Shane refused to be duped by the smooth-talking government type. His foot brushed the stalk of the M-16 protruding from under the couch. He glanced at it, noticing a dime-sized spot of blood seeping through the gauze covering the left side of his chest and shoulder. His gaze returned to the woman. He crossed his arms and ignored the pain, not allowing the injuries to make him look weak.

Her smile promised she had no ill intention, and her expression of concern seemed genuine, urging the scared little kid inside Shane to the surface. He gritted his teeth and kept his expression firm.

"You can bring the gun if you want, but we do have to get going." Her brow furrowed with solemnity. "There are a lot of kids to rescue and too few of us left to do it. Many of them are too young to care for themselves—infants and toddlers abandoned in their homes."

Shane studied her honey-brown eyes. She could've been trained to lie for all he knew, but his instincts told him she had good intentions. What did she have to gain by taking them in anyway?

An irregular thumping of footsteps carried through the quiet house.

"Did you see the helicopters out...?" Tracy limped through a door on the left. The pistol in her hand started to rise, its barrel coming to bear on the stranger.

"It's okay, Tracy," Shane said, not taking his steely gaze off the woman. "We're going with them."

The gun stopped. Tracy studied the woman, and her face twitched like she too experienced conflicted feelings about seeing an adult alive. Before the limbic manipulator killed her family, she had been bent on following in her stepdad's footsteps and joining the military. He'd seen the pain in her eyes after they'd heard the message from Dr. Gunderson, telling them the government was responsible for all of those deaths. Those same emotions showed in her face now, along with a hint of relief that Shane expected only her closest friends could pick up on. Funny how much he'd learned about her in such a short time. She shifted her gaze, fixing questioning eyes on him.

Last night's shower had done her wonders. He'd forgotten what she looked like when her face wasn't covered with dirt and blood. She must've found some clippers in the house too; her crew cut was freshly trimmed. Still, her eyes were bloodshot and had purple bags beneath them.

He remembered waking up during the night to go to the bathroom. When he'd walked down the hall, he heard a lot of the kids crying. Shane was still a little numb. He hadn't come to terms with all the deaths, but he wasn't immune to the dark cloud of grief hanging heavy over the home.

Tracy leaned over slightly, the gunshot to her leg and stab wound on her back obviously causing her discomfort. He remembered pointing his M-16 at her in the underground battery compartment just before they shut down the limbic manipulator weapon, how he was so certain killing her was the right thing to do in that moment. It wasn't his fault—the weapon had scrambled his brain. But that fact didn't ease the guilt.

Jules stepped through the door behind Tracy, a shotgun held ready and the same fresh crew cut replacing her brown mullet. She was a couple of inches taller and leaner, able to eye the woman over the top of Tracy's head, and Tracy was almost as tall as Shane. He hadn't talked to Jules much in the short time they'd been acquainted, but he knew she was as tough as Tracy. Jules fought like a cornered mountain lion against Shamus and his gang of thugs in Atlanta. Her eyes had no redness in them. Maybe she was numb too. Her eyebrows rose upon seeing the woman, but her expression remained stoic.

Tracy's eyes narrowed, and she lowered the pistol. This blonde, fair-skinned JROTC commander was a badass for sure. Shane was glad they were on his team, especially now in his weakened condition. If he gave the order, these girls would rip the woman to shreds in an instant.

"Get everyone up and outside," he said, and then made a move toward the door.

The woman smiled at the girls and turned around, leading the way onto the porch. Tracy and Jules' eyes followed her, a look of relief on their faces when they turned to execute Shane's order. They might be free of the burden of responsibility for everyone's protection soon, but Shane was determined to make sure they were truly safe before he'd relax.

Turning her back on him showed an awful lot of trust—he wouldn't afford the woman the same leap of faith until he knew more. So many of the kids he and his friends encountered over the last two days would stick a knife in her without a second thought. What made her think he wouldn't?

Six dark green military helicopters waited in the field a hundred yards away, their rotors lazily spinning to a stop. A woman wearing the exact same black pantsuit and a man wearing matching garb stood by the open door at the side of each aircraft. They wore stern expressions, not smiling and compassionate like the woman. He was immediately struck by how similar they all looked, at least from a distance.

His escort stopped and turned to Shane, her hand extending.

"I'm Lilith, by the way. But my friends call me Lily. What's your name?"

Lilith was unique, but it seemed too simple a title for her. He expected her to introduce herself as Agent So-and-so, or at least Ms. Someone Important. Irradiated by the soft morning light, her tanned skin was unblemished—not a single freckle marked her face. Her features were perfect—high cheekbones, long, curved eyelashes, plump, red lips, and yet she didn't appear to have on any makeup. She was too... too symmetrical or something. Shane had trouble putting his finger on it. Her smile almost seemed to glow, chiseling away his doubts about her sincerity.

But he still had trouble coming to terms with the idea that these adults actually came to rescue them. Remembering his manners, he started to reach out and take her hand. Pain flashed through his shoulder, the laceration stretched by movement.

"Sorry," the woman said, a frown expressing her empathy. She extended her other hand.

He took it with his good side, wondering if she'd prompted him to shake with his injured arm just to remind him how vulnerable he was.

"Shane."

"Pleasure to meet you, Shane."

"Same," he said automatically, hoping it would indeed be a pleasure, that her intentions weren't malicious.

Her palm was dry and cool, reaffirming her honesty. Cold hands, warm heart—at least, that was what Granny used to say. He wished she were here now. She could read a person's character from miles away.

"Where are you taking us?" He didn't let go of her hand, fighting the desire to give up and trust her. With his eyes, he conveyed he wouldn't be pushed around, wouldn't allow her to bring his people to harm.

"To a hidden base north of here."

Lily didn't pull way, seeming content to endure his interrogation. She kept her eyes locked onto his, inviting him to search them for any sign of deceitfulness.

"And then what?"

"Then we can try to stop the people who killed your parents, before they kill anyone else."

Forcing himself to remain on guard, he embraced skepticism. Every word coming from her mouth could be a lie. He tried to nurture the idea that she might be weaving an elaborate snare.

"I thought the government was responsible for killing our parents," he replied, trying to sound the way Principle Collins had last year. She'd found out it was the footballers who'd turned her car sideways in its parking space—Steve and Aaron's brilliant idea—and was looking for necks to stretch.

The sleep had done Shane good, but seeing his aunt and father killed, seeing the rest of the adults slaughtered, fighting off the criminals at the gym, and then battling his way downtown, only to have the death match of the century with Steve, weighed heavily on him. The exhaustion of forty-eight hours of the worst experiences imaginable made his body and mind seem filled with lead, though the pain of his injuries gave him a degree of clarity. Hoping he didn't look half as bad as he felt, he eyed her like he'd eye a defensive tackle that wanted to take his head off during a game—warning he was more than she could handle.

"It wasn't all their fault," she said, not appearing intimidated. "We'll explain more once we get you to safety and have your wounds treated."

Lily's focus shifted to the old, plantation-style mansion behind him. He followed her gaze, not letting go of her hand although it was becoming awkward.

Tracy, Kelly, Steve, and Laura stepped out of the house, a mob of younger kids in tow. All eyes darted between Shane, Lily, and the choppers. Their faces were slack with shock, like they were having trouble comprehending that some adults were actually here. Several of the girls who'd been assaulted in the gym and most of the younger children's chins wrinkled, and tears began to flow.

Once in the yard, James and Sara, the two little kids he rescued behind the grocery store in Leeville, broke away from the group and ran toward Shane and Lily. Nat and several other children followed. Kelly attempted to grab her sister. After missing, she glanced at Shane with a desperate look on her face. There was nothing he could do. The children bypassed Shane and gathered around Lily, pressing between them such that it forced him to relinquish her hand. They hugged her and wept, looking up at her with relief in their wet eyes.

"It's okay, children," Lily said with a nurturing tone. "It's all over now."

Emotion and concern swelled in him. He was the one who'd kept them safe while these adults hid from the weapon's effect. He and his friends had risked their lives, and Matt and Aaron had given theirs, to keep these kids alive. This woman showed up, and they acted like their parents had returned. He glanced back at his friends, trying to decide if he should have them step forward and separate the children from Lily.

He hadn't determined it was safe to trust her yet. Most of the younger kids still stood behind Kelly and the others with conflicted expressions on their little faces.

A glance at his friends told him he had to place his faith in this woman. They were in desperate need of medical care. Steve looked bad, his face swollen from the brawl with Shane. He imagined he must look about as good. Although Tracy's hidden injuries probably posed a greater risk of infection, Laura looked the worst. Her left eye had a makeshift patch over it, and gauze was wrapped around her head to cover scratches caused by the crows.

Maurice and what was left of his gang, forty or so teenagers and only a few youngsters, had spilled out after the original group from Leeville. The city kids appeared more skeptical than those from his hometown. They spread out across the front yard, most of the older kids clinging to their guns. Their eyes shifted nervously from the helicopter and the black-suited adults to Shane. When they looked at him, they seemed to beg for him to tell them it was okay to surrender, that these adults were indeed the good guys. Even in the presence of these authoritative people, his friends and the other kids looked to him as their leader. Before, he had resented his role. Now, however reluctant, he'd come to accept it and was determined to keep them safe.

The peaceful and calm morning fueled the little flame of hope their rescuers inspired in him. The sky took on a light yellow color, the sun just peeking over the trees and chasing away the cool night air. When the ominous, green clouds had dominated the heavens over the last couple of days, he feared he'd never see a normal sunrise again. Birds sang a welcome to the new day, innocent and beautiful. Those feathered musicians were ripping the eyeballs out of adults not so many hours ago. A cow mooed from the field where the now-silent helicopters waited, and he wondered if its hoofs were stained with the farmer's blood.

From the other side of the house, Shane heard a loudspeaker calling for kids to come out of their hiding places. He glanced at the road and saw two green military buses roll slowly by. Suddenly, his army of teenagers seemed a lot smaller.

"They're with us," Lilly explained, her smile exuding compassion. "Here to help."

He gave her one more drilling inspection over the heads of the kids that still surrounded her. Nat and James clung to her hands and looked happier than they had since he'd rescued them, like somehow this woman could reunite them with their parents. A wave of dizziness washed over him, and he worried he might collapse if he stood much longer. He maintained a stiff posture in spite of it and took a deep breath, trying to stay strong as he turned to address his people.

"If y'all are okay with it, we're gonna go with these people," Shane announced, his voice not coming out as loud as he intended. "They're taking us to a military base where we'll be safe."

CHAPTER TWO

"Should we leave our weapons?" Maurice asked, lifting his black rifle into the air.

"No—bring them," he replied coolly, glancing at Lily to give her another warning. She didn't flinch, seeming unconcerned his people would be armed—another notch in her favor.

His friends and the other kids looked at one another, then at Shane. Steve moved first, taking long, confident strides across the yard toward the field. Kelly was second, and then everyone else started walking. Excited chatter erupted amongst them. As much as he wanted to embrace the atmosphere of relief, it made Shane nervous. He feared if something did go wrong, it might be hard for him to regain control.

When he spun and fell in step next to Kelly, her hand slipped into his. Her touch gave him lucidity, subduing his pain and calming his mind. The sun shone through the few strands of golden-blonde hair she'd missed, her ponytail pulled together in a hurry. Concern polluted her expression, her blue eyes shifting from Lily and Nat to the choppers. Her scrutiny didn't harbor the fear of a naïve girl who might easily be deceived. Instead, she appeared to size up the situation—a soldier preparing for multiple contingencies in case things went wrong.

Her gaze fell on him, and she squeezed his hand. No hint of awkwardness showed in her delicate features, like they'd walked hand in hand a million times and it was perfectly natural. Her eyes conveyed the trust and confidence she had in him—she'd follow him anywhere. The pain from all her loss and the horrors she'd seen made her look ten years older than she did in church a week ago.

It hurt to remember her coming down her driveway with her T-shirt covered in her parents' blood, calling for his help. But now she was wise to the harshest of realities, battle-hardened and capable of unrestrained violence if the situation demanded it. There was still kindness in her expression when she looked at him. Beneath her cautious and tired exterior was the sweet, Sunday choir-singing, varsity cheerleader he'd had a crush on for years. Though he admired her strength and only liked her more because of it, he intended to nurture that happier girl in her until it dominated her personality once again.

They passed through a bent, red metal gate and into the pasture. His brow grew moist with sweat, and it got harder to ignore the dizziness and the pain from his injuries. Approaching the choppers, Shane got a better look at the other CIA types standing by the open side doors with their hands clasped behind their backs in a nonthreatening manner, presumably waiting to help load the children.

Maybe it was because of the black suits and matching hairstyles, or maybe he was just growing delirious, but they all looked so much alike—he imagined they could be siblings. He stopped twenty feet from the aircraft and turned to Maurice.

"Divide your best fighters so all the kids have someone older with them." His voice sounded hoarse. Kelly put her arm around him, discreetly helping him to stand tall.

"Don't worry," Maurice replied, putting a hand on his good shoulder.

Jules stepped next to him. "We'll make sure some loaded guns are on every one of these helicopters."

The squat boy and the tall, wiry girl cast stern glances at Lily. They clearly perceived that he didn't want them to drop their guard until there was no doubt about these adults' motives.

Shane wanted to supervise himself, but he feared he'd collapse if he didn't sit down soon. Leaving Maurice and Jules to tend to the rest of the kids, he followed the group surrounding Lily to the first aircraft. It was only thirty feet away, but it seemed like a mile. His hearing was muffled, and it felt like his brain was spinning in his skull, but he kept it together and took each step methodically.

After lifting Nat aboard, Kelly climbed in and offered her hand. He must've looked pretty bad; her face expressed her fear that he couldn't make it. Her kind gesture only added to his nausea. After hesitating, he took her hand. He mustered his last bit of strength and stepped up without using her help.

Her needing him was okay, but him needing her was frightening. Every woman he'd needed help from in the past was dead.

The effort it took to get in the helicopter was too much. He collapsed into one of the canvas seats. Gritting his teeth to keep from vomiting, he clung to the sides of the seat. He was vaguely aware of her settling next to him. Being off his feet, the dizziness passed and he regained control of his senses. Kelly had taken the seat between him and Nat and had a hand on each of their forearms.

Steve and Tracy joined them in the aircraft, along with James, Sara, and a bunch of the other kids. Some of the little ones sat two in a seat and shared a seatbelt. Once the aircraft couldn't hold another passenger, Lily and her male counterpart closed the sliding doors on either side, climbing into the cockpit without another word to Shane or his friends.

"Sikorsky UH-60 Black Hawk," Tracy announced enthusiastically, buckling her seatbelt. "Looks like the rotors have been modified to make them stealthier. No wonder we could barely hear these babies when they landed."

Although he was sick from the constant pain of his injuries and was uncomfortable with the idea of flying, Shane couldn't help but smile. Tracy would find delight in military toys no matter how bad things got.

The whine of the engine and the rotor slapping the humid air quickly made conversation impossible. Vibrations in the aircraft amplified the pain coming from his shoulder, and he leaned forward to find comfort. Kelly put her hand on his back, eyeing him with concern. He gave her a weak grin, her touch soothing him. The helicopter lifted off the ground and climbed just above the trees, its belly scraping the forest canopy and its whirling rotors quieting to a whisper as it accelerated north.

Although his injuries were distracting, he kept his attention on Lily and the pilot. Their black suits made them seem as out of place in the cockpit as they did on the farm. People in Leeville only wore suits for church, weddings, and funerals, and nothing as fitted and fancy as these folks sported.

Shane's wariness kept him on edge and gave him the strength to stay vigilant. If they had bad intentions, why bother loading him and his friends and taking them somewhere else? They could have easily disposed of them back on the farm. Heck, if they had these helicopters, it was likely they had access to some bombs or rockets. They could've just blasted the farmhouse and killed them all while they slept— unless maybe they were taking them to a labor camp.

Images of concentration camps he'd seen in movies swam in his head, of starving prisoners forced to do slave labor until they died. Then there were the buses that passed the farmhouse. They might be picking up kids with the promise that they were taking them to a better place, only to deposit them behind barbed wire.

Feeling silly for the thoughts, he leaned back and took as deep a breath as his wounds permitted. It was irrational to be too suspicious of their rescuers. They had let him and his friends bring their weapons after all. Just because he wasn't used to people wearing fancy clothes, he didn't trust them? How backwoods of him. But then again, if they were part of the same government who'd mucked up and killed the adults, how could they be trusted?

Blank expressions on their tired faces, Steve and Kelly looked out of the windows. Ever the maternal type, Laura shushed some of the younger kids who were frightened by the helicopter ride. Given her jet-black hair, painted black fingernails, and pale vampire complexion, he never expected her to be so nurturing. Tracy scanned the inside of the aircraft, a mild look of awe in her usually stoic gray eyes. She was leaning forward, probably trying to keep the pressure off the stab wound in her back, but she didn't look as faint as he felt.

The helicopter's engine revved, and it climbed the ridgeline into the Appalachian Mountains, going further north than he'd ever been. Shane knew there were areas of these woods where no one lived, though rumor had it moonshiners still hid out there, cooking up their poison to sell to the old timers down in civilization. It didn't surprise him that there was a secret base in this wilderness—it was the perfect place.

After an hour of flying above what he imagined was the wildest country on the East Coast, the helicopters came over a large mesa that was cut into the side of a mountain, a clearing amongst the ancient trees. They settled on an asphalt runway, and Shane could see a several-acre military base stretched out around them.

"Here we are," Lily announced cheerfully, climbing out of the cockpit as the rotors spun down.

She opened the side door and helped everyone out. Upon standing, Shane grew dizzy and his knees buckled. Steve caught him before he crumpled to the ground.

"I think we'd better get you to medical," Lily said, looking in his eyes. "Those wounds are getting the best of you."

Shane shook his head. "Not until I know all of my people are safe," he replied weakly.

"They will be well cared for," Lily promised. "It's time for you to trust us, Shane. You need help."

"Don't worry, man," Steve said, nodding toward the other choppers. "Maurice and his gang have them."

Following his gaze, Shane saw Maurice ordering the armed teenagers to round up all the children, keeping them together so he could look out for them.

"I'm going to take Nat and go with them," Kelly said, patting the strap of the rifle that hung off her shoulder. "Let them treat you, or you're no good to any of us."

Shane glanced at the kids and then Kelly one last time before nodding to Lily.

"Follow me," she directed, starting across the tarmac.

"I got you," Steve said, slipping his thick arm around Shane's back. "I feel like a sack of shit for cutting you like that."

"Wasn't your fault," he replied weakly, feeling less guilty about Steve's bruised and swollen face.

Beyond the shadow of the chopper's main rotor, the sun shined full in his face, blinding him. He closed his eyes and tilted his head, his eyelids glowing red and his face absorbing the warmth. His foot caught on a crack in the blacktop, and the jarring sent pain blazing from his shoulder. Sweat wept from his forehead, and the world spun around him. Gritting his teeth, he tried to focus on Lily's back. Keeping it together and standing tall was all that was important at the moment.

He wasn't going to look weak in front of their hosts. He also didn't want the kids spilling out of the helicopters to be alarmed, though they'd seen so much horror that he doubted they'd flinch even if he dropped dead.

"Damn you, Steve." He made an effort at chiding for a distraction. "You could've found a smaller knife."

"Hey man, go big or quit, right?" Any humor in Steve's joke was lost, his voice ripe with worry. "You want me to carry you, man?" he whispered.

"No way—I'm cool."

A bent shadow lay on the ground ahead. Seconds before, the sun had felt wonderful. Now, the tarmac was an inferno. Shane looked up at a metal building, its roof curved and corrugated like it was made out of half of a huge drainpipe. A white door with a red cross on it graced its otherwise olive-green exterior. Lily opened it and stood by, and Steve helped Shane into the air-conditioned interior. The cool air reviving him, he passed through a small, outer waiting area, down a narrow hallway and into another room.

"Put him there, and I'll go get the doctor," Lily said, pointing at an examination table.

Steve guided Shane to the table, and he sat on the edge. As soon as Lily stepped out, he leaned over, too dizzy to keep his head up.

"Whoa," Steve exclaimed, catching him before he could roll onto the floor. "She's gone. You can lie down, tough guy."

Shane didn't resist Steve pushing him onto the padded table. The pain and dizziness faded when he lay down. He closed his eyes, taking deliberate slow breaths to try to regain his strength. If things suddenly went wacked, which had happened a lot lately, he needed to be ready to fight. Right now, he felt absolutely useless.

The door opened, and a brunette woman wearing a white lab coat entered.

"Lily?" Shane asked, confused as to why she'd step out saying she was off to get the doctor and return wearing a lab coat, like it was some kind of a game.

"No—I'm Doctor Blain," the woman replied.

CHAPTER THREE

"What—are you guys twins or something?" Steve asked, confusion clear in his voice.

"Something like that." The woman smiled at him, and Steve blushed, glancing down.

Shane was still suspicious of their rescuers; too many people's safety was at stake for him not to be. He realized he couldn't rely on his big friend's help in figuring out what was going on, at least not with the ladies. Steve could face down a herd of the most vicious footballers without flinching, but he always turned to mush in the presence of a pretty girl.

Dr. Blain was an exact replica of Lily, identical in every way except one of her eyes was an icy blue color, the other the same honey brown as Lily's. A wave of nausea washed over him. It must've shown on his face because the doctor rushed to his side and put a hand on his forehead.

"You've got an infection," she observed with concern. "We need to seal your wounds and get some antibiotics in you."

She gently helped roll Shane onto his side and used scissors to cut his shirt off.

"If you've got a weak stomach, you may want to step out," she said to Steve without looking away from her work.

The door opened and shut, Steve clearly taking the invitation to leave, probably too embarrassed by his squeamishness to say anything about it to Shane. In his weakened condition, with his shirt off and the laceration in his shoulder exposed, he felt nervous being left alone with this slightly less perfect clone of Lily.

"Relax," she said softly, her attention on his wound. "I'll get you fixed up and out with your friends before lunch."

Not like he had a choice. He felt like crap and could tell he wasn't going to get any better without help.

"What about my friends? They've got injuries too."

"I'll get to them all, but Lily seems to think yours are the worst and need immediate attention," she replied.

He hadn't thought so earlier, but with the way he felt right now, he was starting to agree with her.

After cutting his shirt to shreds and removing it without making him move his arm, she prepared two shots on the bedside table.

"One of these will ease your pain, and the other will knock out the infection," she explained, inverting little glass vials and filling the syringes.

Of course, she could be filling them with poison for all he knew. Keeping his face blank, he stared at the ceiling. He didn't want to let on how much he hated needles—he'd rather be punched in the face than get a shot. The first injection in the shoulder must've been the painkiller, because he didn't even feel the second one. The doctor moved around the examination room, gathering supplies to treat his injuries. By the time she returned to his side, Shane felt a million times better. The pain medicine didn't cloud his consciousness. He was fully awake and a bit nervous as he watched her remove the last of the blood-soaked gauze from his chest.

"At least you got some betadine on this," she said. "It might've gotten a lot worse otherwise."

Thanks to Tracy's first aid knowledge, Shane thought, trying to ignore the smell of blood and keep his eyes on the ceiling.

Dr. Blain squirted a numbing solution on the wound and dabbed it with clean gauze. Curiosity won out, and he got a clear view of the jagged cut Steve gave him. It was a bloody mess, like two long strips of poorly butchered steak lay on his chest and shoulder. What appeared to be a rib was visible at the bottom of this meat valley, and his collarbone had to be exposed at the top. Nausea returned in a hot flash, his mouth filling with metallic saliva.

"Maybe you should look the other way," Dr. Blain advised.

Rolling his head toward the wall, he closed his eyes, breathing slow and deep to recover. He felt no pain as Dr. Blain scrubbed his wound, though the sound of the bristles on the brush she was using to scrape it clean only increased his nausea. Then came a humming sound accompanied by soothing warmth around the injury. He kept his eyes closed, his teeth clamped shut. Determined not to get sick, he thought of Kelly, of being strong for her. He wished she were here with him now, but he also didn't want her to see him acting so weak.

Daring a glance at his chest, he saw Dr. Blain moving a pencil-sized tool over his gash. It was white, with a silver button near its tip, which she depressed with her forefinger. Blue light projected from a small, glass ball floating an inch in front of the device, fanning out and illuminating his injury.

Amazement swept away his nausea and disgust at viewing his insides. Under the effervescent light, the damaged tissue in his shoulder and chest regenerated. Lacerated blood vessels elongated and reconnected, muscle tissue reformed, and the jagged sides of the wound rejoined from the bottom up. Dr. Blain moved the light slowly over the area, and the laceration closed, leaving fresh, unblemished skin in its wake.

Although he experienced no pain, the sight of his miraculous healing was more than he could bear in his weakened state. He fought to stay alert, but a haze closed in on his vision, and then darkness.

Opening his eyes, Shane glanced frantically around the white walls and ceiling of the room. It took a second for him to gain his bearings, to remember he was in the medical clinic on a military base hidden somewhere in the Appalachian Mountains.

Dr. Blain sat on a stool a couple of feet from him, typing on a computer that seemed entirely created of light. A holographic screen hovered in front of her, both it and the keyboard projecting from a dice-sized silver cube. Technology he'd never seen or heard of. He expected the government had things they didn't share with the public, but the advanced computer she used and the healing pen that closed his wounds were full-on science fiction.

Glancing down at his bare chest, he was stunned by her work. The cuts and bruises Steve gave him were gone. A streak of white, hairless flesh was where his injuries had once been. His new skin looked like it belonged on a baby, all soft and delicate.

Shane pivoted, the padding of the examination table squeaking under him as he sat upright. He braced himself, expecting to feel dizzy and weak. Instead, he was refreshed, as if he'd woken from a good night's sleep, and the trauma to his body had never occurred.

"All better?" Dr. Blain asked, smiling at him compassionately and sounding a little proud of herself.

"Uh," he glanced down at his rejuvenated body once more, "I reckon so."

"See—told you. And well before lunch."

He had trouble focusing on her different colored eyes. His stomach growled, and he realized he hadn't even had breakfast.

"I don't get it. How did you do this?" He ran his right hand over the smooth place were the laceration had been.

"Let's just say we have toys not everyone is familiar with." Dr. Blain grinned. "Here are fresh clothes for you. If you'll get dressed and go to the waiting room, I can patch up your friends."

Pushing off the exam table, his bare feet landed on the cold, tile floor. He hadn't noticed until this point, but he was only in his underwear. During the helicopter ride, blood had leaked out of his bandage, dripping all the way down to his knee. She must've thought his leg was injured and had cut away his pants to treat him.

Embarrassed, his hands shot down to offer some extra coverage, but Dr. Blain was focused on her typing, so there was no cause for alarm. On a chair at the foot of the exam table sat neatly folded clothes. Fresh socks, underwear, running shorts, and a T-shirt, all black, awaited him. Glancing at the doctor once more and satisfied she wouldn't look his way, he turned his back to her and slipped out of his skivvies—which also had blood drying on them. He donned the new clothes as quickly as possible. Black running shoes lay on the floor in front of the chair, the last things he put on.

Once dressed, he looked at the doctor. She didn't turn away from her computer, affording him the same trust Lily had in turning her back on him at the farmhouse. She was using her finger to mark the areas where his wounds had been on a holographic image of him. Embarrassed at how detailed his likeness was but also in awe of the advanced technology, he slipped out of the door and into the waiting room.

"Wow," Steve exclaimed, his eyes wide with disbelief. "You look like a new man."

"Yeah," Shane said, plopping into a chair next to him. "That woman is a magician. You're next, big guy—get in there."

Steve gave him a worried look, and Shane nodded toward the examination room.

"Don't worry—she doesn't bite," he said, smiling. "Though I bet you wish she did."

"You're an ass," Steve replied, the reddening in his cheeks obvious, though his face was bruised and swollen.

The linebacker rose to his feet with a grunt. His injuries

may not have been as visible as Shane's were, but with the way he staggered to the exam room door, he reckoned Steve was in no little amount of pain. Shane remembered hitting him hard more than once. He expected Steve had a few broken ribs, not to mention his nose was pointed in the wrong direction.

Alone in the air-conditioned waiting room, Shane revisited the questions lingering in his mind. He leaned back in the chair, embracing the opportunity to rest his eyes for a second.

Although they seemed extremely nice and had done nothing but good to this point, something was off with their rescuers. He guessed they'd get some answers soon. There was no way they'd keep him in the dark for much longer, or they had to know they'd have trouble on their hands. After all, Maurice and most of the others in his group still had their guns, and the black-suited adults on this military base seemed unarmed and well outnumbered. Shane wished he still had his M-16, even if his instincts told him he wouldn't need it.

A noise roused him—Steve strolling out of the exam room. Shane sat upright, studying his friend. His nose was straight, and his facial bruises gone.

"She's freaking awesome!"

"Told ya," Shane replied, jealous that he got to keep his clothes. The black shorts were rather thin and didn't cover much—good for running, but not much else.

The white door leading to the tarmac opened, and Tracy and Laura entered.

"Holy crap!" Tracy stopped, her eyes wide. "How'd you

guys get fixed up so fast?"

"You'll see," Shane replied, pointing at the exam room. "Let's just say the government has been hiding more than advanced weapons from the public."

Lily stuck her head in and looked at him.

"All better?"

Shane and Steve nodded to her. He was struck once again by how similar she looked to Dr. Blain.

"Great. Then come with me," she said cheerfully. "I expect we'll be able to answer a few questions that must be eating at you."

CHAPTER FOUR

"See you guys in a bit," he said to Tracy and Laura, giving them reassuring smiles. Laura stood taller, her mood clearly lifting at the notion that the damage to her face could be reversed.

Shane and Steve followed Lily out of the medical building. Shane's step was light. He felt better than he did before the world went to shit. It was great how Lily's twin healed him, but in the absence of suffering, even more questions and suspicion sprouted in his mind. Why did Lily and her counterparts look so much alike? It was even more obvious to him now as they passed by four men and women in black jumpsuits who were refueling the helicopters. Why did they bring him and his friends here? What could they possibly want? Lily had said something about stopping the people who'd killed the adults, but that didn't give him much to go on.

They walked by a row of hangars. Shane didn't have any more dizziness, but he broke a sweat. It was late morning now. It had to be well over ninety degrees—one of those long, scorching summer days where he'd usually be found by the lake. That life seemed gone forever now. He bit his lip. The absence of his physical pain allowed his suppressed grief to surface. Taking a deep breath, he pushed the emotions aside. There was no time for them now—he had to keep his focus.

The first hangar's doors were wide open, helicopters undergoing repairs inside. The next four were sealed, so he couldn't see what they held. At the fifth hangar, they stopped. Lily opened the door and led them into the relatively cooler interior.

Once his eyes adjusted to the fluorescent lighting, Shane saw four large aircraft in the middle of the hangar. He assumed they were fighter jets, but green canvas covered them from their lofty tails to the shiny, concrete floor, so he couldn't be certain. Lily walked halfway through the curved-roof building and stopped at a door leading into a long room with mirrored windows looking into the hangar. Opening it, she held her hand out to indicate they should enter.

An oak conference table dominated the air-conditioned, rectangular room. The smell of fresh-brewed coffee invited him in. It looked like a war room, and he imagined many generals had rested it in the worn leather chair cushions, discussing clandestine operations in far-off deserts.

"There are refreshments over there." She pointed at a kitchenette on the side. "I'll be back with the rest of your friends."

She slipped out of the door before they could respond, closing it behind her. Shane wondered what she meant. His and Maurice's group combined were far too many to fit into the room. Steve looked at the snacks, a gleam in his eye. He glanced at Shane and nodded toward the little table.

"Looks like they have donuts," Shane mused, his stomach growling.

Starting toward the kitchenette at the same time, their shoulders collided and Shane nearly knocked over a chair. They pillaged the food, bringing several pastries each to the conference table and sitting down before devouring them without fanfare.

"Dadgum." Steve leaned back, emitting a satisfied grunt. "I love donuts."

"What do you think is going on here?" Shane spoke in a quiet voice, wiping the crumbs off his mouth.

"Don't know," Steve replied. "I'm glad we aren't on our own with all those little kids anymore, but these folks are weirder than a snowman in July."

"Right?" Shane took a sip of coffee. He wasn't much for the stuff. With a lot of sugar, it wasn't half bad. The caffeine sharpened his mind, making up for his sleep deprivation. "They all look so much alike. You think they're clones?"

"Why not?" Steve scratched his short, brown hair. "With all the crap I've seen in the last couple of days, I don't think anything could blow my mind."

The door opened.

"We'll see about that," Shane whispered.

Lily entered. Laura and Tracy followed her in, their wounds miraculously healed. They were smiling and lighter on their feet, their recovery clearly raising their spirits. Still carrying their guns, Kelly, Jules, and Maurice came in next.

Kelly's eyes brightened when she saw Shane, and she rushed to him. She leaned her rifle against the table and hugged him.

"Wow, you guys look brand new," she exclaimed, glancing from him to Steve with disbelief. "How'd you get fixed up so fast?"

"Lily's sister is a medical magician," Steve replied, casting a sideways glance at the woman in the black suit who was fixing herself a cup of coffee.

"How are the others?" Shane inquired. It worried him to see they'd left the kids.

"There's a big building set up with lots of bunk beds in it," Kelly replied. A miniscule tremor in her voice hinted at the conflict she'd endured upon deciding to leave Nat and join him here. She might be second-guessing herself, but he knew she wouldn't have left her sister unless she was one hundred percent certain it was safe. "They had toys and books, and promised they'd start schooling the children right away."

"We left armed guards around the building," Maurice said in a threatening tone, loud enough for Lily to hear. He leaned closer and whispered, "Though I don't get the feeling we'll need them. These people seem like decent folks."

Lily and the doctor hadn't said or done anything to give him an argument against Maurice's estimation of them. Shane expected his stout friend was generally a good judge of character, but he was glad for the armed teens. It seemed wise to be prudent—at least until they learned more about their new guardians.

"Why don't you guys grab something to eat and have a seat?" Lily advised, stirring her coffee with a red, plastic straw.

"We have a lot to talk about."

"Nice shorts, by the way," Kelly whispered and smacked him on his butt before heading toward the food. His breath caught, her unexpected flirtation sending a surge of heat through him. He glanced around to see no one had noticed, and then took his seat.

Having missed breakfast, Shane's friends didn't need a second invitation. They crowded around the refreshments and came back with stacks of bagels, pastries, and donuts, settling in chairs on either side of Shane and Steve.

Cradling her cup of coffee as if to warm her hands, Lily walked around the long conference table and settled in a chair on the other side, directly in front of Shane. It seemed she'd decided he was in charge as well. He looked at her and she smiled, the same kind and caring grin she'd afforded him all morning. Then she looked up and down the table, silently watching them eat.

Having already finished his breakfast, he grew impatient. He was about to start asking questions, but then Lily cleared her throat, capturing everyone's attention.

"You kids have had to grow up quite a bit in the last forty-eight hours," she began, "and unfortunately, we're going to ask more of you—a lot more."

The preface of dire news stopped his friends from eating, their eyes locked on Lily. Shane couldn't hear anyone breathing, and the tension was immediately palpable.

"The weapon that killed your parents was just the beginning of what we expect will be a much larger attack."

"I thought that was the result of a military experiment

gone bad?" Tracy said, a measure of aggressiveness in her voice.

"What gave you that idea?" Lily's tone was inquisitive, her eyes widening as if she hadn't expected them to have a clue.

"We found an army radio and tuned it to a message recorded by a scientist who said so," Shane replied, worried he was giving away too much too soon.

"Dr. Gunderson?"

"Yes," he said, surprised.

"We intercepted the same message," Lily replied. "Before we could figure out a way to get into Atlanta to shut the weapon down, someone else did it for us."

"That was us," Kelly exclaimed. "We shut it down."

"Really?" Lily said, her eyes filled with astonishment. She leaned back in her chair and looked at each of them, fresh awe in her expression. "I guess we've found the right group of teenagers then."

"Why?" Shane asked, scrutinizing her. "What do you want with us?"

"Well," she said hesitantly. He could tell she was about to drop a bomb on them. "We're here to help you save yourselves."

Lily didn't add anything else, perhaps waiting for them to get what she was saying.

"What do you mean?" Kelly demanded, her tone frantic. "We shut down the stupid weapon—what else could we possibly have to do?"

"Unfortunately, the weapon wiped out all the adults. There is no one else left to defend this planet. If you don't want to become slaves, half of you dying in the process, then you're going to have to fight back."

The room fell silent. Lily's expression transformed from compassionate to steely, letting them know the dire seriousness of what she was saying.

"But apparently all the adults *aren't* dead," Shane objected. "You're here, and you seem to have a few friends. Why can't you fight?"

"Oh, don't worry, we'll be fighting too. But there are not many of us, and the enemy will see us coming from miles away." She took a sip of her coffee, sadness creeping into her eyes. "I don't want to give you false hope. We've failed before. You're going to have to face an extremely powerful foe. But we believe, with our covert help, they'll never expect an attack to come from you. Besides, this is not our planet in the first place—it's yours. It's your duty to defend Earth."

"What?" Tracy snapped, incredulous. "What do you mean—it's not your planet?"

"That's right," Lily continued, eyeing her unemotionally. "We aren't from here."

"You're aliens?" Steve asked, chuckling skeptically.

"Not a label we care for," Lily countered, offense apparent in her voice. "But yes, I suppose you could call us that. We're from a planet about a hundred light-years from here—a planet to which we can no longer return." She glanced down into her coffee cup and then took another sip, her composure visibly shaken.

"How come you look so human?" Kelly asked more gently.

"Many species on other planets do," Lily replied, looking at her. "Evolution is not as random as humans believe."

"Wait." Shane captured her gaze. He was confused and starting to get upset at the idea she might be messing with them. "If you want our help, stop talking in riddles. Tell us what you mean."

"Okay, but I must warn you—it's a lot to swallow," she said ominously. "The Anunnaki came here two hundred thousand years ago and mixed their DNA with that of the Neanderthals. Humans were the result."

She stared at them, her eyes wide like she expected their heads to explode—like she'd seen this news blow up heads before. Shane didn't know what to think. It sounded like a load of horse crap. Bat-shit crazy or not, they had her talking, and he didn't want her to stop.

"Go on," he encouraged, hoping they hadn't been picked up by some powerful cult that had taken this base after all the soldiers stationed here had died. He couldn't deny that the miraculous healing he and his friends just got did give credence to her words. "We're listening."

"They came back six thousand years ago and enslaved humans, which was why you were originally created," she said. "They used humans to build extraction sites for precious materials hard to find elsewhere in the universe. During that time, they also further tweaked your species' DNA to make sure humans evolved as planned."

"Anunnaki?" Maurice asked, his brow furrowing with disbelief. "You don't mean the gods of ancient Sumer?"

"Yes," Lily replied, sounding impressed. "I'm surprised

you know about them."

"My father was a historian as well as a pastor. He used to talk about this stuff all the time," Maurice explained, glancing at his friends. "How are the Anunnaki tied to all of this?"

"They leaked technology to your government, who believed they'd gotten lucky and stumbled upon something not intended for them. What they actually found were the instructions for the creation of the limbic manipulator weapon. Unfortunately, they decided to keep the information from us, or we would have warned them."

She paused, and the silence tore at his ears. His mind struggled to grasp what she was saying.

"We believe it's all part of an invasion the Anunnaki have been working on for years. Brilliant really, to destroy the adults before a single ship lands. By the time we figured out what was happening, it was too late. And we had no idea where the weapon was hidden until we intercepted Dr. Gunderson's message the night before last."

"Just before we shut it down," Tracy mused.

"Exactly," she replied.

"So you're saying we're half caveman, half Anunnaki?" Maurice asked, incredulous. His usually confident and certain demeanor vanished, and he looked like a kid who'd just been told Santa Claus doesn't exist.

"Yes," Lily replied. "I know it's a lot to take in, but you have to understand me. They're coming back, and this time, they will enslave the human race for good. The human crop is ripe, and they're returning to Earth to harvest you."

Chills ran through Shane.

"Yeah, but who are you?" Steve asked with suspicion. "You said you're not from Earth. Why should we trust you?"

"We were Anunnaki as well," Lily replied, disdain clear in her voice. "We rebelled against our people hundreds of years ago, because we believed it was wrong to infringe on the rights of other intelligent species in the universe. We fought our government and lost." Her lips compressed, and her eyes grew wide. "But we are here now to take another stand, to stop them from taking Earth."

"What'll they do when they get here?" Shane asked, anxiety and confusion knotting his stomach. His head did indeed feel like it might explode. "How can we stop them?"

"They need soldiers and slaves," she replied curtly. "They'll take the remaining teenagers and children on this planet and pit them against each other in a global war to find the best warriors amongst you. They'll record and publicize the battles on their home planet for entertainment. Then they'll reap the survivors." The contempt in her voice increased with each word. "Because of their imperialistic behavior, the Anunnaki have made a lot of enemies throughout the galaxy, and they've been at war for thousands of years. You are the secret weapon they plan to use to turn the war in their favor. They exterminated all the adults first, because older humans don't make ideal slaves—they're not as malleable and don't receive the mental reconditioning as well as younger humans."

"How will they enslave us?" Tracy asked angrily. "They'll have to kill me before I do what they say, and I'm guessing there are a lot more people like me."

Shane nodded to show he agreed with Tracy and noticed

his friends doing the same.

"Which is one of the reasons we truly believe you have a chance," Lily replied, admiration flashing across her expression as she looked up and down the table at each of them.

"Unfortunately, when they created humans, they inserted an obedience gene into your DNA. The limbic manipulator already activated the gene—it won't be long before the remaining humans will do whatever they're told. Their memories will be modified, and they'll believe they owe their allegiance to the enemy. They will fight for the Anunnaki with as much devotion as if they were fighting to protect their homeland. This aspect of their reconditioning will make them extremely formidable soldiers and loyal servants. You see? Humans were designed to be the perfect slaves."

"So you're saying this gene is already active in us?" Jules asked.

"Yes, but we have a way of suppressing it."

Recalling the fight with Steve in Atlanta, Shane wondered how the gene was affecting them now. He remembered being confident that killing Tracy and then Steve was the right thing to do, and he wouldn't have stopped trying to end them if Tracy hadn't disconnected the battery. There hadn't been a doubt in his mind that they were meant to die.

Was his desire to trust Lily now because of the gene's influence? He worried about how they could be enslaved and still believe they had their freedom. Such a master could make them do horrible things with conviction and a smile.

"That sounds foolish," Jules countered. "If they can wipe memories and control us through our DNA, why would they kill off the adults? Wouldn't they want to keep some of them alive? Especially those that were already trained as soldiers, like in the army and stuff?"

"Yes, that would make more sense," Lily replied. "But over the last two hundred thousand years, mutations have led to a flaw in the slave gene. About ten percent of the children and teenagers will suffer a dangerous form of mental psychosis, usually leading to sociopathic behavior. The older the humans are, the higher this percentage. In adults twenty years and older, the psychotic response is upwards of ninety-five percent.

"So you see, if the Anunnaki didn't arrange for all the adults to be killed, then they would have likely turned on each other and on you when the gene was activated. The adults would have killed off the rest of the crop. You are likely already familiar with this psychosis, many of the serial killers who have gained repute for their crimes suffered from a rare auto-activation of their slave gene. Some, such as Adolf Hitler, were even able to recruit other humans to help them commit their crimes on a much larger scale."

"But can't you talk to them?" Laura chimed in, sounding desperate. "There must be a way to stop them peacefully."

"No—they will not negotiate," Lily replied coldly. "As I said, the Anunnaki created humans. They believe they own you—that they have a right to enslave you."

"But if your people couldn't stop them," Shane said, trying not to succumb to the feeling of impending doom, "what makes you think we can?"

"Honestly, Shane?" Lily leaned back and gave him a stern

look. "I think you have about a snowball's chance in hell of succeeding, to use a human cliché. But that doesn't mean you should just lie down and die, does it? After all, you're supposed to be dead now. By our calculations, the limbic manipulator might have killed everyone fifteen and older before its battery ran out."

No one responded. Shane bit the inside of his lip, frustrated with what Lily was telling them. His friends' heads drooped, like the Anunnaki already had them in chains.

These kids had survived the impossible; they'd fought through an army of thugs and shut down the limbic manipulator. But that wasn't an advanced alien race they were up against.

"Well, I reckon we've been through the wringer these last two days, and we survived." He spoke to his friends as much as to Lily, the quarterback in him taking charge. "Our odds of success had to be less than zero, but we shut down that stupid weapon, and here we are. We sure as hell aren't gonna give up now. Are we?"

Steve looked at Shane first, and the rest followed. They appeared less defeated, shaking their heads and agreeing they would never quit.

"I didn't expect you would," Lily said admiringly. "We've been living amongst humans for seventy years, and if we've learned anything about your species, it's that you don't give up without a fight."

"How did you get here?" Steve shifted the subject. "Why do y'all look so much alike?"

"You've heard of the Roswell, New Mexico crash?"

"Yeah. We live in the woods, but we ain't stupid." Steve chuckled, turning red under her gaze.

"Well, it wasn't little green men they pulled from that spacecraft," she replied. "My co-pilot and I were in a fighter ship, trying to overthrow the supremacist government in charge of our home world. The Anunnaki army used a rather nasty implosion weapon to destroy the rebellion. It created a temporary wormhole, and my spacecraft was pulled in and spit out near earth." A sad frown crossed her face. She glanced down, the weight of the memory seeming to crush her. "There were only two of us onboard. As far as we can tell, no one else survived."

She looked up again and added, "Your government was kind enough to take us in, provided we share some technology with them and keep our existence a secret from the general population."

"Such as the limbic manipulator weapon?" Tracy challenged without a hint of reservation in her voice. Shane appreciated her assertiveness. He didn't trust the alien yet, and he wanted her to know they weren't to be pushed around.

"We brought you into the computer age. The silicon chip, cell phone, internet—all us. As I said before, we had nothing to do with the limbic manipulator. We had lots of advanced technology to share in exchange for being provided a place to live, but we made your government agree to let us introduce it to them slowly."

"What about all your brothers and sisters out there? How'd they get here?"

"Clones." Lily picked up her coffee cup. "It's how we've

procreated for a long time. Our Anunnaki ancestors played with our DNA a little too much, trying to prolong life, increase beauty, intelligence, and create perfect children. The same sort of stuff your scientists were starting to tinker with. They rendered my people sterile, and so we have to make our babies in a lab. Your government was kind enough to permit us to create more of our own, and we shared some of our cloning technology with them."

"Dolly the sheep?" Laura asked.

"Exactly," Lily smiled. "We've been able to create a couple of phenotypes, but we have a limited gene pool to work from, so a lot of us do look very similar."

"So against all odds, we have to fight these Anunnaki," Shane said. "Won't they be attacking with spaceships and weapons far more advanced than we have?"

"No." She sipped her coffee and set the cup down. "It will be a bit easier than that, though still a daunting mission. As far as we know, the Anunnaki haven't realized we escaped during the rebellion. They'll come here expecting no resistance, and they'll bring humans into their ships to arm and program them for the cleansing war. You will be amongst the kids who initially enter the recruit ships, and you will attack them from the inside."

CHAPTER FIVE

"Like the Trojan Horse," Steve mused, rubbing his chin. He straightened in his seat, pushing his chest out and resting his big forearms on the table. "I got no problem kicking the crap out of these An-hacky."

"An-un-naki," Lily corrected. "Don't underestimate them."

She pivoted her chair to the right and pressed a button on a remote control. The TV on the other end of the long conference table lit up, and images of a battle flashed onto the screen.

"I don't want to make you feel hopeless—we do believe you have a chance. But you must understand your enemy to be effective. These videos were taken by my ship's onboard camera." Her voice cracked. "After all these years, it's still hard to watch." She blinked quickly several times, seeming to struggle to restrain her emotions. "My people are the ones organized on the ground below."

The screen was filled with an army, charging silently up a gentle slope. Leaving shadowy trails in a calf-deep sea of lush, green grass, the soldiers all wore shiny, red armor from head to toe. It first struck Shane as medieval. But they didn't move slowly, like knights wearing heavy plates of steel over shirts of chainmail. They were swift, the armor appearing not to hinder them, or perhaps even enhancing their movement.

Coming within ten yards of the rebels' crimson helmets, the ship shifted upward, aiming its camera at a jagged wall of gleaming, white skyscrapers that formed an abrupt end to the verdant plain.

"The only way to get past the city's defenses was on foot. When they designed it, they never expected an attack to come from the ground," Lily said with melancholy. "They weren't supposed to know we were coming until it was too late. Somehow, the enemy discovered our plan to take the capitol. They were ready and waiting for us."

The tallest of the buildings reached up through gray clouds, pillars holding the angry sky aloft. Kelly let out a nervous sigh, and her hand slipped into his. He squeezed it, beginning to realize everything he and his friends had survived and accomplished to this point was nothing compared to what lay ahead.

Although their tops were crowned with thunderheads, the lower parts of the cylindrical buildings reflected the sun, which Shane guessed set in a clear sky behind Lily's ship.

"I was supposed to stay back," she explained somberly. "To provide air support until they were in."

A dark line drawn across the foundations of the city grew thicker. The camera zoomed closer, revealing thousands of soldiers, covered in the same angular red armor as the rebels.

Unlike the rebels, many were unprotected from the neck up.

"They could have just killed us all right away. But first, they marched on us with no helmets, so we could look our executioners in the eyes," Lily explained as the camera panned over the angry faces. "It was the worst kind of war—families divided, brothers and sisters on opposite sides."

The ones without helmets looked similar to Lily and her counterparts, all with tan skin and dark hair. The Anunnaki raced down the hill toward the rebels, shouting and waving their weapons.

"An army straight out of Hell," Tracy whispered.

When they were a football field's length away, they stopped. The camera on Lily's spacecraft scanned left and right, up and down the enemy's ranks. In the center, a soldier was pushed ahead of the rest by two of his comrades. One of them kicked him in the back of his legs, and the other pushed him so he fell to his knees. His comrade stepped beside him, raising his glowing weapon, which appeared to be some kind of a plasma sword.

Clasping his brethren's hair with his free hand, the soldier dropped the curved blade and swept it horizontally to slice through his neck. He lifted the head into the air, blood dripping onto his armor. Horrified gasps erupted from Shane and his friends. The body swayed for an instant, and then fell forward into the grass.

"He was one of our spies," Lily said softly. "He infiltrated their army and made it to a lofty rank before they discovered him."

The soldier swung his arm in a circle and threw the dripping head high into the air. It landed amongst the red-clad soldiers beneath Lily's ship, and the Anunnaki charged.

Lily's people resisted, firing laser guns with plasma-bladed bayonets, but he could tell by how disorganized they were that the Anunnaki had effectively reversed the element of surprise on the rebels. The Anunnaki broke their line, attacking with such violence that it appeared each of the warriors had a personal vendetta. They shot and stabbed the rebels, even after they had to be dead, and then stomped on the bodies to get to their next victim.

Blasts of green energy emitted from somewhere near the camera, decimating a cluster of soldiers.

"That blast came from your ship. Did they retaliate?" Tracy asked, sounding more analytical than excited.

"Yes—watch."

Lily got off a couple of more shots before an aircraft, the size of a passenger jet and shaped like a cigar with no wings, came barreling at her from the city ahead. The image jerked left and right as she evaded blasts from the ship, and then it leveled off.

"They stopped attacking. That's when I knew we were doomed."

A massive, golden ship, shaped like an Egyptian pyramid, settled on the hillside behind the red army. Firing their weapons to keep the rebels at bay, the Anunnaki retreated into an opening in one of its reflective, slanted faces. The surviving rebels stood stunned, their weapons drooping as if they couldn't understand what they'd done to cause the sudden retreat. Once all the Anunnaki were loaded, the gold ship lifted into the sky. The camera on Lily's spacecraft followed it, blasts of green energy directed at the vessel coming from her cannons.

When the big ship's pointed apex impaled the clouds, it emitted a beam of bright white energy from its square, black bottom, directing the blast down amongst the scattering rebels.

"We didn't consider the ship to be a threat, didn't expect them to use the weapon so close to the capitol. They were willing to risk everything to destroy us."

The craft lifted higher, and the ground collapsed inward where the beam impacted the battlefield.

"They created a temporary gravity well amidst our soldiers." Lily's voice cracked. "We didn't have a chance."

"A black hole?" Laura asked with terrified awe.

"Something like that," Lily replied.

Her craft moved closer to the beam and then spun away. The camera captured a double sunset, one yellow sun slightly above the horizon and the other orange one half below. The camera rotated down and back, filming the rebels as they fell and clawed at the green plain, trying to resist being sucked toward the beam. When they got close to it, their armor imploded, their bodies crushed and violently ripped apart before vanishing into the light.

"I tried to fly away, but it pulled me in."

There was no sound, but Shane imagined the engines on Lily's ship were screaming against the irresistible draw of gravity. The light picked up by the camera grew brighter and brighter until the TV screen was white. Then it went dark for a few seconds, and the image changed. An image of North America from space appeared on the screen, and the image began to rotate, slowly at first and then faster until it was a blur.

"We were pulled into some sort of wormhole created by the implosion. The mouth of the wormhole must've been high enough above the plain that it only captured our ship, protecting us from the most destructive gravitational forces generated by the weapon. While everyone on the ground was being crushed, we passed through unscathed. We came out over New Mexico, our engines shut off by the space-time distortion," Lily said. Flames engulfed the image as the ship passed through the atmosphere. When the fire retreated, the tan, spinning desert rushed up to meet the camera, and then the screen went blank. Lily turned the TV off and looked at Shane and his friends, her eyes moist.

"It didn't seem like you had a chance," Jules said distantly. "I don't see how we can possibly fight them."

"They knew we were going to attack." She regained her composure. "Their spies must've infiltrated us."

"Looked like they really hated your people," Tracy mused, staring at the dark screen.

"We resisted the idea that Anunnaki are the supreme beings in the universe. We believed all sentient beings should be treated with respect and allowed their freedom," she explained. "We destroyed numerous factories and training facilities that were preparing for attacks against planets like your own. The Anunnaki government called us traitors and wanted us all dead."

"What makes you think we'll do any better?" Shane had heard enough. He wanted to know what their chances were. The rebels had advanced weapons and an understanding of their enemy he and his friends couldn't gain in a lifetime. He didn't feel overly confident at the moment.

"Although you are not as technologically advanced, humans are a lot tougher than the Anunnaki, as is your design. Your people have been fighting constantly for thousands of years—it's in your DNA," she replied. "Humans have created heroes and gods in myth, attributing great strength to them and telling stories of how they overcame impossible obstacles. In Anunnaki lore, humans fill the roles of our children's heroes. We have always admired your strength and willingness to fight when the odds are against you. In combining the primitive, though physically powerful, phenotype of the Neanderthals with the intellect of the Anunnaki, my people created the perfect warriors."

"We're not all violent monsters bent on killing each other," Laura objected with disgust.

"No, you are not," Lily confirmed apologetically. "Humans have a great capacity for love and creation. It's another reason my people are so fond of you. Humans are the greatest achievement of the Anunnaki—both sides agree upon that. You also desire peace, and we rebels expect one day your people will stop fighting each other. But for now, your intelligence, primal aggressiveness, and propensity toward war make you ideal soldiers. You are their secret weapon, and they expect you'll help them overthrow their enemies. These same characteristics may save you and your planet from them."

"But our armies are gone. We're just a bunch of kids," Jules said. "What do you expect us to do?"

"Based on our calculations, we have between four and six months until the Anunnaki arrive," she replied. "It's not much time, but we can train you. My partner and I had a long history of executing covert operations against the enemy before we came here, and we helped train lots of recruits."

"Yeah," Steve said, "and you lost."

"Remember," her enthusiasm was undeterred by his pessimistic response, "unlike the multitude of successful attacks we rebels made during the war, the enemy won't be expecting you. They don't know we are here. You have surprise on your side. Yes, the odds of success in this mission are dire at best, but we believe in you. And you have to believe in yourselves."

Lily studied them, admiration and optimism in her eyes. Shane fidgeted with his cup, his head aching from all the new information. He glanced at his friends. They had to fight— what else was there to do?

"We've been dealing with the impossible for the last two days, so I guess we're used to it," Shane said. Then he faced Lily, resting his elbows on the table. "What do we have to do?"

"A small fleet of Anunnaki ships are coming to earth," she began. "Their mission is to enslave the remaining kids. They'll use the slave gene in the kids to make them pass through seven main recruit ships, which will land in different parts of the world. They'll equip the kids with armor and weapons. You will be with the enslaved kids. You and six other teams, en route to this base now, will enter the ships, appearing to be under Anunnaki control."

She paused and looked up and down the table, like she was making sure they were following what she was saying.

"We already got that. Go on," Shane demanded, his head spinning.

"Once you're equipped, you'll slip away from the rest of the recruits and make your way to the ship's engineering department," she said, now speaking directly to him. "We will teach you how to input a sequence into the control panel that will destroy the primary reactor."

"And then what?" Steve asked. "Sounds like a suicide mission."

"Everyone in the reactor chamber will die. But if you can get out before the reactor goes critical, then your odds of survival are actually quite high," Lily said, though Shane wasn't convinced this part of the plan was a priority.

"The Anunnaki use the energy from the ship's reactors to power their strength-enhanced armor, and they need it to boost the control signal to the human slaves. With the reactors destroyed, the enemy will be thrown into chaos, and the slaves will be freed. Then we have a chance of defeating them."

Lily wanted to beat the Anunnaki—that much was clear. Whether or not she cared if Shane and his friends survived was yet to be determined.

"Well, if it's the only hope we have," Tracy commented. "We have to at least give it a try."

"We knew you would," Lily replied. "Which is why you are here."

"And you think we're the best people for this mission?" Shane asked, skeptical.

"Well, you managed to shut down the limbic manipulator weapon, didn't you?" Lily looked up and down the table, her eyes wide as if to invite an objection.

"You didn't know that when you selected us," Shane said, his gazed fixed on her. Had he caught her in a lie? "Why did you choose us?"

"We have neural scanning equipment that is beyond your understanding," she replied, not acting the least bit suspicious. "We scanned you before we met you at the farmhouse, when we flew over in the helicopters. The results of the scan are what led to your, and every other teams, selection. We were surprised that you didn't seem to have any special training, but now that I know what you've done, the scan results make perfect sense." Lily paused, her expression becoming more sincere. "You may not have the training of some of the other groups, but you've got a fighting spirit that few can match. You're the type of people that don't give up, and that's what we need if we're to make it through this situation."

CHAPTER SIX

"Judging by what you must've gone through, I doubt those pastries have done much to curb your appetite." Lily stood and came back around the table.

He felt more at ease when she approached him, beginning to come to terms with the idea that they were on the same team. She had suffered too, had lost her people and her home. He couldn't ignore the irony of having the rebels land on a planet destined for harvesting. What were the odds? And even if the enemy was as formidable as she made them out to be, the notion of destroying them from the inside seemed viable. He wanted to believe she was good, and her plan could work, but he reminded himself to stay cautious.

"So, about these guns," Lily said, looking at Kelly's M-16, which was propped against the table. "I won't order you to relinquish them, but I do worry about an accidental discharge. You brought a lot of kids with you, and it concerns me to have these weapons everywhere."

The teens were silent. Shane stared at her, hesitant to

take the final leap. He glanced at his friends—all eyes were on him. They expected him to make the decision; otherwise, they would have said something by now. Biting the inside of his cheek, he looked at Lily once again and sighed.

"Yeah, I think it's okay to leave them here," he said.

Lily smiled. Relief settled on everyone's face except for Tracy and Steve's. He sensed neither of them had misgivings about parting with their guns for fear of Lily. They glanced at the weapons with longing—children forced to surrender their favorite toys.

Aside from football, Steve's other great passion was hunting. He wasn't good at school, just barely making the grades so he could play sports, and he wasn't particularly successful with the ladies, who probably didn't enjoy that he only talked about these two things.

Tracy loved anything military related. Her stepdad had been a Green Beret in the Army, and she seemed to want to be just like him. The JROTC program at Leeville High had been an obscure club with a few oddballs in disheveled uniforms when Shane was in the ninth grade. With her stepdad's help, she revived the unit in less than two years. She even had the soldier wannabes marching during halftimes and twirling rifles.

Grinning at their discontentment and satisfied his friends felt he'd made the right decision, he followed Lily out of the conference room and onto the tarmac. She pointed the hungry teenagers toward the base cafeteria and went back inside.

He and his friends walked across the base in silence, and

he expected they, like him, were contemplating all Lily had just said to them. She'd mentioned six other teams were on their way, and his imagination conjured three dozen teenage commandos with tattoos and battle scars being scooped up from the darkest corners of the globe. It made sense to get the best kids alive on this mission. But, if the rebels initially weren't aware his team had shut down the limbic manipulator, why had they chosen them? It wasn't like they had any special training that would make them better candidates. The whole neural scan from above explanation she gave wasn't easy to believe. Maybe Lily did already know what they'd achieved and was just trying to boost their egos by acting amazed when they told her.

The cafeteria was inside a squat, rectangular building, a contrast to the curved half-pipe or taller, blocky structures making up much of the perimeter of the airfield. Passing through the glass doors, Shane immediately got a sense that the ceiling was too low. It gave the windowless dining room a dark and claustrophobic feeling, despite the lines of fluorescent lights breaking the monotony of the acoustic tiles. It had more rows of tables than the Leeville High lunchroom had, and a long, stainless-steel serving area took up the entire wall opposite the entry.

"Some rescue," Maurice grumbled, setting his tray down across from Shane. "When they plucked us off that farm, I thought things might get better."

"I'm not ready to give up," Shane replied, trying to maintain a semblance of courage. He looked across the room at Kelly, who was in line getting food.

"Me neither—I'm with you," Maurice said unconvincingly. "It just sucks, that's all." His head drooped, and he shoveled a bite of tuna casserole into his mouth.

Although he'd only known him for a couple of days, he felt close to Maurice. The short, thick kid was willing to give his life if that was what it took to win. He was a great orator, brave as hell, and strong as an ox. Shane didn't know much else about him. In the short time they'd been acquainted, he'd never seen the boy carry his head so low. He usually stood proud and seemed taller than he actually was, but now something was undermining his confidence.

"What was your family like?"

Maurice glanced up, his eyes wide like he was taken off guard by the question.

"They were the best kind of people," he said earnestly. "My dad was a preacher in a church in Stone Mountain. Mom was a nurse. All they ever wanted to do was to help others, to make the world a better place." He looked at his tray, chasing a brussel sprout around it with his fork.

"Did you have any brothers and sisters?"

Shane didn't want Maurice to dig up painful memories, but it had made him feel better when he talked to Kelly about those he'd lost. And if he was going to continue to fight alongside these kids, he wanted to get to know them.

"Yeah, a grip of them." Maurice gave a little smile. "I was the youngest. I had a sister and two brothers who were in college and two other sisters who were all grown up and married." He paused, his eyes glistening. "Veronica, the oldest, was pregnant." His voice trailed off.

"I'm sorry," Shane said quietly, hoping he hadn't asked too many questions.

"It wasn't so bad before this morning." The thick kid's lower lip trembled. "I had my faith—believed they were all in heaven."

"What changed?" Shane hated to see Maurice so distraught. The kid had been a rock through the battle in Atlanta. Shane needed him to be strong now.

"Lily said we were made by aliens," Maurice replied, sounding disgusted. "Don't you see? It defies everything we learned in church. Makes me feel like my whole religion is a farce."

"I don't see it that way," Shane replied. "Just because there's more to our history than we knew before doesn't mean heaven doesn't exist. I know my granny, my mom and dad, and everyone else is up there looking down on us right now. I can feel it. Just because some of what we've been taught might be wrong doesn't mean what you feel in your heart isn't true."

Shane was half impressed with what he'd just said. It sounded like some of Granny's counseling. Looking at Maurice, he smiled, but inside, he felt a twinge of shame. Maurice seemed way more qualified to give spiritual advice. Shane wasn't even sure he really believed what he'd just said. He was trying to make Maurice feel better, and his own doubts made him feel like a liar and a hypocrite.

"You know what?" Maurice raised his head. "You're right." He reached across the table and put his hand on Shane's forearm. "Thanks, brother."

He nodded and then glanced around the room, unable

to keep looking into the boy's brown eyes with the uncertainty eating at his insides. However, he knew he'd done the right thing. If he was going to lead these people, he had to put their well-being and peace of mind above his own.

The cafeteria had at least sixty tables in it. Red-haired Rebecca and another girl who'd been a victim in the assault at the gym monitored the youngsters, sitting at a table on the other side. That corner of the room had more chatter and even some laughter coming from it. He envied the little ones, some young enough that they'd forget most of this in a few years if they survived what was to come.

"What about you?" Maurice looked at Shane, his eyes showing compassion and an innate desire to ease the suffering of others. Fitting for the son of a preacher and a nurse. "What was your family like?"

"Mine was a bit of a mess, but I loved them just the same," Shane replied honestly.

He told Maurice about his mom, and how she'd died of cancer a while back. Then he talked about Granny before mentioning the weapon killed his aunt and father. Maurice was easy to talk to, and he didn't feel as much pain as he expected while recanting the story. Perhaps he was starting to get over their deaths, or maybe it was the numbness haunting him from the moment his aunt died—he couldn't tell which.

"Y'all got something deep going on there?" Maurice said, a mischievous grin on his face.

Shane realized he'd been looking at Kelly as he told the last half of the story. She was heading across the cafeteria toward their table. He felt his face get warm and returned his attention to Maurice.

"I reckon we might," Shane replied and cleared his throat.

"Well, that's a good thing as far as I see it," Maurice said. "As long as we got love, we'll be alright. That's what my pop used to say."

"Hey guys," Kelly said, walking around the table and sitting next to Shane. She forced a smile at them, and he could see she was having trouble digesting everything too.

"Hi Kelly," Maurice replied, smiling in return.

Shane was glad the old Maurice was back. His steady and ever-present cheerfulness was good medicine.

"At least they have decent food here," Shane said, watching Kelly dig in.

He took a bite of his roll and imagined what it would've been like to have her cut through the crowd in the high school lunchroom so she could sit next to him. It would've been insane. Shane would have risen from near obscurity to the height of teenage royalty had this captain of the cheerleading team chosen him over all the other boys in school. He chuckled at the thought.

"What?" Kelly glanced at him.

"Nothing," he replied, embarrassed.

"I'm so hungry," she said with an apologetic tone, and then started eating slower.

"Me too," he replied, trying to convey he wasn't laughing at her.

The funny thing was that Kelly was probably oblivious to the power she'd had in high school. Like a fairytale princess, she was humble and sweet to everyone. Before, Shane sometimes wondered if it was just an act, if maybe she was being condescending. Now he realized she was genuinely a kind person. Although, she had a mean streak of which he never wanted to be on the receiving end.

Steve and Laura came to the table, followed by Jules and Tracy. They finished lunch without much talk. Once in a while, one of them would look up from their food over to the other tables, perhaps envious of the higher spirits of the little kids or just checking on them to make sure they were all right.

These were good people. Each had proven they would fight alongside him. They'd give their lives if necessary. This was Shane's team, and he wasn't going to let them get manipulated by anyone. But Lily might be telling the truth—she sure seemed to be. He had to build up their confidence, make them believe they could stop the Anunnaki. A lover of proverbial quotes, Coach Rice had told him confidence was the ocean on which the victorious sail. Even if Shane didn't think they had a chance against the Anunnaki, he had to make his team believe he thought they would win. His own fears and concerns must be suppressed, and he had to help them overcome theirs.

"So what are we gonna do, boss?" Steve asked, wiping his mouth with his hand and then rubbing it down his shirt.

"We're gonna train," he replied firmly. "We're going to practice and learn everything these rebels can teach us. We've got to bust our asses every day until the Anunnaki arrive."

"We should act like a military special forces unit if we are going to have a chance," Tracy interjected. "We should wake up early and run. We need to get in the best shape we can."

"Agreed, and we should do some calisthenics too," Shane added. "At least some push-ups and sit-ups." He'd played sports long enough to know being in good shape would only help them. And the less time they spent thinking about how impossible their mission was, or about lost loved ones, the better.

"Who are we kidding?" Laura said, hysteria pitching her voice. She was sitting on the other side of Steve, hidden behind his massive frame. "I don't mean to be a downer, but how can a bunch of teenagers defeat space soldiers who have been traveling around the universe for thousands of years, kicking the crap out of entire worlds for fun? I mean, has it occurred to you guys that it sounds like no one has ever beaten them?"

"Yes, Laura, that has occurred to me," Shane replied quickly. He could see Tracy was about to snap at her, and he knew it wouldn't help. "But we are different. The Anunnaki have never fought humans, so we don't know what our chances are." He gave each of his friends a stern look. "No one ever wins a fight going into it thinking they're gonna lose. We have to believe in ourselves, or we definitely don't have a chance."

Laura didn't respond, but her comment put a dampener on the mood of the kids around the table. After a moment, Shane stood and lifted his tray, taking it to the window on the right side of the cafeteria and dumping the remains of his meal into a trashcan. Sliding the tray through the window into the kitchen, he could see some of the kids from his and Maurice's groups washing dishes and helping to prepare food.

When he turned around, Kelly, Steve, Laura, Maurice, Tracy, and Jules were behind him. They all dropped their trays in the window and gave him a *what's next* look.

As if cued, a man in a black jumpsuit entered the cafeteria and glanced around. When his eyes found Shane's, he walked briskly toward them.

"I'm Jones," he growled, glaring at them like they weren't worthy of his attention. "I'll be in charge of your training."

Other than a large scar running from his temple to chin, the alien resembled the other male clones. But his facial features were where the similarities ended. Jones' broad, muscled shoulders threatened to burst the stitches of his black shirt. He wore his dark hair in a crew cut like Tracy, and he stood tall, with his big chest thrust forward.

"Is it just the seven teams who'll be attacking the Anunnaki?" Tracy asked, unmoved by the alien's drill sergeant demeanor. "Won't we be getting more troops?"

"We're recruiting as many kids as possible for the fight against the Anunnaki. On hidden bases around the world, teams will be trained to attack different parts of the Anunnaki ship. This base is being used to prepare the special attack squads that have the most important role in the mission— destroying the reactor. Here, your group will compete with the other six teams to determine which is the best and, therefore, which will attack the Anunnaki flagship," Jones rumbled.

After barely taking a breath, he continued, "Each human opposing the enemy must be given an earbud to suppress the slave gene. We have a limited supply of the earbuds, but we'll give them to as many kids as possible to build several small forces for an exterior attack on the remaining Anunnaki after you and the other teams have completed your missions.

Once the reactor is destroyed, and they are released from the enemy's control, you will also recruit the humans who were enslaved. The Anunnaki will be outnumbered. Now, if you'll follow me, I'll take you to the barracks." Jones spun away, putting an abrupt end to the questions.

He led them out of the cafeteria and onto the tarmac. The lush treetops reached up behind the hangars to their left, the forest of the Appalachian Mountains stretching away from the base. Shane imagined there was nothing but wilderness for hundreds of miles in every direction.

The thought of all of that uninhabited forest comforted him. He used to spend hours in the woods when he was younger, his imagination turning trees into skyscrapers and his arms into wings. Granny descended from Irish hillbillies who tamed this forest and lived off the land. She taught Shane how to run a trout line in the crisp, cold rivers and make a rabbit box to catch a meal. Intent upon keeping her family's history alive, she even showed him how to create medicine from the wild ginseng and herbs that took an experienced eye to find.

He wished he could remember more of what she taught him, but he was confident he could survive out there just fine. If only he could flee with Kelly and his friends. They could build log houses and live peacefully amongst those towering pines—could try to put their broken lives back together and find some resemblance of happiness.

The video Lily had shown them warned that any such escape to isolation would be short-lived. The enemy was too advanced and Earth too small for them to hide. The Anunnaki would find them. No—Shane, Kelly, and his friends had no choice but to fight.

"Why do you guys have names like Lily and Jones?" Jules asked, walking in the shade of the half-pipe-shaped hangars with Tracy separating her from Jones. "They don't sound like names for extraterrestrials."

"Most of us were born, or should I say cloned, on Earth," Jones replied, sounding annoyed with having to answer another question. "Lily was one of the original two who crashed in New Mexico. Lilith is a popular name on our world."

"An interesting choice, if you know anything about the biblical legend of Lilith," Maurice mused. "The original disobedient wife of Adam turned baby killer."

"This is our home now, and we're willing to die for it," Jones growled. He seemed easily annoyed by trivial conversation. "Though we will never be human, we don't want to be thought of as alien either, so we've chosen earthly names."

"I meant no offense," Maurice murmured, his eyes wide as he looked at Jones.

His comment got Shane wondering. Lilith the baby killer—he wasn't familiar with that story. It renewed his suspicion, but a thumping coming from the west distracted him.

A Black Hawk appeared above the treetops, flying so low that the tallest pines scraped its belly. Clearing the buildings, the helicopter dropped to the tarmac. Lily came out of the hangar where she'd met with Shane and his friends earlier, jogging across the fractured blacktop to greet the new arrivals. She slid open the side door and seven Asians, four guys and three girls, stepped out, all wearing matching blue tracksuits with red stripes down the arms and legs. Seeing these kids and recalling what Jones had just mentioned about the contest against the other six teams, Shane's competitive nature took over, distracting him from all other thoughts.

"It's the Koreans," Jones explained once the engine on the helicopter spun down enough for him to be heard. "They're a very promising group of teenagers, all part of the South Korean National Tae Kwon Do team. They were slated to be in the next Olympics."

"How are we gonna compete with that?" Laura asked.

"They are formidable, but each of the teams has characteristics that give them a distinct advantage," Jones reassured. "Don't forget—we might not even have a chance if it weren't for you." A hint of admiration took the edge off his gruff tone. Judging by his drill-sergeant behavior thus far, Shane reckoned it was a rare occurrence. This dude preferred one-way conversations, with him yelling the entire time.

Shane stared across the tarmac, studying the new team. The shortest of the girls stepped ahead of the group and bowed to Lily. Unheard greetings were exchanged, and then Lily turned and led them to the building, where she would undoubtedly show them the same video he and his friends saw.

The short girl at the head of the Koreans—who he reckoned had to be their leader—looked at Shane as she walked. Her steely expression promised she would not be an easy adversary. Shane met her gaze, knowing looking away would give her confidence. He wasn't about to do that. They passed each other before their eye contact broke.

CHAPTER
SEVEN

"Did you get a look at those guys?" Jules asked once they entered the barracks.

"Yeah," Kelly replied. "I hope our little competition doesn't involve fighting each other."

"Right?" Laura seconded with a chuckled.

"Hand-to-hand combat is part of your training," Jones corrected.

"How's that?" Steve asked, sounding less intimidated. Not a single member of the Korean team looked like they weighed half what he did, and Steve was solid muscle.

"We'll be using an advanced form of MAC training, which stands for Modern Army Combatives." Pride entered Jones' gruff tone. "The version we will train you with is a hybrid between what was used to train your Special Forces and CIA teams and the training system used to prepare rebels for missions on our home planet. The training is designed to nurture your inborn warrior instinct and help you face the enemy with fearless aggression. The contests will motivate you and help us determine which group will have the highest probability of success on the mission, so we can determine who to send against the flagship. While much of the score will be accrued by tests of strategy and mental endurance, two major components are physical and combative."

"Damn, you're screwed," Tracy said, looking at Laura.

"What?" Laura glared at her. "You don't know me."

"You're right," Tracy replied, condescendingly. "I don't."

Shane looked back and forth between the girls, uncertain as to what was going on. Before the world fell apart, he'd only known them in passing and hadn't really ever hung out with either of them. He'd never seen them interact at school and, as far as he knew, they'd just met two days ago. For some reason, Tracy didn't seem to like Laura. It was like the quiet Goth girl had done something horrible to her in the past, or maybe Tracy just sensed weakness in her and didn't think she belonged here. They glared at each other for a moment, and then turned their attention to the lodgings.

The barracks was a long, rectangular room with two doors, the one they'd entered through and another twenty-five yards down.

"Bathroom, beds, study area." Jones pointed from the second door at the far end to the two rows of bunks taking up either side of most of the room, and then at the brown, metal chairs in front of a flat-screen TV that hung on the wall to their left.

It reminded Shane of a chicken house, long, narrow, and designed to pack in a bunch of birds, or in this case, people.

"Wow, this is much more than we need," Shane observed,

concerned.

"All seven teams will sleep in here," Jones explained.

"I was afraid of that."

The ill-tempered alien didn't acknowledge him, walking to the TV and picking up a remote.

"Battle videos, audio files, interviews with soldiers and civilians, physiological analyses, engineering lectures on spacecraft and armor—everything you need to know about the Anunnaki plays in a loop here."

He touched a button on the remote and a leaner, unscarred version of Jones appeared, but the sound was muted. Shane selected a set of headphones from a basket to the side of the TV with a tag that read "English" on it. He slipped them on, and the alien's voice played in his ears. It was a lecture on Anunnaki anatomy, talking about their muscle connections and how they made most Anunnaki physically weaker than the average human. But, he warned, their armor more than made up for the difference.

Taking off the headphones, he returned them to the basket. Five other baskets hung on the wall, each with a different language tag on it. Shane gathered at least one other English-speaking team would be joining them. There were twice as many headphones in that language than the rest.

"The loop takes seventy-two hours to get through, and then it replays. You should spend as much of your limited free time as possible viewing these lessons," Jones advised. "The more you learn, the more effective you'll be when the time comes for you to try to save this world."

"No pressure," Maurice said, laughing nervously.

"I'm sure Lily made it clear, but to put it in words you can understand, we don't intend to sugarcoat anything. You must fully grasp the magnitude of this situation, so the only one surprised during your attack is the enemy." Jones shifted his cold gaze from Maurice to the rest of them. "We want you fully prepared. If you lose, we lose—my people have no place else to go either," he added, no less aggression in his voice.

"Come this way, and I'll show you the quads."

They followed him past the TV area and between the bunks. Once they were in the aisle, Shane could see narrow panels separated the beds, creating cubicles that slept four people per section. The quads opened onto the aisle, affording no privacy from the people on the opposite side. In each divided area, four metal lockers sat under the high windows on the exterior walls. There were no locks on them to secure valuables, not that Shane or his friends had any. All they had left at this point was each other.

"This first set of quads belongs to you," Jones growled. "Boys on the left, girls on the right."

"I guess that means we get an extra bed," Maurice said, cheerful in spite of the gruff alien's condescension.

One of the bunks had stacks of black clothing on it—seven piles of sweatpants, shorts, and T-shirts—all the same as the ones Dr. Blain had provided for him.

"Looks like we all have to wear butt-huggers," Steve complained, picking up the running shorts from the stack with the largest-sized clothing in it.

"They suit some of us quite nicely," Kelly whispered to Shane.

"Yeah." He chuckled. "I can't wait to see you in them." He shot a grin at her, and she was the one blushing this time.

There was also a small, clear plastic case with an earbud in it that looked like a tiny, transparent hearing aid, and a paper cup with five large pills in it.

"What's this?" Jules asked, picking up the earbud. "I didn't think we'd need to wear it until we attacked the Anunnaki."

"It is the device that will suppress the slave gene, but it's also a translator and the simulator interface," Jones explained. "You'll need to wear it at all times during training so you can understand the non-English speaking teams."

"What about the Anunnaki?" Jules asked. "What language do you speak?"

Shane tried hard not to smile. She was pithy and aggressive as any of them—a fitting complement to his team. Jones' face twitched—he clearly didn't enjoy the label.

"*They* speak a universal language everyone on this planet will understand. To you, it will be English. To the Chinese, it will be Mandarin," he replied. "You'll understand the Anunnaki, and they'll understand you."

He wondered why the alien kept the scar on his face. After what Dr. Blain had done to the gash in Shane's chest, he was certain she could fix anything. Perhaps the captain was just trying to look as intimidating as he sounded.

"And these?" Laura asked, poking her finger at the horse pills.

"Your training will be exceptionally vigorous," Jones replied. "Those contain a special mix of amino acids, super nutrients, and vitamins Dr. Blain put together to help your body and mind recover quicker. If you don't take them, you will fall behind."

Not allowing for any more conversation on the subject, he turned away and led them past six more identical sets of quads to the door at the end of the barracks. He pushed his way in and held it open.

"Here's the bathroom. To the left of the sinks are laundry machines and a locker filled with cleaning supplies. You and your roommates will be responsible for keeping this barrack spotless."

"Great," Kelly said apprehensively. "So is this one for the girls or the guys?"

"I'm sorry," Jones growled, his voice getting louder. "Perhaps I haven't spoken clearly. You will all share this barrack."

"With only one bathroom?" Kelly sounded incredulous and unintimidated.

"Yes," Jones replied curtly. "Sharing berthing and bathing areas will help us evaluate you."

"That's just wrong in every way," Laura objected, putting her fists on her hips and donning a defiant scowl.

"Wrong?" Jones said, enraged. "The survival of your species, of this very planet, is at stake! The seven groups of seven who will train here are our only hope. Is it not worth a bit of suffering so we can prepare you for the single most important mission your species has ever attempted?"

The veins in his thick neck bulging and his face red with passion, Jones glared at each of them. Shane cast nervous glances at his friends. He could tell no one liked the situation any more than he did, and they seemed weary of the alien's constant yelling.

The barracks didn't look like a haven for rest, and Shane expected it was part of the plan. Other than the coed factor, it was a lot like football camp. Coach Rice used to give lectures to the football team to explain their training. In one, he mentioned the body and the mind best learned reflexive action, such as leaping to the side in an instant to avoid a tackle, when both were completely exhausted. He said this was why he made them run and lift weights until they nearly dropped and then had them practice plays on the football field once their eyes were drooping from fatigue and their arms and legs felt like jelly.

Shane and Steve were familiar with the aggressive approach, but he wanted to quit all the time when he first started. They were going to have to help the others along until they got used to it.

After impatiently staring at them for a moment, seeming to give Shane's now gloomily introspective squad a chance to ask some final questions, Jones pivoted sharply on his heel and marched back through the barracks. The seven teens shot wide-eyed *dude's crazy* glances at each other, and then followed him.

"If you need anything, dial one," he said, pointing at an old, green, touchtone phone to the right of the front door. "Each team has a number. From this point on, you will be referred to by that number. You are Team One."

"I can live with that," Steve said cockily. "I like being number one."

"It has no reference to your rank as related to the other

teams." He looked at each of them in turn, his brown eyes narrow, and his brow wrinkled with intensity. "If you have no further questions, I will leave you to get situated. We start training at zero four hundred hours tomorrow. The rest of the squads will arrive today." Jones walked, or rather charged, out of the building, the door slamming behind him.

Shane's mind was a whirlwind, trying to process everything he heard and saw since arriving to this hidden base. His blurry gaze remained locked on the exit until Tracy cleared her throat. His friends looked just as dazed, but their attention was on him.

"This ain't gonna be easy," Shane said, breaking their catatonia. "But we can handle it."

"How'd he know we shut down the limbic manipulator?" Jules asked, pinching her chin thoughtfully. "An hour ago, Lily acted like she didn't know when we told her. Now it's common knowledge?"

"Maybe the room where Lily met with us was being monitored too," Tracy murmured covertly, glancing up at a camera in the corner to the left of the door. "They're probably studying us already and planning our training."

"I'm not sure we're the right people for this." Laura crossed her arms and rolled her shoulders forward, seeming to get smaller. "I mean, what experience do we have? Those Koreans have been practicing martial arts all of their lives."

"Look," Tracy snapped. "These aliens brought us the internet, computers, cellphones—hell, they came here in a spaceship. They're way more advanced than we are, and I'd have to say a heck of a lot smarter. I don't think they'd have chosen us if we weren't good candidates. Out of all the billions of kids left on the planet, they picked just forty-nine. Why waste their time on us if we couldn't hang?"

"She's right," Maurice seconded, though with more compassion than Tracy would ever manage. "We may not be the ones who'll take out the flagship, but we have to do our absolute best. Those kids we fought so hard to protect need us now more than ever. According to Lilith and her friends, the whole world needs us."

"And Aaron, Matt, and Billy gave their lives," Steve said mournfully, eyes heavy and somber. "We owe it to them to do our best."

"I'll die before I let anyone hurt my sister," Kelly snarled. "If there's a fight that's going to save her, I have to be in it."

The rage and aggression he'd seen when they fought Shamus' gang in Atlanta entered her eyes. She was a cornered lioness, ready to use tooth and claw to protect Nat. The look was the opposite of the one the sweet girl he'd gone to church with on Sundays and had a crush on for most of his life had worn. Her ferocity would cause even the bravest man to cower, and it was hard to hold eye contact with her for more than a couple of seconds.

"Give it a few days, Laura," Shane said. "I think you may surprise us all."

"Yeah," Kelly agreed, her features softening. "We just have to stick together, and we'll do fine."

It was abundantly clear to Shane—their ability to transform from quiet, humble kids from Leeville into violent warriors was why they were here. He wasn't proud of what he'd done—the lives he'd taken. The thought of hurting anyone or anything else made his stomach turn. But as much as he hated the realization, he was good at killing when the situation demanded it. Not something he would've thought to put on his résumé until recently. Aliens indirectly murdering his dad and coming here to enslave the girl he loved were situations that justified some killing—that was for damn sure.

Laura must have the same strengths, but she hadn't gone downtown with them. According to Jones, the rebels were going to put them through some vigorous training. He reckoned they'd soon learn what Laura was capable of, and then her doubts would fade, and Tracy would show her more respect.

CHAPTER EIGHT

"I'm stepping out for some fresh air," Shane said, overwhelmed and exhausted from being around them. "You guys should do as Jones said and settle in."

He didn't want to appear weak to his friends, knowing they would look to him for leadership, but he needed a moment to clear his mind. Without giving them a second glance, he headed out of the barracks.

The door squeaked closed, and he stood on the edge of the tarmac. The hot August sun shined full in his face. He closed his eyes and tilted his head back, letting the distracting heat soak him.

Opening his eyes, he noticed a narrow egress between the barracks and the hangar next door. He strolled into it, searching for what he hoped was easy access to the woods. As he walked the length of the paved alley, the sappy and earthy smell of the forest grew in intensity, displacing the diesel fuel and tar odor that polluted it on the tarmac. At the rear of the buildings, Shane crossed a narrow strip of fescue-riddled gravel and pushed through the briars. Eight feet in, the undergrowth cleared. The mingling canopies of old oaks and pines blocked the light such that only ferns, poison oak, holly, and other shrubbery could survive on the shadowy forest floor.

The moist fragrance of the forest initially swept away his stress. He stretched his arms upward and rose onto his tiptoes, sighing deeply like he'd just returned home from a long day at school. This very same forest reached all the way down the spine of the Appalachian Mountains into Leeville.

The base sat near the top of a mountain, and a few yards into the forest, the grade dropped off steeply. Shane came to the first tall oak, its girth fifteen feet around, and its roots stretching out through the soft soil, creating ridges between piles of leaf litter and acorns. The majestic tree had to be over two hundred years old. He put his hand on its coarse, gray bark, his fingers digging into the soft moss clinging to it. Closing his eyes, he imagined his ancestors walking through this forest. They may have touched this very tree. He could feel its old soul, shushing him and telling him everything would be all right.

Drinking in deep breaths of the sweet forest smells, he hiked down for ten minutes. He opened his eyes just wide enough to keep from bumping into the trees. The leaves crunching under the running shoes provided with his black garb covered all other sounds.

It didn't take long for him to feel he was much farther away from the base than he actually was. When he came upon a thick tree fallen across his path, he climbed onto it and sat, facing downhill. He closed his eyes and let out a long sigh. It felt like iron bands fell away from his chest and stacks of cinderblocks rolled off his shoulders. He hadn't realized how stressed he'd become and wondered how much more a person could take before breaking.

It was the first time he was able to relax in… what? Well, he reckoned it was just a few days, but it felt like a lifetime. Being an only child, he wasn't used to having people around him all the time. Usually, he got hours alone each day, and he needed those moments to recharge.

The chirping birds and the rhythm of a woodpecker's hammering shattered his tranquility. Squirrels rustled through the trees above him, bringing a surge of fear. These animals might have killed some poor moonshiner in these woods. What if they had a taste for human blood and came after him? He was unarmed and too far from the base to outrun them. They'd tear him to shreds, and no one would hear his screams.

Focusing on how the alligator-skin bark of the old pine pinched his bottom for a distraction, he tried to ignore the absurd rush of terror. But then he started worrying the carpenter ants might attack him. Their powerful mandibles could take a tree apart—what could they do to his flesh?

He wanted to be lulled by nature's soothing chorus, but he feared it might never sound as pleasing to him as it had before the critters went berserk. *It wasn't the animals' fault*, he told himself. They were forced to attack the adults and would never act that way in the absence of the limbic manipulator. As usual when he kept still in the woods, the sounds grew louder and the animals became comfortable with his presence. Determined to face this fear head-on, he resisted the urge to shout and clap his hands to chase them away. He closed his eyes and forced himself to listen.

Ten minutes may have passed, or even a half hour, in his struggle to find peace, Shane couldn't tell. A subtle crunching sound sent a surge of panic through him. He opened his eyes to a deer, nosing around in the underbrush for a snack. Scanning its hoofs, he was relieved to see they weren't stained with blood. Shane tried to remember how he used to enjoy seeing deer in their natural habitat, doing what they did when no one was around.

Staring at the animal, he started to convince himself to ignore the irrational fears. But then the animal made him think about Aaron. A rush of grief obliterated his calm. *Damn death.* He missed his best friend. Before, he'd hated the idea of killing such a pretty creature, and always got nauseous when Aaron or Steve bragged about one of their hunting trips. But now, he'd be glad to see a thousand deer die if he could get his friends and family back.

The doe raised her head, as if sensing the eruption of his inner turmoil. She looked past him, stiff, with her ears perked and trained up the hill. He held his breath, worried she might try to leap on him. Lifting her head higher, she seemed to pick up a sound he couldn't perceive. In a flash of chestnut, the doe darted through the trees, flagging her white tail. The report of her pointed hoofs piercing the leaf litter receded until all evidence of her presence vanished.

Shane kept perfectly still, wondering what he'd done to

startle her. Did she pick up on his anxiety over remembering Aaron's death? He'd heard dogs and horses could sense human emotion, but he never suspected wild animals had the same ability. A noise behind him solved the mystery. It was a delicate sound, seeming to come from two feet and not four. The only animal who made that sort of noise in the woods was a human, though the person was moving with the stealth of a prowling cat.

Hoping whoever walked down the hill behind him would find their own place of solitude and not discover his, Shane kept still and didn't look back. The birds and the squirrels grew silent, wary of the new trespasser. In that moment, he felt like one of them, wanting to dart up a tree and hide until the human passed and the wild symphony could crescendo once again.

"Shane?" Kelly's honeyed voice carried through the trees, timid, like she worried he may not want to be disturbed.

"Yeah." He twisted on the log and saw her fifteen yards up, peering between the thick trunks. He was awash with relief. It didn't bother him that she'd followed. "Come on down and sit for a spell."

More adept at walking quietly in the forest than he would have ever expected, she made her way to his log. He helped her climb on. After sitting, she inched closer until she pressed against him and then stared off into the forest, perhaps sensing he didn't come out here for conversation.

They sat hip to hip and shoulder to shoulder, neither saying a word. The animals resumed their song, growing accustomed to the new visitor. Shane's pulse kicked up to a gallop, this time not because of fear of the animals.

"I love the woods," Shane stammered, trying to control his excitement at being alone and so near to her. He wished he could be cool and suave like the dudes he'd seen in the movies, but he could barely think.

"I used to," she replied. "It used to make me feel closer to God when I was in the forest."

"Yeah." It was something Granny would say. No wonder he liked Kelly so much. "What's wrong now?"

"Guess I'm weirded out by the animals." She glanced around, her eyes wide with concern. "I don't think I'll ever be able to look at them the same."

"Don't worry, Kelly," he said, grabbing her hand. "That was all because of the limbic manipulator." He didn't let on that he'd been thinking the same thing, wanting to be strong for her.

"I know," she said, looking at him bashfully. "It's just hard to forget what I saw. That horrible day when it all started—it's like the images are always there in my mind, waiting for me to blink or go to sleep so they can torment me."

He pushed the hair out of her face and gently rested his hand on the back of her neck. "I didn't let the critters get to you in Atlanta, and I won't let anything hurt you now, or ever."

She smiled, the corner of her lip trembling like she might reply. An unexpected look of concern showed on her face, like she didn't like what he'd just said. He looked at her, nervous he'd done something wrong. She leaned closer and pressed her soft lips against his. Lingering in the kiss, she slid her free hand up, resting it on his chest. Shane was sure she could feel his heart pounding. Her touch and the taste of her mouth ignited a fire in him that burned away his anxiety.

His attention was drawn from everything around him, entirely focused on her. He wanted more than just the kiss, his head spinning with desire. He wanted to touch her, to press her against him, but he held back, afraid of moving too fast and pushing her away. She pulled her lips from his and smiled, sighing like she was resisting the urge to do more. Laying her head on his shoulder, she pulled his hand into her lap, squeezing it between her thighs, most of which were left exposed by her black running shorts. Her skin felt like heaven, and it made him dizzy to touch her. The flowery smell of whatever shampoo she'd found in the barracks mixed with the piney fragrance of the forest.

He struggled to relax and just sit quietly next to her, but the inferno she'd ignited in him made it hard to keep still, made it hard to breathe. Being this close to Kelly Douglas, inhaling her fragrance and feeling her touch—his wildest fantasies were coming true. He resisted the urge to turn her toward him and kiss her again, afraid of coming on too strong.

Kelly sighed, sounding like she might be as breathless as he was. Squeezing her legs together tighter, she pressed the soft inner flesh of her thighs against his hand. His heart raced even faster, and his stomach felt like it was filled with helium. A surge of heat started him sweating, and then he remembered the itty-bitty running shorts he was wearing. Suddenly terrified of what she'd think of what was happening, he cleared his throat and forced himself to think about the forest animals attacking, hoping fear would be a sufficient distraction.

"What?" Kelly lifted her head and looked at him, her cheeks flushed and her pupils dilated. Was she thinking the same thing?

"Awe, nothing," he replied, gazing into the forest.

"We're gonna be alright," she whispered. "I don't know how I know, but it's for certain. I can tell you that."

"For some reason," he said, "I think you're right."

She laid her head on his shoulder again, and he leaned into her, forcing his mind to go blank and trying to just enjoy being near her. They sat in silence for a long time, until the shadows grew inky and began to spread through the forest, taking over as the light of the sun diminished. Shane smacked a stinging on his bare leg.

"We'd better head back," he said. "The no-see-ums are comin' out."

"That's the only thing I used to not like about the woods," she replied, swatting at her face. "The darn bugs."

The darkness concerned him too. Even if most animals wouldn't attack them in the absence of the limbic manipulator, there were coyotes in these mountains. Even worse, there were cougars, though he'd only ever seen their paw prints. They stood on the log and jumped onto the hillside above, then blindly made their way between the trees back up to the base. About halfway back, Kelly slipped, and he grabbed her hand to keep her from falling. Once she regained footing, he loosened his grip so she could let go, but she didn't. Instead, she clung to him until they made it to the thick brush at the edge of the forest.

Shane pushed ahead and held the briars aside so Kelly could pass.

"Why, thank you, sir," she said with an accentuated southern-belle drawl, then curtseyed once she was beyond the thorns and on the gravel.

"My pleasure, ma'am," he replied, tipping his pretend hat.

They laughed and walked through the narrow space between buildings, just as another helicopter came over the trees on the western side of the base. Shane shielded his face from the wind created by the chopper and watched it touch down. A shadowy figure, presumably Lily, crossed the tarmac and met seven more kids.

"I wonder how many are left," Kelly said.

"I don't know," Shane replied. "I'm betting we've got a few new roommates inside."

He opened the door to the barracks and followed her in, blinking at the stark fluorescent lighting. Tracy and Jules were sitting shoulder to shoulder in front of the large LCD screen, headphones on and eyes wide as they watched the Anunnaki annihilate a primitive army on some forsaken planet.

It really hadn't sunk in that humans weren't alone. There were other intelligent species on planets similar to Earth scattered across the universe. Shane diverted his gaze toward the back of the long room, unable to stomach any more information today. He and Kelly walked to the first set of quads and saw Laura lying in her rack, staring up at the bunk above.

"Any info on the new arrivals?" Shane asked.

"What?" She blinked and looked at him and Kelly. Her eyes were damp. He wondered if she'd been thinking about her parents, and felt guilty that he'd never cried over losing his dad.

"Oh, yeah." She composed herself. "The Koreans moved in next to us, and a Russian team showed up shortly after."

"Where're Maurice and Steve?"

"I believe Maurice went to the chapel, and Steve's grabbing a shower."

Just then, a loud, metallic bang came from the bathroom, followed by a shout.

"What the heck?" Shane said, trotting toward the other end of the barracks.

He burst through the bathroom door, almost tripping on overturned metal shelves. Towels were scattered, and the room was filled with steam and Steve's curses. The damp floor was tinged pink with blood.

"I'll kill you if you ever do that again," Steve yelled, his eyes wide with murderous fury.

He stood beyond the shelves, butt-naked and dripping water. The shower behind him still ran. Blood trickled out of his nose and hung off his chin. He had a tall, wiry, blond kid, who was wearing a towel around his waist, pressed against the white, tile wall, his forearm crushing the boy's neck. Two other new boys were standing by, cheering them on and smiling wildly.

"Steve! Let him go," Shane shouted.

"This piece of shit?" Steve returned, his eyes filled with murderous rage. "This piece of shit turned the cold water off while I was in the shower. I had soap on my face, and I got scalded. Can I ask you? What kind of an asshole does that? I'm gonna kill him."

CHAPTER NINE

"No, you're not," Shane said firmly. "Now let him go."

The other two backed up, mischievous grins on their faces. Steve looked at Shane, his expression wild and dangerous. He tensed, about to launch onto his friend to keep him from committing manslaughter. Steve took his weight off the boy's neck, and the blond kid dropped to the floor, gasping for air and groping his windpipe.

"We meant no harm," one of the shorter, dark-haired boys said with a thick accent. "This just good Russian greeting, that's all."

The other boys cackled like hyenas. Shane had seen Steve murderously angry before—these boys had no idea how close they'd come to getting killed.

Steve snatched a towel off the pile on the floor and wrapped it around his waist.

"Well," he snarled, glaring at them. "If you do that again, I'll give all three of you a good American broken neck!"

"Okay, okay, big, strong guy. We are sorry. Congratulations on your shower."

The two smaller guys lifted their friend to his feet and walked into the shower stalls, laughing and speaking loudly in Russian to each other.

"Are you good?" Shane asked.

"Yeah, I'm good," he replied. "But don't look at me like that. I didn't start it."

"I didn't say you did," Shane replied. "I just want to make sure you're alright, and you ain't gonna kill anyone when I walk out."

"I said I'm good," he snapped, wiping his nose.

"What happened?" Shane asked, nodding toward the blood.

"I slipped when those bastards shut off the cold water and damn near cracked my skull open."

"Well, looks like you gave them a good scare," Shane replied, confident Steve could've destroyed all three of them if it turned into a brawl. He wondered if the aliens knew what was happening and would've come to the foreign boy's rescue if he hadn't. Would they have let Steve kill the Russian for training purposes? "I'm guessing they won't mess with you again."

"They damn well better not," Steve shouted toward the other end of the bathroom, where the Russians were showering. He stepped into his shower stall, jerking the curtain closed.

Shane shook his head and walked out. Going from the excited bliss of being alone with Kelly to this scene of anger and violence was about the last thing he could take. He headed to the quad, looking forward to lying down and closing his eyes.

"Let the games begin," he said exhaustedly once he got back to the quad.

"What happened?" Kelly asked.

"Let's just say the Russians wanted to give Steve a warm welcome, and he wasn't having it."

"Was he hurt?"

"His nose got busted, but I'd say he won the fight. I'd have stayed in there if I were worried about him." He decided to leave out the details.

"Shhh." The sound came from the next set of cubicles, the Koreans trying to sleep.

"They sure go to bed early," Kelly said in a quieter voice.

"I guess we should turn in as well," Shane whispered. "I get the feeling the morning is going to come too soon."

Kelly's hand brushed his, and her eyes said she wanted to kiss him again. Too bad there was no privacy in the barracks. She gave a sweet smile that sent a passionate surge through him and turned toward her bunk.

Warmed by her hints of affection, he headed toward the boys' side of the barracks, pausing in the middle of the aisle when he saw Steve come out of the bathroom. Steve glared into the Russians' quad as he passed, challenging them to another tussle. But then his expression softened in an instant, like he didn't want to offend one of the people he saw. When he faced forward, there was a slight grin on his lips. There was only one thing that could turn the ferocious linebacker from anger to sheepishness so fast—a girl.

Shane continued across the aisle and stopped in front

of his rack. Steve entered and stepped next to him, reaching up and pulling back the blankets on his bunk. Deciding his friend had been picked on enough for one day, he didn't ask about his mood-shifting encounter at the Russian quad.

"What do you suppose these'll do?" He picked up the little paper cup.

"They'll make you a badass," Steve replied cheerfully. "Like me." He did a couple of quick boxer's hops and threw a punch at Shane.

"Yeah, right," he replied.

"No really, man," Steve continued. "They smell and look just like the supplements I take all the time, though they are probably a better version."

Shane stared at him.

Steve laughed. "Not steroids, dumbass. It's just amino acids and stuff to help your muscles recover. I get 'em at the mall for crying out loud."

Shane knew a lot of the guys on the football team took nutritional supplements. He couldn't afford them or he might've too.

"The darn things are so big," Shane said, swirling the cup. "How the hell do you get them down?"

"Come on, dude," Steve teased. "We all know you're a swallower."

"Jackass." Shane elbowed his friend.

"I already took mine, and I'm fine," Steve said, shrugging his shoulders and leaping up onto his rack.

"Yeah, I saw how fine you were just a few minutes ago in the bathroom."

"Night, man," Steve said, laughing and rolling toward the wall.

"Goodnight," Shane replied, looking down at the pills again.

What did he have to lose? And why would the rebels go through so much trouble just to poison them with these chokers? Everyone else was crawling into their racks, so he assumed they'd all taken them. He walked over to the water fountain and forced the pills down, one at a time, and then returned and rolled into his bunk.

He lay awake, listening to the Russian boys whisper and laugh two sets of cubicles down. They were a jovial bunch; he had to give them that. But their merriment was of the mean sort, and he worried they were the types that got their kicks by hurting others. A stoic, female voice finally snapped something in Russian, and they fell instantly silent.

Shane reckoned it was around nine or ten o'clock when the lights were shut off. His eyes adjusted to the soft moonlight filtering in through the high windows, and he saw Tracy and Jules go into their quad and crawl into bed. They'd been watching the Anunnaki reel the entire time. Admirable. He'd have to pick their brains tomorrow. Maurice came in a short while later and climbed into his rack.

It was getting late, but Shane's brain wouldn't stop. Expectations of what lay ahead, horrible flashbacks of the last few days, and more pleasant thoughts of Kelly took turns whirling in his head. His team consisted of four girls and three boys. Granted, Steve was a tank and Shane was six feet tall, and both had been lifting weights for years for football, but he worried the girls might put them at a disadvantage if some of the other teams were all male. Then again, he knew better than to be sexist. After all, Tracy had proven to be tougher than any boy he'd ever met.

Maurice wasn't as tall as Steve or Shane, but he was stocky and strong as an ox. And, the cheerful preacher's son wasn't easily intimidated. Shane saw Jules in action during the fight in Atlanta, and that she was still alive was a testament to her capabilities as well. The only person he was really worried about was Laura. She was definitely smart and compassionate to a fault, but could she fight?

Damn it, stop thinking and go to sleep!

He rolled onto his belly and tried to clear his mind, but it didn't slow down or make any progress toward resolving his concerns. Time passed at a blistering rate, and the door to the barracks squeaked open just as he was about to drift off. The patter of footsteps made him look to the aisle. Seven Asian kids, five boys and two girls, walked quietly by his quad. Must be the Chinese. He listened to Jones whisper the same introduction to the barracks he'd given the Americans. It sounded like he spoke in English, but Shane knew it had to be Anunnaki. It was unlikely they'd understand him otherwise. Jones left, and they settled in their bunks. Soon, the sound of heavy breathing dominated the barracks once again.

Exhaustion made every part of Shane feel like he'd doubled in weight, though his mind refused to let go of consciousness. His eyes finally grew heavy, and soft emptiness crept through him.

"Wake up! On your feet!"

Startled, Shane tried to open his eyes, the lights blinding him. He squinted and rolled to his side, realizing he must have drifted off. Was it an hour ago? It felt like five minutes.

"Get out of your racks and put on the clothes and shoes provided in your locker. If you haven't already, insert the translator bud into your ear. Do it, and do it now!" the gruff male voice coming from the front of the barracks yelled.

It was Jones, and he sounded like someone had pissed in his cereal.

"What the hell?" Steve grumbled, sliding out of the rack and hitting the floor with a heavy thud. "Did I fall asleep and wake up in the Army?"

Maurice laughed groggily.

Shane was jealous that the big guy had gotten sleep. Already wearing the black T-shirt and boxer briefs, he rolled out and put on his running shorts. He opened the small, plastic case holding the earbud. The inside of the lid contained a picture with instructions on holding and inserting it. It wasn't much bigger than a broken-off pencil lead, and a wire was attached to the thicker end for a handle.

He ran his free hand down his face, tugging his eyelids further open to wake up. There was an allure to the tiny thing in a secret agent sort of way. He carefully pinched the wire, lifted the earbud, and stuck it in his ear. It slipped deep into his ear canal, poking his eardrum. Shane winced, jerking it out. Holding his other hand over the insulted ear, he studied the wire handle held between his fingertips. It had come loose, leaving the device well out of reach inside his ear.

"Your bud will translate so you can communicate with

each other, and it'll prevent the enemy from messing with your brain. Do not lose your earbud!"

How could he? He wondered if he'd ever be able to get it out again. From across the aisle, Shane and Tracy's eyes connected. She held just the wire in her fingers too. Her expression was all seriousness, but he detected a little gleam in her eye, the same one that was there when she found the Stryker and rode in the Black Hawk.

"There is a line on either side of the barracks in front of your bunks. When you are dressed, stand on it. The last team on the line loses two points."

"Get up, Laura!" Tracy snapped.

Her aggression was unnecessary, but they couldn't afford to lose any points, of that he was certain. Shane slipped into the running shoes and stepped to the line at the same time as Maurice and Steve. Across the way, Kelly, Tracy, and Jules were already on their line, but Laura was still tying her shoes.

To the left, Shane saw the other six teams spilling out. The Koreans, Russians, and who he guessed were the Chinese, all stood at a position of attention, like they'd been doing this for years. Between them, a group of kids with a mix of ethnicities stood looking up and down the barracks, their eyes half open and disgruntled expressions on their tired faces. They blocked his view of the last two squads, those closest to the bathroom.

To his right, Jones strode into the aisle, unmistakable from his cloned counterparts because of his broad shoulders and the scar on his face.

"Stand tall and stiff, eyes straight forward, hands at your

sides," he bellowed, and Shane thought he heard the high windows rattle. "From now until you save this planet, you are all soldiers destined to die."

Shane kept his eyes forward, but he could feel Jones glaring at them.

"We have chosen some of you because you are the best of the surviving humans on this planet. The rest were chosen because of your association with these few. We will train you and make you all the best of the best. We will teach you how to stop the enemy, and we will teach you how to stay alive. Do I make myself clear? Say, sir, yes sir!"

A chorus of scrambled responses came from up and down the aisles.

"Now louder and all together!" came the order.

"*Sir, yes sir!*"

"On your faces. Push-up position."

Shane and Steve dropped, Maurice following.

"So much for getting up and exercising on our own," Steve whispered.

"This works too," Shane replied, grinning.

"No talking," Jones yelled.

Shane realized the rude way the alien spoke to them yesterday was the nicest he'd probably be for their entire training.

"Most of you know by now—my name is Captain Jones," the man continued. "I earned the title by working with the U.S. Navy Seals. I'll be in charge of your training while you are here. Straighten your backs and stay off your knees!"

Shane glanced across the aisle and down the barracks. Laura and several others struggled to keep good push-up form.

"I am your drill sergeant, your asshole father, and that coach who kicked your butt every day after school. I'm here to break you down and rebuild you into a stronger person than you ever imagined you could become. I am not here to listen to your problems. I am not your shoulder to cry on. If you don't want to be here, you can be replaced at any time. The survival of your species depends upon you, and there is no room for weakness, no time for sniveling or complaining. Do I make myself clear?"

"Sir, yes sir!" everyone shouted.

"Now, push-ups. One, two, three, four, keep your bellies off the floor," the alien drill sergeant sang. "Five, six, seven, eight, keep your backs and legs straight."

It felt good to do the push-ups, and Jones' military-cadence style of counting forced a smile onto Shane's face. Getting his blood pumping took the edge off the exhaustion. He never minded a good workout, but he could see Laura and Maurice weren't as enthusiastic. After ten push-ups, Laura dropped to her chest and laid there, her arms trembling with a futile effort to lift her body once more. Her surrender contagious, Maurice collapsed next.

"What is your problem?" Jones stepped between them, rage in his voice. He squatted down, glaring at them. "You give up like that on the mission, and we are all goners. Push-up or get out!" He pointed toward the door.

Shane feared he was about to lose two teammates, and the first day had barely started. To his surprise, Laura growled angrily and, under the gun of scrutiny, they both shakily lifted themselves off the floor. Jones moved down the line, yelling the entire way.

"You all have strengths that set you apart from the rest of the kids we could have chosen, but you also each have weaknesses." Spittle flew from Jones' mouth. He shouted in such a guttural way, Shane thought for sure Jones' voice would give out. "I intend to flush out those weaknesses, and together, we will crush them. Do I make myself clear?"

"Sir, yes sir!"

Laura dropped every few minutes, seeming done. Then, after a quick rest, she'd press on. Probably not wanting to be beaten by the girl, Maurice kept pace with her. Shane guessed there was more to Laura than he or anyone else realized, now that she'd have a chance to show it. Underneath her ghostly pale skin and jet-black hair, the same determined spirit everyone else on his team had simmered.

"On your backs! Crunches—begin!"

Jones had them do crunches and flutter kicks until Shane's tailbone was bruised. Then he made them plank until his stomach and arms were on fire, a puddle of sweat forming on the floor under him.

"Time to freshen up your pretty little faces, and then get out on the tarmac. If anyone is left in this building after exactly fifteen minutes, you will all have hell to pay. Go!"

The barracks erupted into chaos as everyone dove for their toothbrushes and charged to the end of the room. Shane expected an all-out brawl, making it to the bathroom with the surge of kids. To his surprise, people seemed respectful of each other. Guys and girls—people from different nations from around the world—lined up behind toilet doors and crowded around sinks. Jones' threat temporarily unified them, or they were just too tired for conflict. Shane finished and rushed out of the bathroom, making room for the others.

Shouting and clapping his hands the entire time, Jones encouraged them to exit the building. It was still dark out, no sign of dawn anywhere in the starry sky. The air was warm and humid, and the night critters were singing at full volume. Shane found Steve sitting on the bench to the right of the door.

"Did you even pee?" Shane asked, shocked that Steve had beaten him.

"The bushes." Steve pointed his thumb to the egress between the buildings.

Shane shook his head and plopped down next to his friend. Soon, the rest of the kids spilled out and coalesced into their squads.

"On your feet! Run!" Jones ordered as he burst out behind the last kid.

Shane took off with the rest of his squad on his heels. He reckoned the tarmac was about the size of four football fields, almost a mile around the perimeter. He glanced over his shoulder and tried to set a pace that everyone could handle. But Maurice was already huffing.

"Come on, hang with me," he said. "We have to stay together."

The Koreans passed them within the first minute of the run, and then the Chinese. It drove Shane crazy to see them blow by. He'd been running all summer to train for football, and he was sure he could keep up with them, if not stay ahead, but he wouldn't leave his team.

Laura let out a pained gasp, slowing to a jog.

"Keep going!" Shane ordered. "Whatever you do, don't stop."

She nodded, her face contorted like she might throw up.

The Russians flew by next.

"Damn it," Jules growled. Taking off after them, she pumped her arms and legs like an experienced sprinter. He suspected she was on the track team at her school.

"Stay with us," Shane shouted.

She waved her hand in the air dismissively, vanishing in the darkness ahead.

"Did you see the tattoo on that Russian's arm?" Tracy asked, running on Shane's right side. Like Shane, she didn't seem winded, Laura and Maurice's pace too slow to wear her out.

"No, why?"

"It was the symbol for the Spetsnaz—Russian special forces," she replied.

Shane had seen a TV show about the Spetsnaz. Their training was brutal—some even died during it. He never imagined they were recruiting teenagers as well, unless these kids were some kind of Spetsnaz wannabes or groupies.

"They might not take lightly to Jules running past them alone," Tracy said with a worried tone.

With what they did to Steve last night, Shane feared they'd hurt Jules.

"Damn it," he grumbled. "Go after her, and tell her to hang back with us."

She nodded and sped off into the darkness.

CHAPTER TEN

"I can't make it any further," Laura whimpered, pressing her fists into her sides. Her long, coal-black hair was soaked with sweat, sticking to her forehead and neck. In the dim light, Shane could see her usually pale face was flushed, eyes bulging as she gasped for air. "I'm cramping up."

"You can't stop," Shane said. Frustrated as all get out that his team was the weakest and, on top of that, they didn't have the discipline to stay together, Shane tried to sound enthusiastic to motivate Laura and Maurice. He grabbed her arm and helped her along. "You have to be strong."

Moving just faster than a speed walker, they made it three quarters of the way around the tarmac. Shane saw Tracy up ahead, on the edge of a security lamp's soft circle of yellow light. Jules lay in front of her, holding her knee pulled to her chest.

"What the hell happened?" he asked, releasing Laura and letting her stand huffing behind him.

"It was the Russians," Jules replied, her voice strained and her expression contorted in agony.

Anger boiling in him, Shane got a look at her knee. All the flesh was gone from it, and ribbons of blood hung down her shin. Her hands and elbows were bloody too.

"They tripped you?"

"Yeah, and it wasn't an accident," Tracy replied for her. "That's for damn sure."

"We oughta kick their heads in," Steve growled, searching the darkness with renewed fury in eyes.

"But we shouldn't stoop to their level," Kelly warned.

"Stoop?" Tracy asked incredulously. "I wouldn't call it stooping. I hate them, but right now, they're acting like the top of the food chain. If we're going to get to their level, we'll have to rise, not stoop."

Shane was with Tracy and Steve—he wanted to kick some Russian butt. He was just starting to wrap his head around the idea that these aliens sought to turn a bunch of high school kids into elite soldiers. The people they'd brought to this base to train were supposed to be the best, and these jerks were trying to bully their way to the top? He wasn't having it, but he didn't want to object to Kelly, so he kept his mouth shut.

Looking down at Jules, her face grimaced and her hands and knees shredded, Shane was hit by a surge of doubt. Should they even be here? Maybe he should gather his people and get the hell out before someone got hurt even worse.

"Can you walk?"

Jules looked up at him, eyes damp. "Yeah, I think so."

Shane and Tracy helped her to her feet and guided her toward the barracks. A few minutes later, the Russians came around and caught up with them.

"Perhaps the Americans have gotten too fat and lazy since the Cold War ended, eh?" one of the Russian boys taunted.

"I'll show you fat and lazy, you piece of… " Steve charged their ranks, tackling him.

"Steve," Kelly yelled. When Steve ignored her, she turned and looked at him. "Shane? Do something."

"Steve!" Shane yelled reluctantly. "Let him go."

The big linebacker rose to his feet, hovering over the crumpled boy. Shane feared the other Russians would attack him, but instead, they just laughed. Steve feinted a lunge at another one, and they recoiled, laughing even harder.

The Koreans ran by in perfect formation, followed by the Chinese in similar fashion.

One of the Russians, a girl who was as tall as Jules, snapped for her group to reorganize. She wasn't ugly, but she had chiseled facial features that didn't look conducive to smiling. Following her order promptly, they took off after the Asians.

"You'd better keep running," Steve yelled as if they fled him.

One limping, two exhausted, and the rest angry and discouraged, Shane led his friends back to the barracks and set Jules on a metal bench outside the door.

"What's going on here?" Captain Jones snarled, coming out of the darkness. "You're supposed to be running."

"Yeah," Shane objected incredulously, "but… "

"Excuse me?" Jones glared at him like he'd committed a heinous crime.

Shane stared back baffled and a little concerned. Then he remembered.

"Sir, yes sir," he corrected. "The Russians have attacked my people twice. How can we train with them always trying to ambush us?"

"That's the whiniest, wimpiest crap I've ever heard," Jones yelled, looking at each of them. "You think the Anunnaki are going to drop their weapons, kneel down, and expose their necks for you? If the Russians are giving you a problem, you kick their asses. Do I make myself clear?"

"Sir, yes sir," they shouted, Steve and Tracy more enthusiastic than the rest.

"Now run!" He shooed them with his hands. "We'll patch her up."

"Yes sir," Shane replied, taking off with his squad on his heels.

He knew Tracy and Steve had vengeance on their minds, and he'd be glad to join them. The barrack was going to turn into a very unpleasant place where no one got any sleep. Why couldn't the Russians see they were ultimately all on the same side? The Anunnaki were the enemy. If they messed with his people again, he was going to do his part to beat some sense into them.

They ran around the track, Laura keeping up better this lap. He could tell by the scowl on her face that anger powered her along now.

"We have to start acting like a single unit," Tracy instructed. "Try to run in formation like the others."

No one objected. It seemed most of the competitors had

some military training, perhaps in programs similar to the JROTC Tracy commanded. Shane was certain his and Steve's football experience would pay off, but he knew they also needed Tracy to help them act more disciplined. However, she had a tendency to rub people the wrong way, and he worried his team might fall apart if he gave her too much control.

"We are only as strong as our weakest link," Tracy continued, glancing at Laura. "We have to work together to make ourselves stronger."

They ran in two lines, Shane at the front of one and Laura at the other. She picked up the pace, like she wanted to prove Tracy wasn't talking about her. They did two more laps, Shane reckoned the total was about four miles, and then encountered Captain Jones in front of an open hangar a few buildings past the barracks. He ushered them inside, instructing them to take a seat.

They were the last to enter the building. The other six squads were seated in brown, metal folding chairs, facing an elevated platform with a dry-erase board and a large LCD monitor on it.

"Thank you," Laura exclaimed, finding a bottle of water under her seat. Glancing at the ceiling as if it were a gift from above, she guzzled the entire bottle. Her face was so flush from running, Shane worried she might throw up or pass out.

"You did good," Kelly whispered to her.

Kelly was right. Although they didn't keep up with the others, Shane could see his friends had all the spirit required for success. He'd wager they'd be able to hold their own after a few weeks of exercise. But he still worried they'd never be able to compete with some of the teams. It was undeniable—the Americans were the underdogs here, at least in the running department.

Jules strolled in and sat down at the end of the row of seats, next to Maurice. She crossed her arms and glared at the Russians with such vehemence that he expected she might burn brands onto the backs of their heads. Her knees were healed, no sign of the injuries she'd sustained. She must've paid a visit to the alien-doctor-miracle-worker who'd mended Shane yesterday.

"Great," he whispered. "They can break us all they want, then just patch us up and send us at it again."

Jones strolled around the perimeter of the room and climbed the aluminum stairs onto the stage. All the kids were silent—even the Russians weren't joking around for once. The anticipation of what Jones was about to relay charged the room, though Shane didn't really expect they would get any more enlightened than they'd already become. The world as they knew it was coming to an end, and the kids in this hangar had to save it. The more he thought about what Lily told them yesterday, the hokier the whole thing sounded. Was there any chance a bunch of teenagers could fend off an alien invasion?

Regardless, his people were being fed, sheltered, and trained. And the little kids they worked so hard to protect were safe here. He'd keep his guard up, but for now, he wasn't going to do anything to jeopardize their relatively good fortune.

"This is the first day of your training," Jones growled. It sounded like he was clearing his throat with each word, and

Shane wondered if the alien was in constant pain from the way he spoke. "Points are being tallied, and at the end of each week, we will post the scores in your barracks."

After the morning run, Shane knew his team was at the bottom. His competitive nature made him sick from the thought.

"There has already been some hazing between teams," Jones continued, "and we want you all to know it is unacceptable. However, we don't intend to interfere unless someone is severely injured. So do not come whining to us about your trivial conflicts."

"What?" Kelly whispered angrily.

The tallest blond Russian boy looked over his shoulder and smiled at the Americans, and Shane hoped Kelly was starting to tilt in favor of retaliation.

"When we go into combat simulations, you may end up causing each other injury as well," Jones said. "But it is important to remember we are all on the same side. We can fix your scrapes and bumps, but we cannot bring back the dead. You must control your anger and remember the goal is to all become the best soldiers possible, pushing each other to achieve greatness. When the Anunnaki attack, these childish differences will have to be put aside."

Jones swept the room with a stern look.

"If you're tempted to fight, remember that person sitting next to you, who is your enemy during this training, will be your closest ally during the war. Do I make myself clear?"

"Sir, yes sir!" The synchronized response was so loud that it felt like the building shook.

"Now we will go around the room and allow a representative from each squad to introduce their team and say a little bit about what they can bring to our training, starting with the front row." Jones pointed at the Russians.

The tall girl with blond hair pulled into a tight bun who'd yelled at her teammates on the tarmac stood and spoke in her native tongue. Shane's earbud translated.

"I'm Anfisa Babikov. My squad is from Russia. We were part of the Junior Spetsnaz training program before the adults were killed. We are experienced with the use of multiple types of weapons, tactics, and hand-to-hand combat." She stood at attention and shouted, "Any mission, anytime, anyplace— Spetsnaz!"

"Spetsnaz!" the rest of the Russians shouted in unison.

Shane immediately started worrying about what he would say to try and sound half as impressive. Anfisa sat down, and the short, Korean girl who'd eyed him yesterday on the tarmac stood up next.

"We are from the National Taekwondo Team in Korea," was all she said.

The girl sat down. And one of the kids Shane suspected were the Chinese stood. "We are from The People's Republic of China."

He sat down without saying anything else. His brevity spoke volumes. These were some badass kids who didn't need to brag about their training. He just hoped they had better manners than the Russians did.

While the two groups were a lot quieter, Shane suspected they might be the toughest to beat. He was envious of them—

of the extensive martial arts training he suspected they had. It was something he'd always wanted to do, but his dad never put him in classes when he was younger, and football took over as he grew up.

"We are from Israel," the next kid said. He had olive skin and brown hair, and his shoulders filled out his black T-shirt like he was no stranger to the gym. "We are from Rabin Pre-Military Academy's Advanced Student Early Enrollment Program."

It seemed everyone had an impressive résumé, and he grew more concerned after each team's representative spoke.

"Let me handle this," Tracy whispered to him. "I'll make us sound good."

She grinned, and he nodded, grateful she'd relieved him of the task. He didn't know what he'd say. B-team quarterback at Leeville High didn't sound awe-inspiring after listening to everyone else.

The other three groups were from Brazil, Finland, and Australia. Though they said nothing more than where they came from, he expected there must be something exceptional about them, or they wouldn't be here.

"My name is Tracy Cyrus." She stood tall, and Shane held his breath. "I am the commander of the United States Army Junior Reserve Officer Training Corps at Leeville High School. We were the team who shut down the weapon that killed the adults. Hooah!"

Tracy directed this last shout at the Russians. They were twisted around and looking at her as she spoke. She glared at them and settled into her seat. Several of the other kids in the room cast awed glances at the Americans before facing forward again.

"Dang, girl," Shane whispered. "You did make us sound good."

"Now that the introductions are done," Jones said, speaking from the metal stage, "you guys can go get breakfast. Return here in thirty minutes, and we will begin weapons and armament training."

CHAPTER
ELEVEN

They stood and filed out of the hangar, Shane keeping a loose, albeit tired, eye on the Russians. He wasn't going to let his team fall victim to any more of their cheap shots.

Light blue painted the sky. The sun was not yet visible above the trees, but the birds sang cheerfully of its approach. A pair of ravens flew overhead, and he noticed Laura glance at the sky nervously. She'd probably never be comfortable around the shadowy birds again after how they'd attacked her.

"Feels like we've already had a full day, and it ain't even morning," Maurice grumbled, stifling a yawn.

"I don't know about y'all, but I'm hungry as hell," Steve said, rubbing his belly. "A biscuit or two would put a grin above my chin, that's for sure."

The smell of bacon wafted from the cafeteria, making Shane realize he was starving too. He and Kelly walked at the front of his squad, keeping distance between them and the Russians.

"What's up, mates?" a cheerful, male voice called from

behind.

They stopped and looked back. Smiling Australians in-termingled with them, offering well-mannered introductions.

"Nice to have some other English-speakers here," a broad-shouldered redheaded kid said. "Liam's the name, rugby's my game." He extended his hand to Tracy, his face expressing trepidation that his friendliness might be unwelcome.

"Tracy," she replied warily and shook it.

"You play a bit?" he asked, looking at Shane, and then Steve.

"Yeah," Steve grunted. "Football."

"Like with pads?" One of Liam's friends, a dark-haired Eurasian kid with a wiry build, joined in.

Shane detected a hint of mischief in both Aussies' eyes.

"Yeah," Steve replied. "But we hit harder than y'all do."

"Of course you do," Liam said, smiling and extending his hand to Steve.

They shook, and Shane got the sense his friends would get along well with these witty kids. The Australians were all boys from the same rugby team. Liam introduced the rest of them, saying what each of their positions were. Although they were a bit arrogant about the superiority of their sport, they seemed a heck of a lot nicer than some of the other teams.

"Those Russians are a nasty bunch," Liam said, falling in stride next to Shane. "I figure if we join forces, they won't be so likely to muck with us. If you Yanks are game."

"Yanks?" Shane eyed him, lowering his brow and making an effort to look offended.

"Sorry, mate. That's what we call you where I'm from," he replied, smiling his crooked-toothed smile. "Not a derogatory name at all. We love you blokes, we do."

"Oh," Shane replied coldly. "Some people from the South may not take to the label, that's all."

"That's right," Liam replied nervously, like he was worried he'd just dropped a major insult. "I remember from history class. Yankee was the name for the people from the North during your Civil War."

"Exactly," Shane replied. He scowled for a second longer, but he couldn't keep from cracking up.

Breaking into relieved laughter, Liam caught on that Shane was messing with him.

"I think joining ranks would be an awesome idea," Shane added. They could help each other, though he wouldn't forget they'd still be in competition. He guessed Liam was thinking the same thing.

"Then it's done. Americans and Australians. What should we call ourselves? Team AA?"

Steve and Kelly chuckled.

"I reckon we're too young to be drunks," Steve said. He'd stepped to the other side of Liam. "But if stuff gets much crazier, I'm thinking I might give it a try."

Shane didn't laugh. It made him think of his dad and the last time he saw him alive. He'd been drunk and angry, driving home from Granny's funeral. All he could think of was the argument they had, and how he'd almost punched his dad. He felt ashamed and cheated. Why couldn't his last memory of his dad be a good one? If only they could've had one more day under the hood of a car, working in the shade of the garage. Those were the memories he cherished. He wished he could forget the bad times, which, unfortunately, outnumbered the good ever since his mom died of cancer.

Kelly must've sensed his sudden gloom. She covertly grabbed his hand and squeezed just before they entered the cafeteria. Inside, they got in line and were served biscuits and gravy, scrambled eggs, sausage, bacon, and fruit by many of the junior high and younger high school kids from Leeville. There was also rice, vegetables, and several dishes he didn't recognize—food to satisfy all the international teams. Some of the girls who were attacked in the gym were behind the counter. Shane smiled at them, and they smiled back this time. It warmed his heart to see them recovering—the work had to be doing them good.

Shane watched his friends and the Aussies' spirits lift as they heaped food on their plates. He was the last one to get a tray, wondering how this supposedly small group of rebel aliens had the logistics to supply such a spread.

"I'm going to eat with Nat," Kelly whispered, looking across the cafeteria to the table where the young kids were sitting.

"Okay," he replied. "But steer clear of the other teams."

"Don't worry." She winked at him. "I can handle myself."

He knew she could, but he kept an eye on her until she made it to the kids' tables. And when he sat down with the rest of Team AA, he took a stool on the side that allowed him to face in her direction so he could make sure nothing stupid happened.

"We should say grace," Maurice announced, stopping half the kids mid-bite. He gave them all a firm look. "We need God on our side, now more than ever."

Shane wasn't opposed to praying. His dad wasn't openly religious and never went to church, but Granny always said grace before eating. So had his mother before she died. The Aussies looked at one another, then at the Americans, a mild expression of discomfort and surprise on their faces.

"Sorry," Laura replied sincerely. "But I'm not sure I'm okay with that."

Maurice studied her for a moment, his face blank like he was processing. Without any expression of disappointment, he grinned and said, "Okay."

He lowered his head and interlaced his fingers, his lips moving silently as he said his prayer.

Whether she was accustomed to saying grace or was just trying to make sure Maurice didn't feel alone, Jules also began to pray. Knowing the boy's strength came from his spirituality, Shane wanted to support him. However, when he lowered his head, anger flashed in him. He hadn't given God much thought since the animals started attacking the adults. Then, he'd worried it may be the beginning of the apocalypse mentioned in the Bible. But the things that had happened, the things he'd seen, didn't inspire faith.

He kept his head down, knowing he needed to be careful and not insult anyone else's beliefs. Whether they bowed their heads or not, he reckoned faith might be the only thing to carry some of them through the hardest moments they'd likely endure. It sure seemed to be Maurice's primary motivation.

When Maurice whispered amen, Shane waited a few seconds more, and then lifted his head. A few of the kids in the Israeli group were looking at his table. One of them nodded at him and gave a little grin. Perhaps they were religious too and respected how some of the kids at his table had said grace. If it earned them more allies, Shane would do it at every meal, regardless of how much it pissed him off.

Everyone fell on their food like they'd just been rescued from a deserted island and hadn't eaten in months. No one spoke a word for the ten minutes it took for their plates to be picked clean.

"She have someone over there?" Jake, the wiry Aussie with black hair asked, nodding in Kelly's direction. He had bright, almond-shaped eyes and a splash of brown freckles across his nose and cheeks.

"Yeah," Shane replied. "A little sister."

"Makes it so much harder." The boy's voice cracked. "I've a little brother back home. Miss him so much. She's lucky to have her family close by."

"Is he being cared for?" It stung to think Shane didn't have any family left.

"Yeah. The aliens promised they'd set up facilities to look after the younger kids."

"That's good," Shane said.

"It is. I wouldn't have left my brother if I didn't think he was safe," he replied, a tremor in his voice.

Lily made it seem like there weren't that many of her kind. There had to be more than just a handful in different countries around the world to be able to raise armies and take care of the young. There must be thousands, if not hundreds of thousands.

Shane finished his meal, never taking his eyes off Kelly. He watched her hug her sister and make her way across the cafeteria to his table.

"You okay?"

"Just barely." She used a finger to scrape away a tear. "She seems happy. Apparently, they've set up a building with lots of toys, and they're starting school today."

"That's good, right?"

"Of course. I just miss her so much. I feel like we should be spending more time together, after what happened." Her voice trailed off.

"Well," Steve said, blinking his eyes like he was suppressing a wave of emotion, "let's kick some Anunnaki butt so you can get back to her." As far as Shane knew, he didn't have anyone left either.

The rest of the table stood, and they headed to the hangar where Jones spoke to them earlier. This time, the Aussies sat in the same row as the Americans. The Russians came in afterwards. Tracy sat at the end of the row. She stuck her foot out just as one of the dark-haired, cackling boys who'd harassed Steve in the bathroom walked by.

She locked ankles with him and jerked her leg back. The boy crashed forward, hitting the Russian girl in front of him. Both landed in a pile on the floor.

"Oops. I'm so sorry. Are you okay?" Tracy asked sarcastically.

The Russian girl snapped at the boy and pushed him off

her. He stood and gave a threatening smile.

"Oh yes, we are fine," he said in English with his thick accent.

"Too bad," Steve said hostilely. "Better luck next time."

The rest of the Russians gathered around the two who'd fallen. They glared at Shane's group, perhaps deciding if they wanted a fight.

"You Yanks having troubles?" Liam asked.

"Oh, I'm sorry." Shane couldn't help joining in the fun. "I'm not sure if y'all have been introduced. Australians, meet the Russians."

"Pleasure, I'm sure," Liam replied.

"To answer your question…" Shane looked at the Russian boy and girl, raising his brow. "I don't know. Are we having troubles?"

"Please say yes," Steve said, crossing his thick arms.

They scowled at the Americans and Aussies for a moment, then continued up two rows and took their seats.

"I didn't think so," Tracy said.

"I thought we weren't going to sink to their level," Kelly, who was sitting on Shane's right, scolded.

"I never said that," Tracy snapped. "We have to show those losers we ain't taking any crap, or they'll never leave us alone."

Shane's gaze fell on the kids from Finland. All but two were blonds, and they had pale skin. They chatted quietly amongst themselves, but he didn't see any of them smile.

"Those guys look tough," Liam said quietly, following Shane's gaze.

"Know anything about them?"

"Not much, but I've heard the Finns are not to be trifled with. You know their little country had to fend off the USSR for a long time."

"That's good," Shane whispered, trying to remember his geography. "Maybe they'll side with us if push comes to shove."

"Quiet," Captain Jones ordered, mounting the stage.

His sweeping scrutiny connected with everyone's eyes, as if ensuring he had their attention before beginning the lecture. The effect was immediate. All forty-nine kids fell silent.

"A critical part of your training will be conducted in simulations. The device in your ear will create the simulations in your brain while your body sits motionless in these chairs."

Shane wondered what else the tiny piece of advanced technology could do. Perhaps blow their heads off if they suddenly weren't compliant.

"Once the neural link is activated, you'll no longer be aware of this reality. Through these simulations, you will get an intimate exposure to Anunnaki technology and to the mission in general."

Shane glanced nervously at Kelly. He wasn't excited about having the earbud take over his senses, but couldn't come up with a reasonable objection.

"The first time can be a bit of a shock," Jones warned. "Close your eyes and relax."

He closed his eyes but held his breath in anticipation. Kelly's hand slipped into his, and he squeezed. A flash of white burst through his brain, accompanied by a buzzing sound, like a bee was stuck in his ear. Shane opened his eyes and blinked at the brightness. The light faded to normal sunlight, and he was standing on a flat field with shortly mown grass, like a golf course with no hills, flags, or holes. There was no end to the perfectly level terrain. It stretched to the horizon, meeting a cloudless, blue sky.

"Holy crap," Steve muttered.

Shane rotated toward his voice and saw the other forty-eight kids standing in a cluster behind him. They had stunned expressions, glancing at each other and at the field in bewilderment. They were dressed in the red armor he'd seen the rebels and the Anunnaki wearing in the video of the battle Lily had shown them just after they arrived at the base. The girls' armor had wider hips and a more feminine curve to the chests and shoulders, but otherwise, they were all identical. Shane felt a gurgle in his stomach, and a metallic taste corrupted his mouth. One of the Finns turned and barfed on the grass.

"Gross," Laura hissed, her face green. She pushed by him to get away from the boy.

"On second thought, maybe they're not so tough," Liam observed, looking a bit pale himself.

"This first time in the simulation can cause some nausea," Jones explained, strolling around the perimeter of the group. "Understand that you are not really getting sick. You're still sitting in the chair in the hangar. This field, the armor you wear, and the vomit in your mouth are all a creation in your mind. Everyone take a deep breath. Relax and don't fight the simulation."

Hoping to stop himself from being the next to hurl,

Shane did as instructed and saw the rest of the kids do the same. Jones had them breathe deep for a minute until everyone's pallor returned to normal.

"Wicked," Jake said, examining the red armor.

It was. Shane imagined this was the future of video games—if there was a future at all.

"This is the extent of the simulation today—it is a chance for you to grow accustomed to the artificial environment. Tomorrow, you will begin training for the mission in here. Meanwhile, we are going to introduce some things you will need to become familiar with to infiltrate the enemy.

"The kids who are under the effect of the slave gene will learn to use their armor and weapons via the neural link to the Anunnaki. We're experimenting with a program that may allow you to upload information in the same way, but it is not safe to use yet, and it may not be ready before the enemy attacks. You have to act like you have a similar proficiency or you'll draw unwanted attention to yourselves. For now, these simulations are the only way we can ensure the required level of preparedness."

Holding a crimson helmet under his arm, he stepped into the center of the group, and everyone backed up to give him space. Jones wore the same armor, though the part covering his chest and back was decorated with a large, eagle-dragon emblem where Shane and the others had a solitary, vertical black stripe running along the ridge of their breastplates from navel to chin.

"The Anunnaki have this one uniform for military use. They wear it for ceremony, for training, and for battle," Jones boomed. "It is lightweight, self-cleaning, and the armor can stop a fifty-caliber round.

"Insignia on the uniform shows their rank, what battles they've fought in, and displays their awards." As he spoke, he pointed at the upper right side of the eagle-dragon, the upper left, and then the bottom. "The uniform demands respect and loyalty from the lower ranks. Not only provided for protection, it's designed to intimidate the enemy, to strike fear in their hearts."

Shane knew the red armor, so glossy it appeared to be painted with fresh blood, would scare the crap out of him if he saw an army of soldiers wearing it coming his way. It was complete, from the helmet that had an angry-looking, V-shaped, tented glass visor, to the matching gloves and boots—no part of the wearer's body was left unprotected. Other than the ridge down the center, the breastplate had a smooth construction. It reminded Shane of medieval jousting armor, designed to deflect the impact of a weapon head-on.

"This emblem is worn by the Anunnaki elite Shock Troops," Jones said, pointing at his chest. "Slave soldiers wear the vertical black line on the front and back of the armor that you see on your chests.

"In Anunnaki culture, anyone, regardless of birth, can rise to the highest rank by being courageous in battle. Less than two percent get to wear this emblem, and they lead the lower ranks and are treated with the utmost respect by everyone."

The symbol and the armor looked rather earthly, not

what Shane would've expected invading aliens to wear. After learning the Anunnaki had genetically engineered humans, enslaving ancient societies, he began to wonder how many things stemmed from the influence of these space-traveling conquistadors. How much of mythology was from human imagination and how much of it was based on actual experience?

CHAPTER TWELVE

"The armor has muscle-assisting technology that will amplify your strength tenfold. Park," he said, looking at the Koreans. "Step forward."

A tall, somber-faced Korean kid approached the alien. Jones instructed him to remove his armored glove and handed him a steel ball.

"Crush this. Squeeze it with your hand until it collapses."

Park took the ball and did as he was told. His face contorted with effort, but he couldn't crush it.

"Now, put the glove back on," Jones said, holding the ball until the black-haired kid did as he was told. "And try again."

Park flexed the fingers of the glove a couple of times, his eyes growing bright with curiosity. He took the ball again and squeezed. There was a cracking sound and a squeak as the metal scraped on itself. The sphere, which apparently had been hollow, was flattened in Park's gloved hand. The boy grinned and held the pancaked piece of metal up for everyone to see.

"You and the other humans will be taken into the Anunnaki ships and given this armor. We will provide you with a Shock Troop emblem to apply to the chest and back once you slip away from the enslaved kids. It will allow you to move about the vessel with a degree of impunity. Once you destroy the reactor, the power supply to the armor will be cut."

Bleeping sounds came from everyone's suits, and Shane suddenly felt the weight of the armor. It wasn't much heavier than his football pads, but it must have had some sort of air-conditioning in it. With the power off, it immediately felt too warm inside.

"As you are experiencing now, the onboard computer, environmental systems, and muscle enhancement will cease to function. Once you cut the power, you'll have the physical advantage, but don't underestimate the Shock Troops. They train for combat in dormant armor. Any questions?"

Captain Jones looked around. Most of the kids seemed excited about the new toys, but it reminded Shane of the dangerous job that lay ahead. No matter how much they trained, it was still just a bunch of kids attacking an empire of advanced aliens. Shane had a thousand questions, too many to settle on just one. But then, they'd only been fed bits and pieces of the strategy to this point. He would try to have faith in the training; there was nothing else to be done at this point.

"Next, we will talk about the three primary weapons Anunnaki carry into battle," Jones continued. The power returned to their suits, and he held the helmet out to his side. It vanished, replaced by a high-tech rifle. "This is the standard-issue assault rifle. All soldiers carry this weapon. As some of you might have guessed by watching the battle films, the weapons use plasma bursts, not the bullets you are accustomed to on this planet. The bursts are the size of a large caliber round and carry enough energy to melt through any metal your militaries use on tanks and armored vehicles."

"Can it go through this body armor?" Liam asked, raising his hand.

"Finally, someone speaks," Jones growled. "Yes. The armor cannot resist a direct hit. A shot from this weapon will sear a hole as big as my fist in you, causing unimaginable pain. It is not a pleasant way to die."

"I gotta get my hands on one of those," Steve whispered, eyes gleaming.

"Yes please," Tracy seconded.

Shane wasn't as enthusiastic. He still didn't like guns, knives, or anything else made for killing. He'd learned to use them in the fight for survival that ensued when the adults were killed off, and it turned out he was a pretty good shot. But he'd never get excited like Steve and Tracy.

"Next, we move on to a smaller weapon, carried only by Shock Troops and higher-ranking officials," Jones said. He held the rifle out like the helmet before. It vanished and was replaced by a pistol. The gun was not much larger than the ones police officers carried, but it had a bigger grip and larger trigger, presumably designed to be easy to use with the added bulk of the armored gloves.

"The elite soldiers carry this weapon at all times. It is used in combat and is used to purge the slave ranks of those who are not functioning properly. If a slave disobeys a command in battle, or shows any sign that they are no longer under telepathic control, the Shock Troops will quickly dispatch them."

"Such nice people," Kelly said under her breath, seeming as enthusiastic about the weapons lecture as Shane was.

"While we will be able to provide you with the emblem of the Shock Troop, you will not be issued this pistol. The Anunnaki will only issue rifles to the enslaved humans. Be forewarned, during your mission, this is one of the things that may give away that you are not real Shock Troops."

"Lastly, we get to what you might call the Swiss Army Knife of the Anunnaki soldier." An I-shaped rod replaced the pistol. It was three inches in diameter and about eight-inches long. "This device emits a controlled plasma beam at any desired length up to six feet."

He activated it, and a white rod of energy rose from the front of the device. Jones held it out away from him, grimacing from its brightness and heat. Shane was at least fifteen feet away, and he felt the warmth coming from the beam.

"This is used as a cutting tool in most cases, for breaking into bunkers where their enemy hides, for cutting through wreckage and such, but some soldiers occasionally use it in a fight," Jones explained, deactivating the tool and holding it out so everyone could inspect it. "The blade can be made thinner and curved. It can also be turned into a whip or affixed to the rifle like a bayonet."

"Looks like a freaking light saber," Laura said, and then blushed like she hadn't meant to speak so loud.

"It kind of is," Jones replied, obviously familiar with the fictional device. "But it's not something you want to be swinging around all day, and no one is going to stop a plasma blast from the rifle or pistol with it. It's more closely related to a sledgehammer than a sword, though it's sometimes used for public execution when they desire to dishonor the victim."

Remembering the video Lily showed them, Shane knew he meant decapitate when he said dishonor.

"To make these weapons and to get those massive spaceships to fly, the Anunnaki must have learned to control gravity and use nuclear fusion," Laura committed excitedly, "or some other near infinite power source."

"Insightful," Jones said, giving her a slight, though impressed, grin. "You are correct. They manipulate gravity as easily as humans do electricity. And they use various sources for power, fusion being one of them."

Laura looked suddenly bashful, like her excitement over the advanced technology had brought out a geeky side she usually tried to hide. Shane recognized that she might be the smartest person on his team—it could be the reason they'd chosen her for the mission.

Jones wiped off his brow, the sweat caused by the heat from the plasma beam. The weapon vanished from his hand, and there was a bright flash of light accompanied by the buzzing in Shane's ear. When the light faded, he was back in the hangar, sitting in the metal chair next to Kelly and his friends. They gave each other wide-eyed looks.

"Okay, up and out onto the tarmac," Jones ordered with a gruff shout.

Everyone rose to their feet simultaneously and followed his order. Once outside, Shane looked around at the base, trying to shake the dreamy feeling caused by shifting from the artificial world back to reality.

Jones told the group to form a large circle on the asphalt. The sun was fully visible now, and Shane guessed it was about ten o'clock in the morning. Although they were much further up into the mountains than Leeville, and he expected it wouldn't get quite as hot, the temperature was on the climb, the black pavement and clothing amplifying the heat.

The groups engaged in excited chatter amongst themselves, many of them seeming jazzed about the armor and weapons they were exposed to in the simulation.

"Silence," Jones shouted, stepping into the middle of the ring. "Now we want to assess your baseline knowledge of hand-to-hand combat. While we hope your attack succeeds without issue, if the mission does not go as planned, you may have to fight your way out."

Shane feared this would be where his team was weakest. Steve could hold his own, and he wasn't too worried about himself, but some of the teams were composed of trained fighters. Seeing Dr. Blain standing just outside of the circle, a small medical bag slung over her shoulder, made him worry some people were going to get hurt. His team might be about to get schooled.

"Our goal here is not to have you hurt each other. We want you to become accustomed to combat, and some of you have more experience. This is more about sharing and learning from each other than proving superiority," Jones cautioned. "This is about facing your fears and overcoming them."

Walking around the ring of kids, he picked an attractive Israeli girl, directing her to the center. Then he came to Shane's group, stopping in front of Tracy.

"You. In," he said.

Tracy's brow rose, and then she shrugged her shoulders and strutted out in front of the girl. She was taller and thicker than the olive-skinned Israeli, but Shane feared the foreigner had some skills that might give her the advantage. Jones probably had some idea about each of their prior training. The question was, would he match them up evenly, or would he set some of them up for slaughter? Either way would be a learning experience. He'd lost a few football games to teams that were far superior. Once the sting of the shellacking faded, his team typically found they'd learned something and came out playing harder, but more intelligently, the next game. These thoughts didn't make it any easier to know he might have to stand by and watch some of his friends get their asses kicked.

"Begin," Jones yelled, standing by to referee.

The girl raised her hands in front of her and twisted her body slightly sideways. Not looking intimidated, Tracy lifted her fists and stepped toward her. She threw a left hook, and the girl blocked it, countering with a punch to Tracy's nose. She stepped back, covering her face. When she pulled her hands away, blood ran over her upper lip. Blinking, she looked at Jones, as if to see if he'd call a foul. When he didn't react, her expression contorted into one of rage. She charged at the Israeli and dove for a tackle. The dark-haired girl sidestepped and kicked her in the stomach, a loud thump resonating from the impact.

Shane cringed, watching Tracy lay on the ground doubled over, her face bloody and her eyes wide and moist as she tried to catch her breath. Jones looked at the Americans, raising a hand to warn them to stay out of it.

"Yes—it is as we expected," a Russian boy taunted. Some of the others laughed.

Jules started toward him, and he caught her arm, pulling her back. She looked at him with wild eyes, and Shane shook his head, and then nodded toward Tracy.

Tracy cast a glare in the Russians' direction. When the girl followed her gaze, she rolled left, wrapped her body around the Israeli's legs, and slammed the girl to the ground. Clearly the stronger of the two, Tracy mounted her and started punching her in the face.

"That's enough," Jones said, dragging her off.

The Israeli pulled herself to her feet, her nose bleeding now as well, and her left eye swollen and red. Brought to quiet tears by the attack, she returned to her group. Tracy looked at the Russians again, a warning in her eyes. They chuckled, though with a bit less confidence than before.

A proud grin crossed Shane's face. His squad had been pushed so hard during the assault on Atlanta that they'd nurtured an animal ferocity the other teams might not be able to match. Once the switch was flipped, they'd be able to hold their own.

Tracy came back and stood between Shane and Jules.

"Good job, killer," he whispered to her.

"Thanks," she said, giving him a bloody grin. "That little girl kicked like a mule."

Dr. Blain came around behind Tracy and tapped her on the shoulder. She used the small device she closed Shane's wound with to treat her nose, then went around and took care of the Israeli.

Next, Jones pitted a Chinese boy against one of the Korean girls. An experienced martial arts fight should have been fascinating to watch, but Shane was nervous about what was to come. He didn't care that he would have to fight, that he might get injured and beaten. He sweated from the hot sun beating down and radiating off the blacktop, but also at the thought of Kelly going into the ring. Imagining her getting hit made his stomach twist into knots, his hands tightening into fists.

The two Asians demonstrated the advantage of years of training. They threw beautiful spinning kicks, stopped lightning fast punches with blocks, and tirelessly evaded injury and defeat for five minutes before Jones called the match.

"These are the people you must learn from," he said, pointing at the two of them as they returned to the sideline. "Their martial arts training is an invaluable resource. The Shock Troops are masters in a form they've modified to be used in conjunction with energized and de-energized armor."

"Now you," he pointed at Steve, "and you." He pointed at the tall, blond Russian boy Steve had pinned against the bathroom wall the night before. "Into the center."

"Happy birthday to me," Steve said, smiling broadly.

The Russian showed as much arrogance, his comrades shouting, "Spetsnaz!" as he stepped forward.

The boy raised his hands in a fighting stance that looked

like he may have as much martial arts training as the Asians. There was a glimmer in his eye that made Shane uncomfortable. It might have been a show of his competitive nature, but it looked too much like the meanness he remembered in Shamus' eyes. He had faith in his big friend, but he worried Steve's cockiness might get him into trouble.

Steve bent his knees slightly and raised his fists, looking like a bareknuckle boxer at a honky-tonk. Not wasting any time with dancing around, the Russian charged. Shane thought he was going to make the mistake of trying to tackle the linebacker, but at the last instant, the Russian jumped sideways and brought both of his feet into the air, landing a double kick that looked right out of a Hollywood action movie into Steve's stomach and chest.

CHAPTER THIRTEEN

The assault caught Steve off guard, but he'd taken big surprise hits on the football field. He'd always been deceptively light on his feet, and a few people had even called him graceful. He managed to step back and absorb most of the energy of the Russian's kick, though he grunted loudly and grimaced with pain. Shane expected anyone else would have ended up on the ground with some broken ribs after getting struck so hard.

Having put his entire weight into the attack, the Russian landed on his side on the hot asphalt and rolled back onto his feet. His team cheered him and mocked Steve. Steve huffed as if to breathe off the assault and moved toward the boy. The Russian darted in and delivered a rapid-fire succession of punches into his stomach before he could launch an attack, finishing with an uppercut into his jaw.

Steve stepped back, rubbing his big chin and grinning. "The kick was more impressive." Although his tone mocked, his smile seemed a little contrived. Shane knew he must be hurting.

The arrogant Russian didn't take to being taunted. He charged Steve again. This time, the linebacker was ready. He lowered his six-foot-two-inch frame and accelerated his two hundred and twenty pounds of muscle at the approaching boy. The Russian hit him at full speed, and there was a loud crunching sound, bones breaking. Steve was moving so fast that he had to leap over his flattened target, plowing into two of his wide-eyed comrades who stood on the sideline.

Shane almost felt sorry for the kid, who rocked back and forth on the asphalt holding his shoulder. The doctor stepped in and eased his hands away from the injury. Sunlight glinted off red and white, the boy's jagged collarbone protruding through his bleeding flesh.

"Help me carry him to medical," the doctor said, and two of the now somber-looking Russian kids came out and picked up their friend.

Steve let out a loud primal growl and thumped his chest once, a silverback gorilla asserting his authority. He walked across the ring to his group, the same wildness in his eyes he'd directed towards Shane when they had tried to kill each other before Tracy shut the weapon down. He didn't ever want to be on the receiving end of the linebacker's wrath again. Everyone in the circle was quiet now, all eyes following the enraged victor of the short-lived match. Shane reckoned between Steve and Tracy, his team was quickly gaining points and respect.

"This will help you learn your strengths and limitations," Jones said, selecting two more kids.

The brutality of the early fights seemed to make the kids approach each other with more caution. Other than one more broken nose and a black eye, the next fights ended with less violence. Jules fought a Korean boy and was able to land only one punch. The Korean kicked her multiple times, though he must've been holding back because she escaped with only minor bruising. Then it was Laura's turn against another of the Israeli girls.

Laura got hit pretty hard a few times, and tears started flowing down her face, though she kept it together and didn't cry out. Shane wanted to beg for the fight to be stopped, hating to see her get beat up. But then Laura managed to grab hold of the girl's ponytail and got a knee up into her face. Shane was shocked—Laura had a mean streak. She came back to stand next to Steve, still crying silently but arguably the victor, as the Israeli girl was knocked out cold.

"You," Jones said, pointing at Kelly. "And you." He selected another of the Russian boys, the dark-haired cackler Tracy had tripped earlier.

Acid flooding his stomach, Shane involuntarily stepped forward to object. Kelly grabbed his arm.

"I got this," she whispered, her eyes narrowing as she studied her opponent. Shane had seen the look when she killed in the gym, and when she fought in Atlanta. He knew she was no wimp, but it didn't make it any easier to see her go against the much larger Russian boy who had to be craving revenge.

She walked to the center of the ring, approaching her opponent so casually it didn't look like she was even going to try to fight. The boy smiled wickedly and raised a finger.

"Shall I beat this little girl with one finger, or two?"

Except for Anfisa, who glared at him with her arms crossed over her chest, his comrades laughed. The tall Russian girl seemed disappointed with the performance of her team, and she seemed to be having trouble keeping them in control.

Kelly smiled amiably at him, her hands still at her sides. With no sign she was going to attack, her foot came up between his legs, landing in his groin with a sickening thud. The boy's eyes went wide, and he crumpled.

"Maybe try three fingers next time," she suggested, pushing his head so he toppled to the ground. Then she turned around and walked calmly back to Shane. "And you thought all those cheerleading kicks were just for show?"

"I'll never doubt you again," he said, chuckling.

"Alright," Jones shouted. "Give me four more laps around the tarmac."

Groans came from half the sweating kids. Shane was too tired to be disappointed that he didn't get to fight, though he wouldn't have minded pummeling one of the Russians. The vengeance Steve and Kelly had taken was awesome, but he wasn't sure it was enough to make them leave his team alone. He started around the track, head tilted down to avoid some of the sun's blistering heat. The rest of the kids followed. This time, there was no racing. Everyone stayed behind Shane. Having grown up with sultry Georgia summers, his people might have the advantage when it came to dealing with the heat.

Shane found a groove, cruising along just a little faster than a jog. He glanced over his shoulder at the turn and saw

Laura was at the back of the pack with Maurice, looking slower with each step. He couldn't drag them around on every run, and he wasn't worried about them being attacked in broad daylight, so he let them be.

Kelly, Jules, Steve, and Tracy kept up with Shane, the exercise they did in their respective sports in school giving them an advantage. He turned the next corner and looked back to see the Finns and the Russians looking like they were suffering the most. Their pale faces were flush, and they huffed the hot, humid air vigorously. They probably never experienced such weather where they came from. The other nationalities were doing as well as his team.

By the end of the fourth lap, Shane was hurting. Jones directed them around to the cafeteria, but made Laura and Maurice keep going, as they were only on their third lap. The rest crowded a table with drink dispensers on it, taking turns filling cups with some generic, powdering-tasting sports drink, and sucking it down until they recovered enough to grab lunch.

In the cool air of the cafeteria, Kelly plopped down next to Shane and leaned her head on his shoulder.

"They're gonna kill us." She sighed.

"Or make us much stronger," Tracy observed.

Sweat plastered everyone's hair to their heads, and their black T-shirts and shorts had lines of white where the water evaporated, leaving only the salts of their perspiration.

"What do you suppose they'll make us do after lunch?" Jules asked, supporting her freckled cheek with her fist as she munched absently on her sandwich.

"Don't know," Maurice replied, sitting down with his tray, "but I hope it involves lying horizontally."

Too tired for conversation, they ate in silence, staring absently across the table at each other's wearied expressions. Laura sat down last and, after eating a quarter of her sandwich, she crossed her arms on the table and laid her head on them.

"Everyone up and out," Captain Jones shouted from the door.

Grumbles passed through the room. They'd been eating for only ten minutes, and no one had a chance to finish their lunch. Shane was glad he'd taken the horse pills last night. Although he was exhausted, he felt better than he would expect after such a rough morning. He reckoned they were filled with some high-tech ingredients that would keep everyone going much longer than they could on regular food alone.

"I guess we're about to find out what's next," Liam groaned.

Passing out of the air-conditioning of the cafeteria onto the scorching blacktop of the tarmac, Shane gasped at the harsh climate change. Kelly must've experienced it too. She grabbed his arm and sighed weakly.

Jones led them around the cafeteria, into the shady egress between it and the next building.

"Looks like we're gonna play in the woods," Tracy observed.

"Sounds a heck of a lot better than being on the pavement," Shane replied.

"We'll see if you feel that way in an hour," Jones, who was just ahead of Shane, threatened over his shoulder.

He glanced up into the forest with trepidation. He was nervous once again about encountering the animals. Although he knew the fear was irrational, he couldn't stop thinking about their murderous rampage.

Behind the buildings, the forest grew tall and thick, its shade inviting. A younger version of Jones, minus the muscles and facial scar, stood next to a cart.

"Line up to receive a weapon," Jones ordered.

"A weapon?" Kelly said under her breath.

"That's what I'm talk'n about," Steve added, eagerly stepping to the cart.

The man handed out paintball guns to everyone, and a chatter of excitement arose from the exhausted kids, the prospect of a war game re-energizing them. Jones climbed up the hill a few yards so he stood above them.

"This exercise is simple. There is a flag at the top of this mountain," Jones explained, pointing behind him. "The person who retrieves it without getting shot, and brings it back down to me, wins ten points for their team. If you are shot, you are out of the game and must come back down immediately. Do not cheat, people. We have cameras placed throughout these woods, and we are watching. Understood?"

"Sir, yes sir!"

"Don't we get any body armor or at least goggles?" one of the Finns asked.

"No, of course not," Jones answered abruptly. "So try not to get shot in the face."

He pointed at a small Israeli flag sticking out of the ground. "This is the starting point for the Israeli team here in front of me. Each team has their own starting point. Teams three, four and five are that way," he pointed left, "and the rest of you are on my right. You have three minutes to get in front of your flag. When you hear this," Jones honked a handheld aerosol foghorn, "you may begin. Go to your starting places."

Shane and his group headed west at a brisk pace along the narrow path behind the buildings. The other two nationalities whose flags were in the same direction followed them, the gravel crunching loudly under everyone's feet.

"You ever been hit by one of these?" Steve waved his gun. "No."

"Well, it hurts like the dickens," he replied. "And it leaves a nasty welt."

"Then we'd best not get hit," Tracy advised bluntly.

They found the little American flag sticking out of the leaf litter and watched the Koreans and Fins pass, walking toward their own flags.

"What's our strategy?" Tracy asked in a hushed voice, her eyes on Shane.

"I reckon we should charge straight up and try to get to the flag as fast as we can," he replied.

"Three of us should go in the middle, and the rest should flank them," Maurice suggested. "That way, the people on the sides can act as a defense and give us the best chance of getting at least one person up and down without getting shot."

"Sounds good," Shane said. "Who's in the middle?"

"You, Tracy, and Steve," Maurice replied decisively. "You're the fittest of us, and if we get shot, you have the best chance of fighting your way back down without us."

A flash of insult crossed Jules' face, perhaps because she was the best runner on the team. She kept quiet, and her expression quickly cleared, like she was committed to doing whatever Maurice recommended. Shane was flattered the stout boy had so much faith in him. It reminded him of the trip to the capitol, when he had stepped ahead of Shane to protect him so he could get downtown to the limbic manipulator.

"I don't think I can make it up there," Laura said. She was still flushed red from the run, and her eyes were drooping with exhaustion.

Tracy glared at her, and Shane feared she was about to say something mean.

"Do your best," Kelly replied kindly before Tracy had a chance. "I bet you can if you try."

"I'm not so sure I can get up there either. If you can't make it," Maurice said, putting a hand on her shoulder, "stop wherever you get to and wait for us to come back down. Hide, and be ready to ambush anyone who might be on our tails."

"Got it," Laura replied. A measure of confidence returned to her expression.

"Good thinking, Maurice," Shane said, impressed. "Same goes for everyone else."

"And we need to conserve our rounds," Steve pointed out. "These hoppers hold about two hundred paintballs, and they only look half full."

"So we've got a hundred rounds each," Shane said. "Seems like plenty."

"Obviously, you've never played paintball," Tracy replied.

"The rounds go fast. Don't shoot until you have an easy target."

"If we head straight up, I don't think we'll encounter the other teams 'til we're near the top," Kelly pointed out.

"Right," Jules chimed in. "Let's run with everything we got. Coming back down will be easy."

"If anyone gets shot, someone pick up their gun so we have extra rounds."

The handheld air horn sounded, its mournful note spurring Shane's pulse to a gallop.

"*Go, go, go!*" he shouted, and he and his friends tore through the underbrush into the forest.

CHAPTER FOURTEEN

The mountain was steeper than it looked from below. Shane and his team slipped in the leaf litter and grabbed tree branches to keep from falling. They settled into a clip that was as fast as they could go while still maintaining their formation. Two minutes into the woods, Laura stopped. It would have bothered Shane to see her give up so easily, but then, having her there, rested and ready to shoot anyone following them back down, was an appealing idea.

"Just like running the bleachers at practice," Steve said. He was huffing rhythmically behind Shane. Tracy took up the rear of their center column.

"Yeah, but a whole heck of a lot slicker," Shane gasped.

After four minutes of climbing, Shane's quads were on fire. The hill got even steeper, and he dug the toes of his running shoes into the soft ground for traction. Their crashing footsteps and labored breathing made it impossible to hear if any of the other teams approached, but he expected they'd all head straight up and collide near the top. Steve had the sharpest eyes in the forest, having been a hunter all of his life. He hoped the linebacker would see the other teams before they saw them.

"How much further can it possibly be?" Maurice groaned. He was climbing on the right side, leaning too much and sweating profusely.

"Can't be too far," Jules encouraged, her long legs and wiry runner's body better suited for the task. "Keep pushing."

Orange splattered a tree one foot ahead of Shane, sending a jolt of adrenaline into his blood.

"On your left," Steve shouted.

The Russians ran along the side of the mountain, moving faster than his group because they weren't heading straight up.

"They're coming right at us!" Kelly dropped to her knee, aiming her gun.

"Keep going," Tracy yelled.

Kelly's head snapped back, paint streaking her blonde hair. She screamed and held her face in her hands. Shane pointed his gun in the direction of the approaching Russians and fired. They were hopscotching between trees, hiding before they tried to take a shot. They clearly had more experience in this sort of game than his people did.

"Hurts like hell, but she'll be okay," Steve promised, coming alongside Shane such that he shielded him from the Russians. "We can make it if we don't stop."

He knew his friend was right, but it didn't extinguish his urge to tend to Kelly. Knowing she'd be upset if he stopped, he leaned forward into the mountain and pumped his legs as hard as he could. A splat came from his left, and Steve cursed.

"I've been hit."

He tossed Shane his gun and dropped off.

A few more yards up the hill, he heard Steve shouting, "You already got me, you bastards," followed by wicked laughter from the Russians.

"I'm still behind you," Tracy said. "Keep going!"

Having lost Laura and Kelly on the left side, Shane ordered Maurice to cross over and provide protection. Amazingly enough, the preacher's son was still with them.

"There are four of us left—we got this," he said, trying to motivate his dwindling team.

"I gotta stop here," Maurice huffed. "I'll keep 'em off you." He turned around and sat on the mountain, taking aim downhill.

A few more yards and Shane saw the sunlight showing through the trees above them.

"We made it," he announced excitedly.

"Here come the others," Jules warned.

Shane looked right and could see shadows moving between the trees.

"The flag!" Tracy shouted.

Up ahead, a red flag on a wooden dowel stuck out of the leaf litter. Shane's group had gotten lucky. Charging straight up, they had the shortest distance to the top. The other teams were climbing at an angle to get to the same point. He snatched the flag out of the ground and shoved it into the elastic band of his shorts. Paintballs exploded on the trees around them, and the frustrated shouts of the other kids echoed through the forest.

"Back down, fast," he yelled.

They spun and raced down the mountain. Shane basically let his body fall, throwing his feet in front of himself to keep from landing on his face. He pointed his gun ahead and Steve's to the side where the Russians had come from, randomly firing shots in hopes he'd get lucky or at least keep the other teams at bay.

"Ouch!" Jules shouted. "I'm hit. Keep going."

"I'll cover you," Tracy said, taking Jules' gun. "Let me in front."

Shane slowed just enough for her to pass. It didn't take long for them to encounter the Russians again. He saw them looking up the hill. They shouted at each other and dropped to their knees, firing their weapons at Tracy and Shane.

Their strategy became apparent. They were waiting, rested and ready to attack whoever retrieved the flag and then pick up the fumble. Smart, even if it did stink of cheating.

Although he could easily run faster than she could down the hill, he tried to stay behind Tracy the best he could, firing over and around her. She had two guns pointed straight ahead, spraying out the rounds. Paintballs found one of the girls and the two dark-haired boys, one of which had already been shot and shouldn't have been fighting. Shane recognized the cheater as the boy Kelly had kicked in the balls, worried he might try to take revenge in the woods. They took four vaulting strides and were almost on top of the Russians when Tracy got shot in the face. She lost her balance and slid down the mountain on her belly.

Shane leapt into the air, expecting to land on top of her. His foot touching down between her outstretched arm and her skull, he cleared Tracy's sprawled body and accelerated.

Fifteen feet below, Anfisa, the stoic leader of the Russian squad, was squatting on her knee, her gun leveled at Shane. He was moving too fast, fast enough to break something if he hit a tree. He pulled his triggers, aiming an impossibility. Despite bouncing wildly down the slope, Shane saw her calm, glacial blue eyes focus on him and a triumphant smile rise on her sunburned face. He squinted, bracing for the stinging wallop of a paintball.

Maurice exploded from under the branches of a fallen tree just above her. Anfisa shifted her aim and rounds from her gun splattered his chest and face, but the shouting boy was airborne, and nothing could stop him from hitting her.

"Woo-hoo!" Shane yelled. He leapt into the air, clearing his friend and the tackled Russian.

"Get him!" Anfisa shouted angrily from under Maurice.

Even over his heavy breathing and the sound of his own feet crashing through the leaves, Shane heard a person, or persons, running down the mountain behind him. The Russians had conserved their energy, waiting for his descent. He sensed they were on his heels and kicked even harder, expecting to trip and get a face-full of tree trunk. Paintballs splatted on trees to the left and right, and the shouts grew louder.

Surprise and relief swept away his woes. Laura hid behind a tree ahead, her gun aimed uphill and her hopper still full. He smiled at the thought that the two least athletic people on his team were turning out to be the MVPs in this game.

His pursuers would never know what hit them. She grinned as he passed, and then he heard her targets cursing angrily.

Not certain he was safe but energized by the nearness of victory, Shane ran even faster. The slope diminished near the base, and there was less risk of wiping out. He could see the undergrowth at the edge of the forest, could see the gravel roof of the cafeteria building—and then someone smashed into his back.

He tumbled forward, hammering a root with his knee. The inertia sent him and his assailant head over heels into the blackberry bushes. Thorns sliced his bare arms and legs, then his head hit something hard. Hot pain flashed through his skull. He blinked his eyes, struggling to maintain consciousness. The tall, blond Russian boy scrambled through the briars and jumped on Shane's chest. He punched Shane in the face with his left and then right fist, shouting.

"Give me the damn flag!"

Reaching up and wrapping his arms around the boy's torso, Shane pulled him down. Then he rolled to the right, rose up, and dropped an elbow as hard as he could into his nose. The boy yelped in pain. Shane broke free of his grasp and launched out of the bushes, leaping as high as he could in the air to get through them.

The drop on the other side was further than he expected, and when he landed, he tumbled forward, his head smashing on the concrete foundation of the cafeteria. Shane groaned and gritted his teeth. His mouth filled with blood.

Jones was above him, looking down. His lips moved, but

Shane couldn't hear what he was saying. Tracy's sweaty face appeared. Then Steve, Maurice, Jules, and Laura showed up. They leaned over him, huffing for air and splattered with neon paint, and they smiled wildly.

Shane couldn't stop the world spinning. He blinked, his vision going in and out of focus. Then Kelly appeared. Her forehead had a red welt growing on it, and orange splattered her hair. She was beautiful, even covered in sweat, paint, and dirt. Her sapphire eyes sparkled with joy, something he hadn't seen much since her family died.

Her voice cut through the ringing in his ears, bringing him out of his daze.

"We did it," she shouted. "You did it, Shane!"

They helped him to his feet, and she embraced him. His head hurt, and his legs didn't want to stay under him, but his team had won. It was a sweeter victory than he'd ever earned on the gridiron. He glanced around at the disappointed faces of the foreigners, amazed his team had beaten them all. Kelly grabbed his head and pulled him down to her, pressing her lips against his. His busted mouth stung when she kissed him, but he didn't pull away.

"Do you have the flag?" Jones asked sternly, interrupting their revelry.

The rest of the teens came out of the forest and gathered around, some looking angry and others defeated. Only the Australians, all of whom had paint splotches, likely victims of the Russians' seek-and-destroy strategy, seemed relatively happy about the Americans' victory.

"Do you have the flag?" Jones repeated.

Shane looked down. His black shirt had a viscous wetness near the waistline, different from the sweat saturating the rest of it. Fear that he'd lost the flag in the scuffle with the Russian overcame him. When he lifted his shirt, pain tore across his abdomen.

"Oh, Shane," Kelly gasped.

Cringing, he lifted his shirt higher, and the red part of the flag flipped out. The wooden dowel attached to it was broken, the halves piercing deep into the flesh of his belly.

Seeing the puncture wound made the pain tenfold worse. Shane's head seemed to swell, his vision blurring and the ringing returning to his ears.

"You okay, Shane?" Steve asked, his big hand clamping around Shane's arm.

"I'm... " He collapsed forward, Kelly catching him.

"Bring him to medical," Shane heard Dr. Blain say.

Steve and Maurice slipped under Shane's arms and helped him limp along behind the doctor. She'd just treated him yesterday, and now he already needed her services again. A lot of the kids had seen her today. Shane figured this wouldn't be his last visit.

They stepped onto the tarmac, and the intense heat radiating off the asphalt made Shane nauseous. He gritted his teeth to keep the vomit down.

The air-conditioning in the infirmary hit him like healing magic. He sighed, then sucked in a deep breath of the refreshing coolness and heard Steve and Maurice do the same. Dr. Blain had them take him into the exam room and lay him on the padded table.

"There's a little fridge in the waiting room. Go get yourselves a drink from it, and I'll patch him up," she said cheerfully to his friends.

Steve and Maurice's eyes widened at her offer, and they hustled out of the room.

"Okay, let's see the damage," she said, her tone soft and nurturing.

She cut his shirt off, and he winced when the bloody cloth tugged on the dowel.

"Nice one," she said with genuine admiration.

"I think you enjoy your job a bit too much," he grumbled.

"Perhaps." Chuckling, she moved her little medical device over the wound and then latched onto the piece of wood. "Take a deep breath."

He started to, but then she jerked the dowel out. Shane moaned in agony.

"All done. The rest is easy," she promised, smiling compassionately.

He closed his eyes. His abdomen warmed under her device. After she was done with the wound from the flag, she treated his concussion and the other injuries to his face and head. Moments later, he was mended, but he was still busted from all the exercise.

"I want you to drink this and sit here for a little bit before you try to get up." She handed him a bottle of water.

"I can't argue with that." Shane was parched, and in no hurry to return to the sultry tarmac.

He drank gulps of the water and laid back. Dr. Blain started typing notes on her futuristic computer.

"How many of you are there on Earth?" Shane asked, wondering at how the rebels and this base seemed pretty well prepared for their training, though there was no need for it until a few days ago.

"Not enough." She didn't look up from her work.

He suspected he'd never get a direct answer to that question.

"Why does Captain Jones have a scar on his face?"

Dr. Blain's ever-present smile faded.

"It reminds him of something. But as far as I know, he's never told anyone what," she replied sadly. "He was on the ship with Lily."

Shane's brow rose, the revelation surprising him, though it did make sense.

"They're like parents to us," she added distantly. Then she focused on him, and her expression grew clouded with guilt. "I'm so sorry. I didn't mean to sound insensitive."

"It's alright," Shane replied, glancing down at his hands. "I've had a while to get used to losing my mom, so it's only half as bad for me as some of the kids."

Dr. Blain put her hand on his knee, dipping her head to capture his gaze.

"I know your training is hard, and Captain Jones can be a—well, let's just say—a lot to take in. If you ever need anyone to talk to, I'm here." Her face exuded kindness and concern.

"Thanks," he replied.

She was so human.

Or humans were so Anunnaki…

He suddenly couldn't wait to get out of the room.

CHAPTER FIFTEEN

'"The governments failed you kids," she lamented. He sat upright on the exam table, searching for an opportunity to leave without seeming rude. "Society failed you, Shane."

Doctor Blain paused, her expression growing firm.

"We won't fail you," she said with conviction. "When this is all over, the Earth will be a better place."

It sounded too much like she was saying *your parents failed you*. He was uncomfortable with her sudden familiarity and insulted at the same time. She gazed distantly in his direction a moment longer, then she focused on him again, and her smile returned.

"How are you feeling? Better?"

"Yes—much," he said, slipping into the fresh shirt sitting at the foot of the table.

He stood and moved toward the door.

"Good. Drink plenty of fluids, and you'll do fine."

"Thanks." He grinned, walked into the waiting room, and then out of the building with Steve and Maurice on his heels.

"That was weird," he whispered once they were outside.

"What?" Steve asked, glaring at the late afternoon sun like he was sick of seeing it for the day.

"I had a little chat with the doctor, and they seem to have high hopes for making the world a better place after we defeat the Anunnaki."

"What do you mean?" Maurice asked.

"I don't know, but it sounded like they intend to fill in for the adults. To take control."

Maurice tugged his chin. "Well, better them than us," he said. "I wouldn't want the responsibility of trying to take care of the billion kids left on the planet."

"Maybe the world will be a better place," Steve mused. "I mean, starting over without all the greed and corruption."

Shane wasn't sure. And as far as he was concerned, Earth belonged to humans, not these aliens. If humans were corrupt, who was to say they didn't inherit the trait from the Anunnaki? Rebels or not, they might be much worse. He didn't mind that they were here and needed a home, and he was grateful for their help. But, he wasn't gung-ho about them taking charge.

Everyone else had already had dinner, so the three friends rushed to the cafeteria and ate just before the food was put away. Their bellies full, they found the rest of the teens gathered outside. The sun was starting to set, and though the shadows grew long, it still cast plenty of light across the base.

"Join us," Captain Jones shouted from the middle of the tarmac.

"I ain't running no more laps today," Steve grumbled,

heading toward the circle of kids.

"Hang in there, big guy." Shane slapped his back. He wasn't keen on any more exercise either, especially since he'd just stuffed his gut.

"It's been a long day," Jones growled as they joined the others. "But I want to take a little more of your precious time and have some of the martial artists in the group share their knowledge."

Jones looked around, his sweeping gaze connecting with everyone's eyes.

"Our Chinese friends have extensive martial arts training," Jones continued. "Today, they'll share."

The seven Asians stepped forward and bowed to Jones. Then they politely organized the group into rows, their Mandarin speech translated by Shane's earbud.

He expected to learn some hardcore kung fu. Despite being totally exhausted, he was excited by the prospect. Instead, a Chinese boy named Ling led them through a meditative exercise, teaching them to breathe from the stomach, filling the lowest part of their lungs first. The technique was rejuvenating, though he would have rather learned a tornado kick or something cooler.

"Breathe like this when you are tired and need energy. Breathe like this when you are scared and need courage. Learn to breathe like this all the time and you will be master of your mind and body," Ling said, sounding much older and wiser than he looked. He bowed at the group and bowed at Jones, showing the lesson was complete.

"You are dismissed," Jones announced. "We start again

tomorrow at zero four hundred hours."

"I don't think falling asleep will be a problem for anyone," Jules grumbled. Her shoulders rolled forward, and she seemed to shrink.

The seven groups of seven kids made their way back to the barracks, most emulating Jules' exhausted posture. In murmured discussion and without dispute, everyone agreed to let the girls use the communal bathroom first. Along with about half of the other boys, Shane grabbed a set of headphones and plopped down in a chair to study the Anunnaki films.

The rebel spy in the loop wore a video camera. The TV showed what he saw as he walked through a curved corridor with smooth walls painted flat gray. He passed a round porthole and glanced out. A few stars were visible in the distance, and a tan planet the size of a quarter hung in the infinite nothingness.

The rebel continued up the passageway and encountered three Anunnaki Shock Troops. They stopped and pressed against the curved wall to get out of the way, raising their right fists over their hearts in salute. Jones had said the Shock Troops, with the eagle-dragon symbol on their crimson breastplates, held the highest ranks. The soldier behind the camera must've been some kind of commander or general to garner such respect.

Lily had told them the rebel they saw executed in the battle that brought her to Earth made it fairly high in the Anunnaki ranks. He wondered if this was that poor schlup, destined to lose his head.

The spy paused at a hatch and tapped his fingers across a screen bearing strange symbols. The door sprang open, and he walked down a narrower tunnel with no portholes in it. He glanced over his shoulder to see the door close behind him. At the end of the dimly lit passage, which Shane presumed led toward the center of the ship, he came to another hatch. This one had a bright yellow symbol on it, three spheres connected by the corners of a triangle. The color and design conveyed "warning," and he bet the foreign writing below the symbol did the same. The spy entered a passcode, and the four-foot-thick hatch slid into an even thicker wall.

He stepped into a cavernous, cylindrical room. A massive column of bright white light extended from the bottom, which was a hundred feet below the metal grates he stood on, up to the arched ceiling as high overhead.

"This is the primary reactor for an Anunnaki ship," a female voice said. It sounded dubbed in the film after it was made. "Only engineers are typically allowed in this chamber."

"How can I help you, sir?" an Anunnaki in a white jumpsuit asked. There was reverence in his voice, and he saluted the same way the Shock Troops did in the outer passageway. But it was also clear that this was his area, and he wasn't going to have anyone loitering about who didn't belong. He had a bald head, looking very different from Lily, Jones, and all of their clones. Shane wondered if it was the fashion for the engineers or if they were specifically cloned for this job.

"We need more soldiers," the voice behind the camera growled. "Your department is being cut by ten percent."

"What?" The engineer leaned closer, his eyes widening.

"We were cut by ten percent last quarter. My people are already taking double watches to keep up with the added workload." His tone was nervous, like he feared he might be crossing the line.

"Do you question the orders of the Fleet Admiral and the Prime General?" The spy's voice grew deeper and louder, seeming to take advantage of the engineer's weakness.

"Of course not, sir," the engineer responded. "But we need to stop losing staff, or we won't have enough people to keep the reactor functional."

"Worry not," the spy replied dismissively. "We are approaching a new system. There are two planets whose populations are mature enough to harvest. We'll get the reinforcements we need, and then you can have your people back."

"The ones who survive," the engineer grumbled.

"Don't be absurd," he scolded. "Your people will be used to support the command and logistics teams—they are not fit for combat."

The engineer seemed insulted for an instant. "The enemy gets stronger each time we encounter them," he retaliated.

"They will be stopped," the spy snapped. "Have your volunteers report to the armory at first watch."

The engineer dared a cold glance at the spy, but he brought his fist up over his chest at the same time, his firm salute an affirmation of his obedience.

After a sweeping gaze at the reactor chamber, the spy returned to the outer part of the ship via the narrow passageway. The screen changed to a debriefing of what just played. Snapshots of the reactor and control panel were shown and different ways to destroy the reactor discussed.

The lecture complete, Shane took the headphones off. Clearly, the point of the video was for him to gain an understanding of how to destroy an Anunnaki ship, but the interaction between the spy and the engineer intrigued him almost as much. He wondered about the enemy they spoke of. It must be one or more species like the humans, who were resisting Anunnaki rule, but who also had the technology to fight back with some degree of success.

"The girls are all done." Kelly's soft voice brought him out of his reflection.

"Oh, great." He smiled at her. "Thanks."

Shane collected his towel and bag of issued toiletries, heading to the bathroom. His legs didn't want to move; he was so beat from the day. How many hours before it all started again? He glanced up at the high windows and could see it was dark. If he hurried, he might get six or seven hours of sleep before Captain Jones came in, yelling at them to get on the line.

When he walked by the Koreans' quad, they stopped talking and watched him pass. The same happened at the Finnish and Chinese quads.

"You guys won the day, mate," Liam said, holding the bathroom door open for him. "The Americans are now the ones to beat."

"I'm not sure that's such a great thing since the prize is most likely a suicide mission," Shane mumbled.

"Don't worry, mate," Liam replied with a weary version of his earlier humor. "We'll take the burden from you tomorrow."

Returning his smile, he entered the bathroom. It was filled with steam, the five showers occupied. Shane brushed his teeth, his mind adrift with what he'd done today. It felt like a week had passed since they awoke to push-ups. A shower opened. He stuffed his toothbrush in his bag and rushed to take it before anyone else could.

"Hey look," the tall, blond Russian said as Shane stepped out of the shower. As usual, his two goons shadowed him. Shane had learned his name was Petrov earlier in the day when Anfisa yelled it. "It's the lucky American."

"Yeah." Shane chuckled, throwing his towel over his shoulder and quickly slipping on fresh underwear and shorts. Steve might be cool with fighting these assholes naked, but Shane wasn't. "Keep telling yourself luck had everything to do with it," he said, straightening up and glaring at them.

"Oh, you don't think so?" Petrov made a condescending expression. "Well, we will see. The luck of beginners, I assure you."

"Because you guys did so well when we fought today too," Shane replied, regretting he hadn't kept his mouth shut. Underneath his overconfident, grinning, tough-guy act, Petrov looked pissed. And he was too darn tired to fight right now.

"Be careful, lucky American. We don't want our hero to slip and bump his face like his friend. Eh?"

The three boys broke into their hyena cackling. Shane stared at them until they entered shower stalls. He encountered Maurice and Steve as he headed out of the bathroom.

"Watch your backs," Shane warned, pointing at the showers. "Numbnuts and his losers are in here."

"Maybe I should get an icepack for the little one's giggle-berries," Maurice said with feigned sincerity. "Though I think Kelly kicked him so hard that they may be in the back of his throat."

They laughed, and Shane headed to the quad. He was dog-tired, but not looking forward to sleeping in a room with forty-eight other people.

He rolled into his rack and stared at the bottom of Steve's bunk above him until it grew blurry.

"Everybody, on the line!" Jones' voice jarred him awake.

The lights were on, blinding him. Had he just fallen asleep? Or was it morning?

Shane rolled out of the rack, every muscle in his body sore. He fell into his shoes and stumbled to the line. Kelly stood blinking groggily on the girls' side directly across the aisle. Her honey-blond hair was damp from her shower. Thank goodness, it was still night. He'd only slept for a few minutes.

On his left stood Steve and Maurice, Shane being the first one in the row. He could see Captain Jones in the periphery of his vision and could see someone stood next to him, but he kept his head straight, eyes on Kelly. The right side of her lips turned up slightly—a simple gesture, but it warmed him through.

Jones gave a recap of the day, and Shane barely heard half of it. He hadn't had a chance to stop and just be alone with Kelly since the night before, and the sudden intimacy of being four feet apart, staring into each other's eyes, was invigorating. He forgot about his exhaustion, forgot his sore muscles, suddenly wanting to pull her close and feel her lips on his once again.

"...and we have decided which of you is to be replaced," Jones said.

CHAPTER SIXTEEN

Jones' words snatched Shane's attention.

"We can't afford to keep anyone here who doesn't perform as expected. We must have the best people possible for these missions if we are to survive."

He held his breath. What if they took Kelly? Shane wouldn't be here if it weren't for her. He wouldn't have been motivated to fight—to stay alive.

"Ivan Anitov," Jones announced, "please come with me."

Shane exhaled. It was one of the Russians, thank goodness. He'd rather have seen Petrov, who he considered downright evil, leave, but with one of his cronies taken away, maybe Petrov would mellow out.

Anfisa stepped into the aisle, anger seething in her voice. "Why would you take him? We are the best trained and most qualified people here."

"We will not explain our motives," Jones replied calmly. "You must trust that we know the enemy better than you, and the final teams will be composed of those people who we feel have the greatest chance of success. Return to the line."

Although he didn't move his head to look at her, in the periphery of his vision, Shane saw the hotheaded Russian girl stand her ground for a moment. But Jones' gaze must have been enough to end the argument—without another word, she stepped back in line.

"This is Vlad Poisek," Jones growled. "He is the replacement."

Anitov walked down the aisle toward the exit, his head low, his shoulders slumped with defeat. He was the smaller of Petrov's two thugs, the one who Tracy had tripped earlier in the day and then Kelly had kicked in the balls during sparring. He'd also cheated during the flag-capturing game.

Vlad walked by, heading in the other direction. He was tall and blond like Petrov, though he looked to be carrying at least forty more pounds of muscle.

"The rest of you, get some sleep," Jones ordered, turning out the lights as he followed Anitov out of the barracks.

When the door shut, the kids broke into hushed conversation.

"Where do you think they're taking him?" Maurice asked, clearly concerned about the possibility of being eliminated.

"Probably putting him with the regular troops," Tracy replied casually. "They said they're preparing small armies of teens to back us up."

"He's better off than we are," Laura said. "I get the feeling they're training us to die."

"You don't know that," Jules scolded, frowning at her. "And even if it's true, have you watched any of the loop?" She pointed toward the TV on the other side of the quad. "The Anunnaki will put us on the front lines in a war against their enemies. I'll take the suicide mission over fighting for them any day. Anyone who doesn't agree is a coward."

"What did you just call me?" Laura stepped around Tracy and looked up at Jules. The dim light coming from the bathroom revealed the concern in her eyes transforming into anger. Shane took a step closer, ready to jump between them.

"Nothing," Jules replied, a slight smile on her face. "But your willingness to kick my ass is probably the reason you're here. You've got more fight in you than I think even you realize."

Laura blinked, the comprehension that Jules had just paid her a compliment taking a moment to sink in.

"She's right," Shane said, hoping to get the attention off Laura. "We are all here for a reason. The rebels have a lot of experience in dealing with the Anunnaki, so I think we just have to trust their judgment and do what we're told for now." He wasn't convinced of what he was saying, but he couldn't afford to have his team lose their focus.

They nodded and made sounds of agreement. Shane's eyes found Kelly's again. When Jones was announcing who was to be replaced, he feared it might be her. And now, he felt a surge of guilt for wanting to see her go. If she was replaced, she might live. But if he did anything to get her eliminated, she'd hate him forever.

Down the aisle, Anfisa's voice grew shrill. She was scolding the members of her team, angry over losing Anitov.

"Wow," Steve said, his eyes wide. "Glad I'm not one of

them."

"Yeah," Maurice added. "Not a very warm welcome for poor Vlad."

Chuckling, Shane and the rest of his team crawled into their racks. Soon the barracks grew quiet, the sound of heavy breathing and snores building into an annoying symphony, a constant reminder that he wasn't asleep.

When he closed his eyes, his mind raced, spinning out of control to the point where he was short of breath. Opening his eyes only made him feel how heavy they were, made him painfully aware of his exhaustion and of how he desperately needed sleep.

There was a rustling, and his sheet lifted. Startled, Shane opened his eyes and saw Kelly slipping into his bed.

"Do you mind?" she whispered.

"Of course not," he replied, moving over against the partition to make room for her on the narrow bunk.

"Can't sleep." Kelly pulled the sheets over her and pressed into him.

"So you decided to come over and spoon with me?" Shane teased. The arch of her back fit perfectly into the curve made by his front.

"I guess so," she said. He couldn't see her face, but he sensed her smile. "Your first time?"

He blushed. It sounded like the question might have more to it than just spooning. A fire ignited in him, and he felt possessed by her smell and the delicate texture of her skin. He could barely breathe, but he was also painfully aware of all the other kids around them. Not to mention, the rebels' cameras probably had a night-vision mode, so everything they did was being watched.

"Uh, yeah," he whispered, his lips near her ear. "Aside from a near-death experience under a school bus in a tornado. You?"

"Yeah, me too," she whispered, sounding as breathless as he felt. She pushed her hips tighter against him and sighed.

Shane breathed in the smell of her hair, soothed by her presence but also boiling inside with passion. The turmoil in his mind vanished, all his attention on the areas where she pressed against him, only their T-shirts and underwear between them. As exciting as having her this close was, it also relaxed him. He wouldn't disrespect her by trying anything while they were so exposed in the barracks, but his mind was free to imagine all the things he'd do if they were alone. It took him away from the traumatic past, and it stopped him thinking about what lay ahead. Happier thoughts, of tasting her lips again and of exploring her body, filled his mind. Although his veins pulsed with excitement, having her this close was a comforting distraction that allowed exhaustion to sneak in. Pulling her even tighter to him, he closed his eyes with a grin on his lips.

"Rise and shine, tadpoles. Get on the line!" Jones yelled. "The last one in push-up position has to clean the head."

"Damn," Kelly said, rolling out of bed.

Steve was already up, giving them a mischievous look. Kelly darted across the aisle onto the girls' side just as Tracy rolled out of Jules' rack. Shane, Steve, and Maurice rushed to the line and dropped into push-up position.

"You guys too?" Steve teased quietly, raising his head to look at Tracy, who was directly across from him.

"Shut up, dude," she whispered back, glaring at him. "It's not like you didn't already know."

Steve chuckled again.

"You're having way too much fun over here," Jones shouted. "Push-ups on my count—up, down, up, down…"

The routine was the same as the day before, push-ups and sit-ups on the cool barracks floor until they'd all created puddles of sweat beneath them. Then they were allowed a fifteen-minute bathroom break, where everyone rushed to pee and brush their teeth. Jones yelled the entire time.

It amazed him how no one seemed embarrassed, and everyone stayed out of each other's way. In one day of suffering together, they were starting to become gears in a well-oiled machine.

Petrov even moved to let Shane spit in the sink when he was brushing his teeth. Shane was cautious the boy might be setting him up for a prank. Or perhaps losing one of his buddies humbled the Russian, and he'd play nicer today. Anfisa's scolding last night might have had something to do with it too. Regardless, Shane was glad for it. In the end, Jones was right. They were all in this together.

On the tarmac, the predawn air was cool. Shane settled into a mellow pace next to Steve at the back of their group, ensuring no one got separated and ambushed in the dark again. Cruising around the loop, he tilted his head back and half closed his eyes, wishing he could get a couple of more hours of sleep. Laura made pained grunting sounds every minute, but she kept going. The Aussies plugged along behind them, forming a formidable unit of fourteen people.

Up ahead, he saw the Koreans and the Chinese run through the circle of light cast by the lamp above a hangar door. They cruised along with an appearance of relative ease, their quiet confidence enviable. He hoped his team would adopt a similar demeanor as their training progressed. But then again, they had won yesterday, so he reckoned he shouldn't be too critical.

By the fourth lap, Maurice and Laura were wheezing, barely moving faster than a walk. Steve was still plodding along with his shoulders square and his chest pushed out, as Shane expected he would until his heart burst if he was put to the task.

"Pick up the speed, or I'll run you until you all puke!" Jones shouted at them as they passed.

"Come on, guys," Shane encouraged. "There's a bottle of water waiting for us in the training building and another lap coming to us if we don't hurry."

It was enough to get Laura moving faster. She was at the front of his squad, and set the pace for everyone else. They came around the north side of the tarmac, and Shane was relieved to see Captain Jones standing at the open door to the hangar where they'd had the morning lecture the day before, directing people to enter.

"I never thought one of these metal chairs could be so comfortable." Maurice groaned and tilted up the bottle of water he found under his seat.

"Today, we will do a walkthrough of an Anunnaki recruit

ship," Jones announced, climbing up the metal stage onto the podium. "Place your hands on your laps and relax."

Kelly reached over and grabbed his hand, tugging it between them so she could hold it discreetly throughout the simulation. In doing so, she moved closer to him, causing their bare legs and arms to touch. He smiled at her, his heart threatening to explode and kill them both when she smiled back. When he felt the warmth and softness of her skin pressed against his and she looked at him like she was now, time ceased to exist. The rest of the world vanished, and he felt completely alive again. Her spirit seemed to penetrate into his through the connection of their skin and eyes. Her lips beckoned him like cool water did a man who had went thirsty for days. He had to stop himself from leaning over and kissing her, almost forgetting they were sitting in a crowded room with Jones glaring down at them.

Buzzing in his ear and a flash of bright light tore him away from her. A warm breeze kissed his face, and he opened his eyes, the joy of being so close to Kelly dissipating. He was standing in a field. A large, pyramid-shaped mound covered in neatly mown sod was in front of him. The rest of the students stood on either side. They wore regular clothes, not the crimson armor of the day before. He had on blue jeans and a white T-shirt. Kelly was standing a few people away, like the aliens had separated them on purpose for the simulation. She wore jeans as well, but had on a tight, black tank top that kicked the embers of the fire she'd started, sending a warm shower of sparks through him. They exchanged a heated glance and he sighed, wishing for time they couldn't have.

Lily stood on the lawn in front of them, wearing her usual black pantsuit and a kind smile on her face. Shane liked her. She was the first person from this alien race he'd met. He trusted her more than Jones, though maybe it was just because Scarface never smiled. At the same time, it unnerved Shane how he was willing to trust her so quickly, how he'd wanted to the moment she'd walked into that farmhouse.

Her gaze swept across the group, connecting with everyone. It seemed to convey a mix of admiration, superiority, and concern. He suddenly wondered how old she was. She must have been an adult to be flying the ship that crashed in New Mexico, yet she looked less than thirty now. She was silent long enough to make them shift uncomfortably and glance at each other, like they were unable to bear her omniscient scrutiny any longer.

"You've all seen these before," she said, pointing at the mound behind her. There was a flash of light, and they were suddenly standing in the blazing sun, desert sands stretching out around them.

"They are scattered across the globe."

An Egyptian pyramid was in front of them, twice as tall as the first mound.

"Humans used pyramids for many purposes; burial grounds, temples, and gateways to other worlds," she continued.

Another flash transported them to a jungle. Shane rubbed his eyes and swallowed the nausea caused by the shifts. Monkeys shrieked and leapt through the treetops. Vines entangled a Mayan pyramid whose peak pierced the lush, green canopy.

"Whether the builders had direct contact with the Anunnaki or were instructed subconsciously, they were all driven by the same purpose."

They flashed to another ruin—this one Shane immediately recognized. It was a pyramid in Teotihuacan, the center of the ancient Aztec empire. He'd just studied about the bloodthirsty warriors at the end of the last school year. He gazed up and down the Avenue of the Dead, stepped pyramids of various heights on either side.

The sunlight glinted off something in the clear blue sky. Shielding his eyes, he glanced up and saw a golden craft flying high above the ruins.

"That's an Anunnaki recruit ship," Lily explained, pointing skyward. "The primary interplanetary vessel used by the enemy."

As it drew closer, he could see that the dark bottom of the vessel was hollow.

"Nearly all the pyramids your ancestors built are landing sites, and they are on every continent in the world except Antarctica and Australia," Lily explained.

"Thank goodness for that," Liam whispered.

"The pyramids are docking terminals where the ships can draw resources from the planet," Jones boomed, stepping next to Lily. "A large percentage of the older kids left on Earth are gathering toward these structures now, driven by what to them is an irresistible and instinctive urge. In reality, it is a residual effect of the limbic manipulator, designed to aid the Anunnaki in harvesting their slaves."

Shane imagined the world outside of this base. Without

parents or governments, the good kids must be fighting roving mobs of juvenile delinquents like the ones who attacked the Leeville gym. And gangs like Shamus' would be fleeing the millions of rotting corpses left in the cities, terrorizing the rural areas in search of food. Meanwhile, they all unconsciously migrated toward these ancient sites, their fates decided millennia ago.

CHAPTER
SEVENTEEN

"There are thousands of pyramids on Earth, many of them undiscovered."

"How can we possibly fight that many ships?" Tracy asked, showing no qualms about interrupting Jones.

"Fortunately, the first wave of recruit ships will be smaller," he replied. "Another, larger fleet will arrive to clean up the mess, after the primary recruit ships select their slave soldiers."

"What happens to Earth when they are done?" an Israeli boy asked.

"They will destroy everything that humans have created, returning the planet to the Stone Age and thereby reducing the likelihood that humans will evolve enough technologically to turn on the Anunnaki. Then they'll leave a few kids with wiped brains behind as seed for a new crop to be available in the distant future."

So it was a cycle. Earth was simply a farm. Even if they succeeded at their impossible mission, it wouldn't be the end. There was no happily ever after. Humans were being dragged into a centuries-old rebellion if they destroyed the recruit ships, or an unjust war against other aliens that had been going on for thousands of years if they failed.

It should have scared the crap out of Shane—he expected that would be the normal reaction. Instead, it just pissed him off. He looked around at the other kids and could see most of them seemed to have a similar reaction—another reason they must have been chosen for the assault.

"We should blow up all the pyramids before they get here," a Finnish boy said. "To keep them from landing."

"I like that you are thinking," Lily replied. "But if we do that, they'll know we are planning to resist. It's better they land, thinking there is no threat on the planet and it will be an easy harvest. This will allow us to ambush them. We need to try to capture these ships so we can use them to fight the second wave. Besides, the ships don't need a pyramid to land. They're using them for resource extraction."

"What will happen when the chosen team destroys the command ship?" Anfisa asked, her tone indicating that when she said chosen team, she meant the Russians.

"The other recruit ships all operate on orders from the command ship," Jones answered. "Disabling it will cause chaos, which will allow us to overwhelm and capture all the ships."

"And you know where the command ship will land?" Shane asked.

"That part is easy. The primary recruit ships are the largest in the fleet, and the command ship will be the largest of those. Aside from dirt-mound pyramids, which can't support the ship's resource extraction process, there is only one pyramid in the world that is big enough."

"The Great Pyramid at Giza?" Laura said.

"Exactly," Lily replied. "And two other recruit ships will land in the same complex."

While they spoke, the ship had descended. Nearing the ground, it kicked up gusts, throwing dirt on them and making them turn away and shield their eyes. It dropped down onto the Aztec temple, its concave inside fitting perfectly over the structure. Letting out a final hiss, it fell quiet. The ship itself was a massive pyramid, the same kind that had destroyed Lily's rebel army and created the wormhole that sent her here. Its ominous exterior was composed of what looked like a seamless sheet of gold.

Shane was dumbstruck. Although the vessel had a sinister purpose, it was magnificent. The video Lily had shown them when they first arrived didn't do it justice. It looked ten times bigger than the pyramid it sat on, its apex reaching high into the clear blue sky.

A rising curtain of molten gold, a section of the ship's gleaming surface vanished upward from the bottom. It formed a forty-foot tall opening, looking in on a stark white interior as brightly lit as the world surrounding it. Shane imagined it was a giant tick, landing on its terrestrial host and sucking the life from it. What *resources* besides people were these invading marauders after?

Gazing into the silent, bright interior, he tensed, half expecting an army of Anunnaki soldiers, clad in red armor and sporting plasma guns, to march out and slaughter them.

"This is one of the regular recruit ships. Although the

command ship is larger, they all have a similar design," Jones said, leading the way into the apparently empty vessel.

Shane's neck hurt from surveying the vast chamber just beyond the entry. He was surprised at the ship's inside, expecting it would look futuristic and utilitarian like the gray passageways and the reactor chamber he'd seen on the TV loop in the barracks. But instead, a pyramid with stepped sides that seemed carved from solid marble was hidden beneath the reflective outer surface. The inner pyramid with fluted pillars and statues of toga-wearing deities looked dreamed up by some ancient Roman or Greek architect. Each massive step had guardrails along the edge carved with intricate designs.

Lily and Jones led them to a futuristic escalator that carried them up the side of the inner pyramid. Everyone's jaw was slack, their eyes wide with disbelief as they surveyed the vessel.

"This outer region of the ship contains the Anunnaki living chambers," Lily explained.

The horizontal steps of the inner pyramid had wide boulevards with railings on the edge and elegant apartments forming the vertical part of each step. Fluted marble columns rising at regular intervals along the railings supported the sparse frame of the sloped outer skin, which Shane guessed must be created by some kind of energy field. White sidewalks framed lawns of lush grass, and palm and fruit trees delineated each apartment's square yard. The lavish dwellings were occasionally separated by terraced gardens that ran at an angle up the full height of the pyramid.

"The plants in these outer portions of the ship clean the air of carbon dioxide, make oxygen, and provide food."

Sunlight shone brightly through the golden exterior, which looked completely transparent from the inside. He imagined the views of space must be spectacular from the opulent homes. Shane looked behind him and grew dizzy. They were so high up that a tumble down the escalator would be fatal. He leaned forward so he'd fall up the steps if he lost balance and returned his attention to the stepped living areas they rose past, determined not to look down again.

While all the apartments looked elegant enough for royalty, it was apparent as they went higher that the elite of the alien society lived near the top. The distance between the steps increased by fifteen feet every so many levels, adding a floor to the apartments until they were five stories tall. They had elegant balconies on each floor, and grand entrances with pillars on either side. If the lost city of Atlantis ever existed, Shane reckoned this might be what it looked like.

Three quarters of the way up the golden outer pyramid, the wide escalator brought them to the flat top of the marble inner structure. He stepped out of the way so the other kids could get off and made sure a guardrail was between him and the five-story fall to the highest apartment's courtyard. His jaw remained slackened with awe as he surveyed the city complex that sat atop the artificial mesa.

A grassy park, punctuated by trees, surrounded the city. To accommodate the sloped exterior, the buildings on the edges were shorter, and toward the middle, they were taller. Shane could see a massive, circular structure standing at the center of the city, its outer walls constructed of layers of arches.

"That looks a bit like a Roman coliseum," Petrov mused. He was standing beside Shane, his mouth agape like the rest of the teenagers.

"Unfortunately, it is used for a similar purpose," Lily said. "Anunnaki citizens can buy slaves and train them for sport. Then they enter them into contests for public entertainment."

"It's what they do to pass the time during long voyages," Jones growled, hatred showing on his face as he glared at the massive structure.

"So this whole cleansing war they do to find the best soldiers is probably like the Super Bowl to them," Steve observed with disgust.

Rising above it all, the sides of the outer pyramid continued upward, meeting at the apex hundreds of feet overhead.

Jones and Lily led them through the city along a wide, palm tree-lined street that ended in a loop around the coliseum. Then they took them back down the escalator and showed them the entrance into the slave-processing parts of the ship.

"Initially, they'll bring you and the other recruits into this holding chamber," Jones explained.

Beyond the elegant outer living spaces was a room the size of a football field. Its walls, ceiling, and floor were windowless and featureless, and all the same flat gray color that Shane remembered from the clip he watched last night. He imagined a person would go mad in such a room if they were left in it for too long.

They were shown the route into the ship the harvested kids would take, and where they would be sorted into slaves and soldiers. Those fit for neither would be rejected back out of the ship. Then Jones showed them where they would be given their armor and a weapon and led them into the final holding chamber, where all the kids' brains would be uploaded with their combat training and missions.

"This is where the six members from each team will slip away and go to the reactor chamber," Jones said.

"And the seventh?" Jules asked.

"One person from each team will stay here," Lily answered. "When the reactor is destroyed, and the recruits are released from the enemy's control, that person will get as many of the people in this room as they can to attack the Anunnaki and overtake the ship. At this time, we will send in the other teenagers we're training to overtake the outer portions of the ship."

"All the recruits' helmets will be equipped with a universal translator, so they'll understand you," Jones added. "Whoever is in this room will have to act fast and get as many of the kids to fight as they can. Each second that passes will give the Anunnaki time to regroup and come up with a plan to stop you."

"How are we supposed to get a bunch of confused kids to rally an attack?" Anfisa asked. "That is a ridiculous plan."

"Their brains will already be uploaded with combat training via their telepathic slave link," Jones replied, glowering at her as if to scold for her negative comment. "They will know how to fight and how to use the weapons the Anunnaki issued them, but they'll suddenly have free will. You just have to point them in the right direction and give them the motivation they need. Tell them the Anunnaki are the aliens who killed their parents. They'll do the rest."

The buzzing came in Shane's ear, and a flash of light returned him to the training room. Kelly's hand was still holding his, and his butt was numb like he'd been sitting for hours.

"Go have breakfast. Meet on the tarmac in half an hour," Jones ordered.

Although they all wore stunned looks on their faces from the tour of the Anunnaki ship, apparently everyone else was as hungry as he was. The room cleared like there was a fire in the building.

"Feeling better or worse about this whole thing?" Liam asked as they walked toward the cafeteria.

"Better, because I'm getting a grip on what we have to do," he lied.

"Their plan still sounds like a long shot," Kelly said. She was on Shane's other side.

"It beats having no plan at all," Steve joined in, twisting his big fist in his opposite palm, "and that's what we'd have without them."

It was a good point. The Anunnaki would've enslaved them all before they had a clue if it weren't for the rebels. He mulled over their predicament in silence at breakfast. Even the Russians, who were usually a noisy mess, wore expressions of quiet contemplation as they ate. They'd learned so much new stuff over the last day that it gave him a headache trying to sort through it all.

They were going to have to face down an alien force that

was as old as time. The Anunnaki had been space travelers since before humans existed. What chance did they really have of defeating such an advanced race? Shane didn't mind being the underdog and always felt it gave him an advantage when viewed as such. But this was more like an ant tackling an elephant.

Jones stepped into the cafeteria and ordered them outside. They made a circle on the tarmac, as they'd done the day before. Shane was overcome by dread, but he kept his head up. He couldn't let his teammates sense his gloomy mood, couldn't risk demoralizing them.

The captain stepped into the center of the ring, looking around at each of their faces. He shook his head, appearing disappointed with the morbid attitude that seemed to have infected them all. Even the Finns, who until this point had been the masters of stoicism, stood slack, their shoulders visibly slumping, like they were sentenced to the firing squad.

"The task ahead seems insurmountable," Jones said, his gruff tone softer, more paternal than ever before. "But we know you are up to it. We've run multiple simulations and are confident the humans can defeat the Anunnaki. There is so much riding in your favor. They will not expect an attack. They'll expect absolute obedience from the human population. When using the slave gene, they have never had a recruit uprising. They will be arrogant on that point. This arrogance is a weakness we will exploit."

Jones walked over to Steve, grabbed him by the wrist, and led him into the center of the ring.

"You all must believe you have a chance—you must believe you can destroy this enemy and take revenge on them for what they did to your parents," he continued. His voice grew louder, and Shane noticed everyone stood taller as he spoke. Like a halftime pep talk from Coach Rice, his words infused them with hope. Jones was a model for how he should behave if he wanted to give his team the best chance of survival.

"We train here—running countless laps, fighting each other on this blacktop, and competing to capture a flag off the mountain—to build your strength, your endurance, but most importantly, your confidence. If you doubt yourselves in the face of the enemy, then we don't stand a chance. Humans have a propensity towards arrogance as well, and it can give you an advantage if focused properly. You have to believe you can beat them. "

Pointing at Anfisa, he signaled her to enter the ring and fight Steve. She took a fighting stance, putting her fists in front of her and turning her body slightly sideways. Steve raised his fists as well, each seeming as big as the Russian girl's head. The air of aggression that charged yesterday's fights was dampened this morning. Shane felt closer to these foreigners, the world seeming a lot smaller after being in the simulation of the Anunnaki ship. These were not just his fellow humans, or even his neighbors. Regardless of the differences his team had with the Russians yesterday, the common enemy they shared made these kids feel like his brothers and sisters.

Steve circled Anfisa, and Shane could see his big friend didn't want to attack. He wasn't the type to hit a girl. The calculating look in her eyes made it clear she didn't have the same reservations about assaulting him. Stepping sideways and closing on Steve at the same time, she slipped within striking range. With lightning speed and lethal precision, she punched under his elbow and made contact with his ribs. There was a loud crack, and Steve buckled over, groaning in pain.

Where yesterday, the Russians would have cheered over the victory, this time, everyone remained relatively quiet, aside from the empathetic sighs at hearing a bone break. Anfisa dropped her guard, her expression transforming into one of regret and concern.

"Are you okay?" she asked.

"I think you broke some ribs," Steve said through gritted teeth. He gave her a weak smile, and she helped him to the side where Dr. Blain was waiting. He wasn't the type to stop fighting over a few ribs, but Anfisa's attention seemed to diffuse what little aggression he'd approached her with in the first place.

"You see," Jones said once they were out of the ring, his black eyebrows elevated as he looked at them. "Even the smallest person here can defeat the largest. Steve underestimated his opponent, just like the Anunnaki will underestimate you. Such a mistake rarely happens twice, and I doubt Anfisa will be able to defeat him if we pair them together tomorrow. The lesson is—when you have a chance to attack a larger enemy, you must make sure the attack will lead to their destruction. If they recover and can retaliate, you will lose."

CHAPTER
EIGHTEEN

The fights happened without much cheering or fanfare, the group of kids growing more united in the single purpose of defeating the Anunnaki and less concerned with beating each other. Jones was enraged by the lack of aggression. He made them do push-ups and crunches on the flesh-searing asphalt, yelling at them the entire time.

"We are here to develop the warrior in each of you. We cannot afford you going soft on each other. From now on, you will fight until Dr. Blain says it is no longer safe to continue," Jones growled.

The doctor had a horrified look on her face, and Shane guessed she was thinking of calling each fight before it started. Jones cast a cold glance at her, and her expression changed, revealing that she'd do what he expected of her.

Ordering them to their feet, he pitted Shane against the ornery Russian prankster, Petrov. The boy didn't have the viciousness in his attacks of the day before. He slipped a couple of cautious hits to the side of Shane's head before he got an angle on the boy and drove his full weight into him. The Russian went down hard, and Shane leapt on top of him. He raised his fist, ready to nail the rude boy in the face. Petrov twisted his head and clenched his eyes shut.

"Finish it!" Jones yelled.

It was good enough for Shane—he'd clearly beaten the kid. Knowing they'd all pay for his unwillingness to do what Jones ordered wasn't enough to make him hammer the boy when he was already down. He got off him and offered his hand, pulling Petrov to his feet.

"It's nothing personal," the Russian said, smiling regrettably and not releasing Shane's hand. "But I'm not good at losing."

The big Russian pulled Shane toward him and punched at the same time. His fist smashed into Shane's mouth. He heard bone crunching, and pain exploded across his face all the way to the back of his skull. His vision filled with white and black swirling spots, and his legs went rubbery. He collapsed to the hot asphalt.

Cradling his broken face in his hands, he cursed and moaned. He tasted blood, and he couldn't open and close his mouth. Dr. Blain was over him in an instant. He let her push his hands down to his sides and forced himself to stay still so she could fix him.

The world grew hazy, but he didn't pass out. The aliens' medical technology meant he'd be better than new in less than a minute. It made the pain seem trivial and easier to ignore. As his face healed, he cursed himself for allowing Petrov to trick him.

"Good," he heard Jones saying, his spirits seeming lifted at the sight of Shane's blood. "Attack the enemy when their guard is down. Even if they have you on the ground, ready to destroy you, do not accept defeat. The enemy will lie to you. Even with their dying breath, they will do everything to convince you that they are your friends—that they can be trusted. Let me be the one to warn you, they have no respect for your freedom. You are property to them, another disposable species they plan to use to crush their enemies."

He was mended quickly, and the doctor used a wet towel to clean the remaining blood off his face. When she stepped away, he saw Petrov still standing nearby. He wasn't smiling and laughing as Shane would've expected. He extended his hand to Shane as he got up. Not willing to fall into another trap, Shane didn't take it. He rose to his feet cautiously, wanting to nail the boy but knowing the fight was officially over and Jones would make him pay hell if he did. There'd be other opportunities to take his revenge. He wouldn't let his compassion get in the way next time.

"Forgive my behavior yesterday," Petrov said begrudgingly, casting a glance toward Anfisa and extending his hand to shake. "We are all in this together, and I should have shown more respect."

"Yeah, okay," Shane replied, conveying he didn't believe the boy.

He narrowed his eyes and cautiously took Petrov's extended hand, expecting the Russian would try to coldcock him again. Balling his free hand into a fist, he fantasized about returning the favor right now, of caving the punk's face in.

Petrov looked down at his clenched hand and then back up at him. He didn't retract or appear to plan to try and stop Shane if he hit him. His expression seemed to say, *Go ahead— take a free shot at me. I deserve it.* After shaking Shane's hand, Petrov sighed as if he'd just finished doing something he'd been dreading. Leaving Shane confused, he turned away and rejoined his group. Anfisa gave a slight grin to her comrade as he approached, appearing satisfied by the exchange.

Shane walked back over and stood next to Kelly. It was unsportsmanlike of Petrov to hit him when he was helping him up. But at the same time, the fight hadn't officially ended, and the Russian was just taking advantage of Shane's weakness. Such sly aggression might mean the difference between winning and losing when it came to the fight against the Anunnaki. As much as it hurt his ego, he knew he should learn a thing or two from Petrov.

The sun climbed higher in the clear blue sky, and it grew hotter by the minute on the tarmac.

"Alright people," Jones shouted, "give me five laps, and then you can have lunch."

A wave of grumbles swept through the sweaty crowd, everyone already exhausted by the morning's exercises.

"Excuse me," Jones growled angrily, letting them know that the sensitive side he'd shown earlier was locked away and Drill Sergeant Jones was back in full force. "Drop and give me twenty push-ups first to help lift your spirits."

"Sir, yes sir," came the response.

Where they were all separated into their respective groups for the morning run, now weary individuals took off around the track as they finished their push-ups. The result was an intermingling of the different teams.

Shane was in the middle of the mob, Kelly on his right side. A few people ahead of them, Anfisa ran next to Steve.

"I think there's love in the air," Tracy joked. She was behind Shane and Kelly. "Who knew? You break one of Steve's ribs, and he'll follow you around like a puppy."

Shane laughed, taking a closer look at the pair. Sure enough, he saw Steve glance over at the tall Russian girl and smile. She returned his gaze with a flirtatious grin and sped up. Steve took off after her.

"Oh my gosh," Jules groaned. "It's like a stinking Disney movie. I'm gonna barf."

"Come on, guys," Kelly said, her voice thick with emotion. "I think it's sweet."

Shane just hoped it wouldn't be a distraction, though he wasn't one to talk. Joking around made the laps tick off easier than before, and soon they were in the air-conditioned cafeteria.

"How are you holding up?" he asked Rebecca. She was replenishing napkins in stainless-steel holders near the food line.

"I'm okay, I guess," she replied timidly. Her cheeks turning red, she glanced up at him and smiled. She was not much younger than Shane was, but she made him feel like he was an adult by the way she addressed him.

"So you guys are being treated well?"

"Yes," she replied. "We have to work in here a few hours a day, and then help with the children, but it's not bad."

"Good." He'd gotten used to his little squad deferring to him as their leader, but her reverence made him feel awkward. "How about the other girls who…?"

"Oh," she said, looking down at the napkin holder. "I think we're all getting over it, slowly. Dr. Blain met with us to talk. You'd think you'd just want to forget, but talking with her and the others did make me feel better for some strange reason."

"Good," he said again, the response feeling wholly inadequate. "Well, if you ever need anything."

"Thanks."

She gave him another smile filled with respect and admiration—a look he reckoned was reserved for fathers. Smiling back, but feeling terribly uncomfortable, he spun away and grabbed a tray.

Heading down the food line, he encountered two of the other girls who were attacked in the gym serving kids from the other side. When they put food on his plate, he noticed they were looking at him the same way Rebecca had. She, and probably every other kid who his team protected before the aliens showed up, believed he was strong and smart enough to save them. What they didn't realize was he wasn't all that special. He'd gotten lucky a few times, but he didn't think he was a hero. The responsibility to protect them, to defeat the Anunnaki so that these kids wouldn't die or become slaves, was always pressing on him. But it suddenly seemed to double in weight.

"Want to eat with the little ones?" Kelly asked when he stepped off the end of the food line.

"Uh, sure," Shane replied, sensing that was the answer she expected. He wasn't thrilled about the idea, but he couldn't think of a decent excuse to say no to her.

His stomach twisting into knots from his interaction with Rebecca and the other girls, he followed her. The kids' table was an uproar of laughter and conversation, but when he approached, some of them grew quiet and looked at him. He threw on his best smile again, hoping they couldn't sense the fist of panic tightening its grip around him.

He looked at Kelly, and her expression showed she could see something was wrong. He felt like a teapot on the stove, the pressure increasing inside of him until he feared he couldn't contain it. He remembered trying to save his aunt, and how miserably he'd failed. And that was just a bunch of bees. Images of how her body looked when she died, his dad's cockroach-eaten face, and all the other mutilated corpses he'd seen ripped through his mind. Then he remembered the kids he'd shot in the gym and in the fight in Atlanta, their slack faces as their souls tore away from their bodies. When he blinked, his tormented imagination creating a picture of Nat, Sara, James, and all the other kids at this table, along with Rebecca and the others, dead and swollen like the adults. He looked at Kelly again, afraid of imagining her the same way.

"I'll be right back," he whispered, then sat his tray down on a table and headed for the doors of the cafeteria at a brisk walk.

"Shane?" Kelly called after him.

He pretended not to hear her and stayed on course. Breaking into a run when he was fifteen feet from the exit, he burst through the doors and darted around the side of the building. The woods were too far. Partway through the egress between buildings, he doubled over and barfed up bile, his stomach empty.

When the heaving stopped, he punched the metal wall of the hangar, refreshing pain enveloping his fist. Blinking and studying his hand to see if any bones protruded from it, he leaned against the building and wiped his eyes.

"Shane?" Kelly's concerned voice came from behind him.

Her feet crunched on the gravel as she approached, and then her hand was on his shoulder. His head drooped, his unfocused eyes directed toward his feet. He wasn't proud of himself at the moment and didn't want her to see him like this.

"You aren't alone, you know?" Her touch and voice soothed him like powerful medicine. "We're with you in this."

"Yeah," he mumbled. "I'm trying to be strong, to inspire confidence in the others, but sometimes, it's just too damn much."

"It is too much," she said. "But Steve, Jules, Maurice, and the rest are all here to help you. I'm here."

He let out a long, shaky sigh and raised his head.

"I know," he said, looking at her. "Guess I just got overwhelmed in there."

She pulled him into an embrace, pressing her cheek against his.

"I'd kiss you," she whispered, "but your breath smells like puke."

He chuckled and squeezed her tightly against him. They

held each other in silence, and he could feel her heart beating against his chest. Her touch diffused the pressure that had built in him.

"We'd better get back to lunch," he said, wanting her to forget the whole ordeal. Holding hands until they got to the tarmac, they returned to the cafeteria and made their way over to the tables where the seven teams were sitting.

"Lunch is over," Jones yelled from the door. "Up and out!"

"Ready to play capture the flag?" Steve asked, standing.

"Not really," Liam replied. "Every bleeding muscle in my body hurts."

"Well, it'll make you that much easier to beat," Jules teased, picking up her tray and taking it to the scullery.

Shane's stomach growled. His hunger flared at the thought of not getting to eat until dinnertime. He already felt dizzy because he'd burned off his breakfast. Snatching the remainder of Laura's sandwich from her plate before she could trash it, he stuffed most of it in his mouth.

"I said out!" Jones glared at him.

He couldn't swallow the mouthful fast enough to be able to take another bite, so he slipped the remainder of the sandwich behind his back and headed for the door, acting like he didn't notice the captain staring at him threateningly the entire way.

Liam grumbled about Jones' yelling, walking out alongside Shane. Fortunately, other than Laura, who had looked stunned by his sudden voraciousness, no one seemed to have noticed Shane's moment of weakness. He glanced at the little kids' tables, hoping he hadn't frightened them. Their usual roar of laughter and conversation carried across the room.

The teenagers crowded out of the cafeteria, back into the blazing sun. He stuffed the rest of the sandwich into his mouth, chewing and swallowing as fast as he could. Whether or not he'd end up injured like the day before, it was a relief to think he'd soon be racing up the side of the mountain. For at least a little while, his mind wouldn't be able to focus on anything besides not getting shot and capturing the flag. He just hoped he wouldn't pass out from not eating enough.

"Gather around," Jones shouted. "Today, the game is going to be a bit different. First off, there will be no guns. In the event that you lose your weapon during the mission, this will be good practice. Secondly, there are no teams. It's each person for themselves, and the one to retrieve the flag and bring it to me doesn't have to run at all tomorrow."

A wave of conversation washed through the group.

"Quiet," Jones ordered. "The purpose of this task is to prepare you in case the rest of your team is eliminated and you have to complete the mission on your own. So take this seriously."

Shane looked at Kelly, Steve, and the rest of his team, not wanting to compete against them.

"I'll warn you now, don't hold back on this competition, or I'll make you run double," Jones growled. "Now go!" He pointed up the mountain.

Everyone looked stunned for an instant. Shane's game brain took over, and he darted into the undergrowth, tearing through it into the forest. In a wild stampede, everyone else followed.

The serenity of the woods was disrupted by the shouts of kids and the crunch of leaves under their feet. He didn't dare look over his shoulder, knowing the herd was on his heels and they'd trample him if he lost his footing. Judging by how long it took him to get to the top yesterday, he reckoned it was about a mile climb.

Within minutes, the noise behind him diminished. He could hear kids huffing for air, but it sounded like some of them were dropping off, exhaustion taking its toll. Shane's legs were on fire. His lungs felt like they were bleeding, and he was dizzy from not eating enough lunch, but he refused to be beaten. Using every ounce of his strength, he pumped his legs up and down, all the while trying to watch where his feet landed.

No one passed him before the light showed through the tree trunks ahead, and he knew he was near the top. Then he could see the little red flag. Digging deep for an extra jolt of energy, Shane gave a burst of speed. His foot found a slick root hiding under the leaf litter, and his leg shot out to the side. He went down hard, and several competitors barreled past him.

Cursing and bruised, he scrambled to his feet in time to see Steve knock three others out of the way and grab the flag. The big linebacker gave a victorious shout, pivoted, and lunged back down the mountain. There was only one way to get the flag out of his friend's clenched fist. When Steve passed, Shane dove at him, slamming him into a tree.

"Not today, brother," Steve growled, twisting his body and tossing Shane stumbling headlong down the hill.

Steve charged onward, only a handful of kids on his heels. He knew a bunch of them must be waiting to ambush whoever came down the mountain with the flag. But once the linebacker was on the move, he was like a force of nature— no one could stop him. Refusing to give up, Shane popped to his feet and chased him. Petrov dove out from between two trees and wrapped his arms around Steve. Using a tactic they learned in football, he spun completely around, throwing the Russian off. Then two of the Finns dove at his legs, and the surprisingly nimble boy leapt over them. Shane was almost close enough to try a tackle when they made it to the bottom. Steve burst through the briars and slid to a stop.

"That's right, people," he shouted, prancing around the gravelly area between the buildings and the forest like it was the end zone and the flag was a ball. "This is my flag," he sang triumphantly. "Mine!"

Gasping for air, Shane couldn't help but laugh at his friend's victory dance. He would've loved to capture the flag two days in a row, but he was happy to see a member of his team had gotten it anyway. The rest of the kids trickled out of the forest, mixed looks of defeat and relief that the run was over on their tired faces.

Jones didn't give them long to rest, ordering them out onto the tarmac to run laps. Shane's stomach growled again, and hunger pangs tormented him. Fighting bouts of dizziness, he ran at a slower pace and was tortured by fantasies of dinner the rest of the afternoon.

CHAPTER NINETEEN

The routine was constantly being rearranged and the training seemed to get harder as the week progressed. Jones didn't allow them to sleep more than a few hours a day. On the fourth day of training, he told them to nap in the afternoon and kept them up all night, pushing their bodies to the brink while constantly stuffing their minds with new information.

Kelly didn't join Shane in his rack again the rest of the week, and he wouldn't have noticed if she did. Sleep deprivation and physical exhaustion cured the insomnia of those first nights, and when he was lucky enough to put his head to the pillow, he zonked out within seconds and saw her and the others do the same.

"Friday is fish and chips day," Rebecca said, smiling at him as she piled fries onto his tray. She acted more cheerful than she had earlier in the week. Dr. Blain's counseling sessions and her responsibilities with the children and in the cafeteria seemed to be helping to get her over the trauma she'd so recently endured.

"It's Friday?" In his delirium, he'd lost track of time.

"Yes, silly," Rebecca replied, laughing.

She must've thought he was joking. He smiled at her, looking forward to sitting down for a minute while he ate. His legs felt like jelly. They must've run over fifty miles during the week, on top of climbing the mountain to capture the stupid flag every day.

"Let's eat with the little ones," Shane said wearily, stepping off the end of the line. Kelly had hinted she wanted him to sit with them again, and after learning how much time Dr. Blain was spending with the kids, counseling them like she was Rebecca and the others, he decided it was critical he stay involved and make sure she wasn't brainwashing anybody.

"Are you sure?" Kelly asked, appearing pleased.

"Yeah," he replied, trying to sound as confident as he could.

He had an ulterior motive. She sat with her sister at every meal, and he was sick of wasting that time eating with the others, looking across the cafeteria at her. If he wanted more of Kelly, he was going to have to man up and be the big brother the little ones needed.

It made him ill that he felt he was ultimately responsible for them, and he was still trying to come to terms with the task. Kelly seemed to embrace her role as a guardian of the children, Nat being her primary motivation.

Following her across the cafeteria, balancing his tray in one hand and holding a bottle of water in the other, he thought about the bigger reasons he should eat with the kids. They needed adults, people who'd take a parental role.

It wasn't right for them to get used to looking to the aliens to fill that void, and Dr. Blain seemed all too eager to step in. For now, these rebels were allies. But when this war ended, they couldn't allow them to take over.

It wasn't that he wanted to be in charge, but he figured there were enough smart and resourceful teenagers left to piece things back together once the threat was dealt with. Earth belonged to humans, and it'd be wrong to give it up without a fight.

He did feel a little guilty for not completely trusting the rebels. They'd done so much for him and his people, and they seemed intent upon preventing the Anunnaki from enslaving the humans. However, wanting to be good leader, he'd was determined to never forget that it was his duty to be vigilant and make sure no one was taking advantage of them.

Nat beamed when she saw him coming, and he felt bad for not eating with her earlier in the week.

"How are you, my lady?" he asked, bowing to her.

"They're making us do homework," Nat answered, sounding very disgruntled.

Shane and Kelly sat down, squeezing in on either side of her. Her complaint was refreshingly petty compared to the things troubling him.

"Well, that's a good thing, right?"

"No way," she replied, crinkling her little nose. Her big, blue eyes looked up at him like he was nuts. "How come you guys don't have to go to school?"

"Oh, we're going to school," Kelly replied, sighing. "I assure you of that."

"Why can't we go home?" Nat crossed her little arms over her chest and stared at him.

"Nat, we talked about that," Kelly gently scolded.

Some of the other kids grew quiet and looked at her with respect and affection in their eyes. Kelly smiled at them in a maternal way that made him ache, bringing to mind a memory of his mother.

He guessed Nat wasn't satisfied with what her big sister had told her. Now she was querying him to see if she'd get a different response, attributing to him some authority or power greater than that of her sister.

"I don't want to stay here anymore."

"Yeah, but this is like summer camp," Shane said clumsily, nervous under her scrutiny.

"No, it's not," she objected, glaring at him. "They wouldn't make me do homework in summer camp."

Shane looked over her head at Kelly, unsure of what to say.

"We can't go home just yet," Kelly said to her sister, her voice cracking. "But we'll be able to soon enough. For now, just try to have fun."

Nat stuck her lower lip out, looking like she might throw a tantrum. Worried that maybe his presence was upsetting her, Shane stood to go put his tray away.

"No," Nat pleaded. "Take me home." She slid off her stool and wrapped herself around his arm.

She wasn't crying, just sincerely asking him to return her life to normal. He didn't know what to say. Several of the other children seated nearby stopped eating, looking at him with the same pleading expression Nat had. Clearly, they thought he had the power to fix everything.

"Look, kids…" He paused, searching for something an adult would say. He cleared his throat and glanced at Kelly. She seemed at a loss for words too. They couldn't lie to these kids forever. Their eyes seemed to beg for directness. Most of them already knew their parents were dead, though he'd heard some speak like they were still alive and they'd soon be reunited with them. "Y'all know there are bad guys out there that want to hurt us, right?"

"Sammy says aliens killed our parents," Nat answered abruptly, pointing at a chubby kid with glasses. The boy looked at Shane with an expression that said, *Yep, that was me.* There was a strong glimmer of intelligence in his brown eyes.

"Sammy is right," Shane said softly.

Kelly glared at him, obviously not happy about him being so forward with the children.

"It's a lot to handle for little guys," he continued, knowing he was out on a limb with them. "But we need you all to be tough now and do what you're told. You need to go to the school they've set up for you."

He glanced around the table. More of the children were quiet now, all looking at him like they'd been waiting for this talk. Like the teenagers, these kids had been forced to act more mature than they were. It was hard to look at them, knowing they'd been robbed of a chance at a normal childhood. It made the memories of his time as a kid seem precious. He used to feel sorry for himself for losing his mother, but he'd gotten to have her for far longer than these children did theirs.

"And you need to play and have fun," Kelly said, sounding upbeat. "You're kids after all, right? So try to be kids."

"Are you going to put the aliens in jail?" Sara asked, looking at Shane with wide eyes.

"Yes." He suppressed a chuckle. "Something like that."

"I wanna help." James, the bold little boy he'd rescued behind the grocery store in Leeville, said. "I'm strong." He pulled the sleeve of his T-shirt up and flexed the muscle in his arm while giving Shane a very serious look.

"You know what?" Shane replied, trying to keep as solemn an expression as the little boy wore. "You are strong." He looked at the rest of the kids. "You're all strong. But we need you to go to school so you can learn everything you need to know. Then you can help."

He hoped he and the others would be able to eliminate the Anunnaki threat before James was old enough to fight. Surveying their young faces, he succumbed to the fear that the fighting might go on for much longer than he expected.

James studied him, seeming to contemplate what he'd said. Shane kept his look firm, not breaking his eyes from the boy's. After a moment, James nodded as if they'd made a deal. The other kids seemed happy with this answer too, returning their attention to their food and each other. Shane sighed and looked down at Nat. She gazed back up at him, still holding onto his arm.

"Will you come and eat with me tomorrow?" she asked with her sweetest voice, no sign of the outburst she'd just had. It amazed him how the kids could switch emotional gears so fast.

"Of course, and every day after that if you want me to," Shane replied, smiling.

Apparently satisfied, she released him and climbed back onto her stool. Kelly smiled and winked, a sign that she thought he'd done well. Shane raised his eyebrows and tilted his head, asking for permission to slip away. She nodded and he made his escape, relieved.

A week later, Shane came out of the shower and heard girls shouting in the barracks. He recognized Tracy's voice and rushed to see what was up.

"Your mom moved to Leeville just so she could stalk my dad," Tracy yelled, glaring at Laura. "What kind of a psycho slut does that?"

"What did you call my mom?" Laura screamed. She charged Tracy, murderous intent glowing in her eyes.

Shane got there just in time. He leapt out and caught Laura in his arms, holding her back.

"Your dad led her on!" Laura screamed. She twisted in his grip, trying to break free so she could attack. When she couldn't get out of his grasp, she continued to spit venom. "My mom had no idea that lying, cheating, sack of shit was married. Maybe your mom was batting for the other team like you, and he wasn't getting any at home."

Tracy pulled her fist back and moved in to hammer Laura's face. Maurice was there in an instant, grabbing her around the waist and pulling her in the opposite direction. Shane glanced over at Jules, worried she might try to step in. Jules was wide-eyed, standing back with a worried look on her face. But she seemed to know this wasn't her fight, and she was smart enough to stay out of it.

"Now listen, both of you," Maurice boomed in a voice that sounded custom made for the pulpit. "We are all brothers and sisters here. The crimes of our parents belong to them, not to us."

"Her mom ruined my life," Tracy snarled, only sounding a little deflated by Maurice's words. Shane knew she loved and admired her stepdad, and learning he'd been cheating on her mom must've cut her to the bone. No wonder she'd been so cold to Laura from the start.

"She ruined your life?" Laura pressed against Shane's arm again, trying to break free. "I was pulled out of my school, had to leave all my friends behind, and had to move to Hick Town because your stupid dad couldn't keep it in his pants."

"If it weren't for these other people," Maurice boomed, stopping Tracy from responding, "which is what your mom and dad are, just other people—then y'all would have no cause to dislike one another. Don't let this come between you. As much as it hurts, those folks are gone. We're the only family that matters now. All we have is each other."

Other than the moment of doubt he shared with Shane in the cafeteria just after Lily had met with them the first time, Maurice had continued his pious behavior. He spent what little free time he had in the base chapel. Jones and some of the others even started referring to him as the chaplain, a title he didn't object to. Shane was sure glad he was there to talk these girls down; he wouldn't have known where to start.

The girls glared at each other a moment longer, seeming

to try to come up with more insults to cast since Maurice and Shane wouldn't let them go at it. Maurice's words seemed to sink into them at the same time. Their shoulders drooped, as if accepting that they didn't need to be at each other's throats for what their parents had done was a great burden.

Once he was certain it was safe to let her go, Shane released Laura and slipped away to his side of the barracks, watching and ready to charge back in if it got heated again. Maurice talked with them in hushed tones. Just after the lights went out, they hugged, Laura in tears.

CHAPTER TWENTY

"You have fifteen minutes to get to the training hanger," Jones shouted, rousing Shane from a dead sleep. "Up and out, people!"

Groaning, he rolled onto the floor and raced to the bathroom, bumping into his barrack mates along the way. He'd grown so accustomed to being woken up abruptly—he hardly had to think about his hurried routine. Within the time allotted by the growling and barking captain, all forty-nine kids made it to the training hanger and were seated in their metals chairs. It was still dark out and Shane had a feeling it was only around midnight, though time had become immaterial to him.

"This simulation will feel more realistic than the others you have experienced," Jones began, marching back and forth across the stage with his hands clasped behind his back. "Seven of you are going to experience what it would be like to have the enemy find you out and turn upon you. The rest of you will play the role of the attacking Anunnaki."

Chatter passed through the room.

"And," Jones said, loud enough to silence them, "we are activating an injury simulation program for this scenario. That means you will feel the shot from the plasma rifle if you are hit. This will help you grow acquainted with how your armor's first aid system responds to injury. If you are delivered a lethal blow, you will be pulled out of the simulation."

Shane looked left and right at his friends, confident they could handle whatever Jones threw at them.

"Another little twist for this game," Jones said, sounding a bit mischievous. "We are making a mixed team for the human defenders, so you may have to fight alongside people you've never fought with before."

Jones paused, gazing across the room.

"You will be in full armor. We'll keep the members of the human team's identity secret from everyone else so there's no hesitating during the fight. However, the team who will act as the humans will have a moment alone in the simulation before the attack begins, so you'll have a chance to get acquainted."

The buzzing came in Shane's ears, and then the flash of light. When his senses returned, he was standing in a tunnel in red armor with the Shock Troop symbol on his chest. He and six other teenagers had their helmets under their arms, gathered at a hatch he recognized as one of the entrances to the reactor chamber.

"I guess we're the humans," Anfisa said.

"And I'm betting we'll be surprised at how many guns we see pointed at us when we open this hatch," Ethan observed.

He was a shorter, dark-skinned kid from the Australian team who Jake said was part aborigine. Originally, Shane had thought that Liam was the leader of the Aussies, but over the last few weeks, he'd seen that Ethan, who was typically quiet and always friendly, actually made most of the decisions.

Steve and Jules were also on the mash-up team, along with Petrov and Jake. It struck Shane as interesting that Jones had only selected people from the top three teams, those who'd gotten used to dominating the leaderboard. Knowing the whooping that would likely occur when they opened the hatch, he reckoned they were about to share a slice of humble pie.

Shane hesitated. They had three obvious leaders, and he wasn't sure if he should try to take charge. Everyone else seemed to be thinking the same thing, glancing from him to Ethan to Anfisa.

"Once we get in there, I'm guessing Jones has it set up so we won't even get to the reactor control panel," Shane said, taking the ball to see what happened. "He wouldn't make it that easy for us."

"He never does," Anfisa seconded. "He probably expects us to die as soon as we open this hatch."

"So what's our goal?" Steve asked.

"We still have to get to the control panel and press the button," Shane said. "That part is obvious."

They hadn't learned the complete sequence of codes to put into the control panel to destroy the reactor, so Jones placed a big, red button on the panel and they had to push it to simulate completing that portion of the mission.

"So we charge in with guns blazing," Ethan said coolly. "We hit the control panel and keep going to the other side of the reactor compartment."

"They'll expect us to turn around and fight our way back to this hatch," Anfisa joined in excitedly, apparently getting his plan before the rest of them did.

"Exactly," Ethan replied. "I'm betting they won't be crowded around the main entry hatch on the opposite side. No one would try escaping that way because it leads through the command center of the ship."

"So we hit the control panel and get to the other side without stopping," Shane said. "Then we seal the hatch and wait for the reactor to blow."

"Well," Jules said, rubbing her chin. "It ain't perfect, but I don't think there's a better plan."

Shane glanced around at everyone, making sure no one else had anything to add.

"Then let's do this," he said, "before they have more time to plan their defense."

They all nodded and made sounds of agreement. After putting his helmet on, he turned and raised his hand to the red button that would open the hatch. It wouldn't be there during the real mission either. All the ships hatches had special codes. During the evenings when they had a few minutes to study, he'd been struggling to ingest them with limited success.

He pressed the button, and the door slid aside. As soon as the opening was wide enough, Steve pushed ahead of him, ever the linebacker ready to protect his quarterback.

Shane leapt through after his friend, rolling forward as he entered the reactor chamber. The discharge of plasma rifles sounded all around him. Shane kept firing his weapon as he came to his feet.

"Go, go, go!" Ethan shouted.

The mash-up team charged across the reactor chamber, firing their weapons in every direction as they ran. The task seemed hopeless. The reactor compartment was filled with the other kids, who were also in red armor and stationed around the core. Forty-two opponents didn't seem all that bad until they were pointing guns at him. Some even stood on platforms higher in the chamber, raining plasma bolts down from above.

He realized it would have been better not to start shooting right away, because it appeared the defenders didn't know which hatch they'd come through. They'd attracted a firestorm of plasma blasts. One burned through Steve's leg and he fell, screaming, to the ground. A moment later, he grew quiet and started firing his gun again, the armor having administered pain medication to keep him going.

"Go," Steve shouted, when Shane slowed to help him. "I'll cover you."

A blast hit the floor near his feet, encouraging him to continue toward the reactor controls at full speed.

Shane fired his weapon and saw the blast burn holes through a female who was shooting at him just ahead. His heart stopped in his chest when he saw her drop, hoping he hadn't just shot Kelly. Then again, Jones said if they were killed in this simulation, they'd simply be pulled out of the game. The pain Steve expressed when he got shot sounded much worse than what his victim seemed to experience in sudden death.

He made it to the control panel with Petrov, Ethan, and Anfisa. Hitting the red button, he glanced back to see if any of their teammates were coming behind them. Steve was still on the floor, hiding behind a tool cart and using the sharp-shooting skills he'd honed from years of hunting to hold off the horde of teenagers trying to close in on him. They were gathering between the mash-up team and the exit. On the floor between Steve and Shane lay the rest of their teammates, all ejected from the game by mortal wounds.

"It's going to work," Ethan said. "They're trying to get between us and that exit.

Shane backed up with the survivors, headed toward the hatch on the opposite side. The other teens weren't guarding it because it led through the busiest parts of the ship. It didn't make sense for them to go that way. They would never try it if this weren't just a simulation. Shane saw Steve get hit by a blast that eliminated him just before he slipped around the other side of the core. He knew it was not real, but it stirred painful memories to see his friend get killed.

They made it to the main hatch just as the defenders regrouped, slipping through it under a barrage of plasma rounds exploding against the bulkhead. The hatch closed, and Anfisa fired a shot into the control panel to disable it. They stood huffing for air, looking at each other and listening. The ship trembled, and a loud roaring sound carried through the thick blast door, the reactor core erupting through the apex of the ship. Silence came a moment later.

"Congratulations," Anfisa said cheerfully. "We have won!"

"I'm not sure I'd call it winning," Ethan said glumly. "We lost three people."

"In war, casualties cannot always be considered a loss."

"Not sure I get your meaning," Shane said, shocked at how cold and academic her response sounded.

"This doesn't mean it is good to lose people," she said, not sounding apologetic, "but every mission comes with certain risk, and sometimes the cost of success is lives."

What she was saying made sense, but Shane would rather approach every mission with plans to keep all his teammates alive. He was about to say as much to her, but the buzzing came in his ears. He was returned to his metal chair in the training building, seated next to Kelly.

Her face was pale, her eyes sad. Shane already knew she was one of the defenders who'd died in the reactor chamber. It was apparent by looking at her expression that the simulation did a good job of making the trainees feel their injuries and experience death in such a way that it seemed as realistic as possible. Looking up and down the last row of seats where the Americans and the Australians sat, he could see everyone but Ethan wore the same shocked expression, blinking and looking down at their bodies as if checking to see if their injuries had been real.

"That sucked," Kelly finally blurted out. "I got shot. " She looked at him with wide eyes, and he felt terrible thinking she might have been the girl he took out in the simulation.

"Yeah, it was bad in there," he said nervously.

"Where were you?" Her color began to return.

"Oh," Shane stammered. "I was in there."

"On which side?" she asked casually. "Alien or human?"

"Human."

Her eyes grew wider, like she suspected he might have been the one who shot her.

"You can see, that was a worst-case scenario, with enemy waiting in ambush in the reactor chamber," Jones said, rescuing Shane from answering the next question he expected Kelly to ask him. "In this situation, many sacrifices would have to be made to achieve mission success. The human team did the right thing by exiting through the main hatch of the reactor compartment, though it would have been overrun by Anunnaki on a real ship."

Jones paused, his gaze falling on Ethan, and then Shane. "If you don't go into this mission prepared to give your life and to let your friends die, then it is unlikely that you will succeed."

CHAPTER
TWENTY—ONE

Last night was his team's fourth turn at cleaning the bathroom, marking the beginning of their fifth hellish week of training. It felt like a year had passed. Sometimes, he wished the damn Anunnaki would come so he could fight them, then they could all get some rest.

Shane huffed for air, leaning over with his hands on his knees. They'd just lost the flag-capturing game to the Israeli team. He was glad they'd won—it was their first time, and it was great to see them cheering and laughing. Winning had become relatively common for his team, and they didn't celebrate anymore like they did in the beginning.

Petrov limped through the briars covered in paintball splatters, way more than was required to take him out of the game. People just liked shooting the dude, and everyone was becoming a better shot each day. Shane had learned the Russian wasn't all bad, even though Shane still occasionally wanted to kick Petrov's ass. He was just driven and would do anything to win. Who could blame him for that?

Like a dog in a muzzle, he still barked all the time, talking smack every chance he got, but he didn't bite anymore. Shane guessed it was because the big Russian was scared of his team's iron-fisted boss, Anfisa. Regardless, when they were in the simulations, Petrov was amazing. And out of the all flag-capturing games they'd played, he'd won four times.

The Israelis took turns waving their little red trophy as they led the way along the backside of the buildings toward the cafeteria and lunch. The rule was that the team who got the flag was first in line at the next meal. This was quite the reward, because Jones pushed them so hard that they were always hungry. The highest team on the leaderboard got to eat next, thus the Americans fell in behind the cheerful winners, who normally found themselves further back in the pack.

Lily stepped out of the egress between the buildings ahead. One of Jones' clones was with her, and they wore black suits and sinister expressions. She raised her hand in front of the Israeli team, stopping the procession.

Jones and Dr. Blain went forward and talked to them in hushed voices. Then the scarred alien straightened and looked at the teenagers, his brow furrowing.

"Listen up, people," he shouted, climbing onto the side of the hill high enough for everyone to see him and helping Lily afterwards.

His somber tone capturing their undivided attention, the kids fell silent. Shane worried it was dread stealing the color from Lily's tan complexion, but was also suspicious that this might be just another twist in their training. They'd been kept awake for seventy-two hours last week, so it couldn't be much worse than that.

"There has been a new development," she said firmly, scanning their faces. "We just intercepted a transmission from an Anunnaki ship. They are going to arrive a lot sooner than we expected. We must cut your training short and transport you to your respective landing sites."

"What?" Kelly gasped.

"We're not ready," Liam exclaimed.

Infectious panic swept through the group. Although he did his best to hide it, Shane was not immune. His heart thumped in his ears, and the hairs stood on the back of his neck. He knew this day was coming, had even wished for it at times. Now that it was here, he felt wholly unprepared for it.

"Do not let fear inhibit your ability to carry out your mission," Lily continued. "You were all capable of defeating the Anunnaki without any training. What we've done here will only increase your odds of success." Her voice had a slight tremor in it, and he wondered if she really believed what she said.

"Go to the barracks and clean up," Jones ordered, no measure of sympathy in his voice. "Then muster at the training building where we will do a final mission briefing."

Giving each other stupefied glances, no one moved.

"This is not the time for hesitation. I said go!" Jones shouted. "Do it now!"

Accustomed to obeying his orders, the kids jogged back to the barracks. Although he was worried about what was to come, a surge of adrenaline reenergized Shane. Little was said as they showered and changed. Everyone wore a wide-eyed look on their faces—a mixture of excitement, nervousness, and fear seemed to permeate the barracks.

"We need more time," Kelly whispered to Shane, stepping behind him as he pulled on a clean, black T-shirt.

"I'm not so certain we do," he said, turning to face her. He took her shoulders in his hands and looked her in the eyes. "We didn't have any preparation before taking on that gang in Atlanta and shutting down the weapon. We didn't really have a clue as to what we were doing, but our instincts carried us through. The time here has taught us more than we need. We will win."

Kelly bit the side of her lip and nodded. Shane didn't know if they had a chance, but he did recognize it was time once again for him to be the quarterback. He'd seen the look of defeat on his friends' faces before, and he'd wanted to quit then too. But they'd pushed on, and they succeeded. Regardless of what he believed their chances were, he had to convince his team they could win, or it wasn't even worth trying.

CHAPTER TWENTY—TWO

Nervous chatter rippling across the room, they took their seats in the training hangar. Lily and Jones were already on the podium, waiting for them to settle and wearing grave expressions that charged the air with a sense of urgency.

"As we've said before, each of the seven teams will be assigned to a different Anunnaki vessel," Jones began, speaking loud enough to hush everyone. "You are all well acquainted with the mission plan."

The LCD screen came on, showing a cutaway of a pyramid-shaped starship. Then it changed to a map of the earth.

"The American team is assigned to the command ship. The Australian and Russian teams will attack the two neighboring vessels at the pyramid complex in Giza," Lily explained. She continued, telling each team where their target was. The Chinese would be sent to a Mayan ruin in Central America, the Koreans to Southeast Asia, and the Israelis to the Aztec Pyramid of the Sun in Mexico.

So Shane's team had won this short-lived competition.

They'd get to take on the biggest of the Anunnaki ships. He couldn't find any joy in the victory, fearing the prize might be death.

"The Finnish team is assigned to the Luxor Pyramid in Las Vegas, the most recent example of the Anunnaki's influence on Earth," Lily said. "You will join with the kids gathering near these pyramids. When the Anunnaki ships arrive, they will immediately begin taking on humans, giving them armor and weapons, programming them for the cleansing war."

"Be wary of the humans whose slave genes are being activated by the Anunnaki," Jones warned. "Until they are fully under the enemy's control, they will be swept into a near-psychotic frenzy. They will be suspicious of anyone who is not as enthusiastic about the arrival of the aliens as they are."

Murmurs swept through the room. His mind conjured all kinds of horrible behavior that would constitute a *near-psychotic frenzy*. Kelly looked at Shane, a range of emotions from concern to anger swirling in her eyes. The one thing he didn't detect in those tumultuous blue windows into her thoughts was fear. She was braver than any of them were.

Once again, he was struck by guilt for wishing she would be left behind, that she wouldn't be allowed to go on this mission. They'd already cheated death in Atlanta, and he feared there wasn't enough luck left in the world to get them through this alive.

"You'll get your armor and pass into the programing chamber. Once the neural upload to the slaves is complete, they'll appear to have regained free will, though they will be fully committed to serving the Anunnaki. Then six members of each team will slip away and place one of these on the front and back of their torsos." She held up a small dot, about the diameter of a pencil eraser. "When it comes in contact with the armor, it will unfold and create the Shock Troop emblem, covering your slave stripes. It'll also disconnect your armor's onboard computer from the ship's computer, essentially making you invisible. This will allow you more freedom to move around the vessel."

"You'll slip out of the programming chamber through this hatch in the back and make your way to engineering," Jones said, pointing at the diagram of a passageway that spiraled through the interior of the recruit ship to an access hatch near the center.

"Had we the time to complete your training as planned," Lily said, "you would have memorized the access codes and ejection sequences to be input in the reactor control panel. We would also have taken you through numerous scenarios so you'd be ready for almost anything. Unfortunately, that option is no longer available to us."

Nervous mumbling erupted. Everything they were saying was just a recap of what they already knew. They'd been through a lot of training in the short time they'd been here, had done a different scenario in simulations each day, and had started learning the codes. Apparently, their instructors didn't feel like that was enough. It didn't inspire much confidence in Shane and, by the sound of it, anyone else. He suddenly wondered why they were even saying this to them. Wouldn't it be better to just tell them they were ready and send them onto the field bolstered by confidence?

"However," Jones said, loudly enough to silence the room. "There is a way we can upload the information to your brains via your earbud. We hesitate to do it because it requires the temporary activation of your slave genes, and it could cause injury."

So here was the catch. They didn't need to sell Shane. He'd do anything to increase the likelihood that they would succeed. His fear of losing Kelly and becoming a slave to the Anunnaki trumped all. Although he wondered what injury it could possibly cause that the doctor couldn't heal.

"As a compromise," Lily said, "you must decide if you want us to attempt uploading this information into your brains."

"Be warned," Dr. Blain, who was sitting on the corner of the stage, said. "The upload could cause permanent instability in some of you. There is a risk of brain damage and possibly death."

Shane glanced at his teammates, then down the row at Ethan, Liam, Jake, and the rest of the Australians. They all looked concerned but also had the same so-what-we'll-take-it expressions on their faces.

"To be clear, we've never done this before," Lily added sincerely. It was admirable that they seemed so opposed to activating the slave gene. These rebels really acted like they cared about them, and they had since the day that they met. "Captain Jones and myself were soldiers and pilots, not the neuroscientists the Anunnaki have to program their slaves. We don't have the immense power reserves available to use that the recruit ships' reactors provide. And though Dr. Blain has studied the archives on the subject that were salvaged from our ship, this will be her first attempt at a neural upload."

After delivering this uninspiring disclaimer, Lily and her two counterparts gazed at the teens in the room, perhaps giving them time to contemplate the risks of what they were proposing. It didn't sound intimidating to Shane, not when compared to trying to attack the Anunnaki with the limited training they'd undergone.

"If it works, this will increase your chances of success and survival one hundredfold. If you don't want the mental up-load, leave now," Jones bellowed less delicately than the other two. "The loop on the TV in your barracks will be playing a lesson that will teach you the bare minimum you'll need to get by." He crossed his arms and looked at everyone.

The hangar was dead quiet. Shane swore he could hear Kelly's heart beating next to him, even over the deafening sound of his own. He'd already made his decision—he was in this to the end. But he couldn't help wishing Kelly would walk out. No one moved.

"Very well." Lily smiled kindly. "Dr. Blain, please begin."

"You will be immobilized like in the simulations." Dr. Blain held a thin, transparent tablet, tapping its surface with her free hand. She stopped and looked at them, that caring, maternal expression on her face that unnerved Shane each time she had treated his wounds. "I'm sorry, but this may be a bit painful."

She tapped the screen. A high-pitched whistle blast-ed Shane, and blinding light scorched his eyes. It felt like it would burn his flesh away, and then, as suddenly as the whistling began, there was silence. A wall of colors, thousands of little, flashing squares, swelled up before him and blocked out the blinding light. The wall curved into a sphere around him. Each of the tiny squares looked like a scene from a movie.

With an earsplitting screech, the scenes all pushed in at once, flowing through him in a blur of color. His head seemed to swell under the pressure. He wanted to scream but felt disconnected from his body, like he was only a brain afloat in a storm of memories that didn't belong to him. So much information blazed through him, making his brain feel like it was being poached. The memories forced their way into him, each one becoming his own. The mission to destroy the reactor repeated hundreds of times in fast-forward, though he was painfully aware of the minutest details in each simulation. He saw the reactor control panel, inputted destruction sequences, and died in a blast in one scene, then escaped in the next. He fought Anunnaki soldiers with and without weapons, and saw all his friends die over and over again.

The mix of pain, fear, and excitement made him want to curl into a ball and weep. The grief of seeing his friends die, of seeing Kelly die, was all too real. It intensified until he expected his head would explode, then everything went dark and quiet. He heard murmuring and opened his eyes. His blurred vision slowly cleared. He was sitting in the metal chair next to Kelly. The teens around him groaned, rubbing their heads. Fading terror left their faces pale and slack, like they'd all just awoken from a horrible nightmare.

He felt sharp tingles in his skull, as if the fires lit by

the neural upload had dwindled down to crackling embers. Glancing around, he moved his arms and legs. He seemed to have survived without major trauma. Kelly turned and hugged him, a quiet whimper escaping when he wrapped his arms around her.

"I saw such horrible things," she whispered.

"I know," he said, pulling her tight. Tears blurred his vision. "Me too."

"It worked!" Dr. Blain studied images flashing on her tablet. "And everyone seems to be okay." She looked at them with a broad smile on her face that showed she had no idea how much they'd suffered during the upload.

The painful tingles subsided, and the misery from seeing Kelly and his friends die in different scenarios lost some of its grip. A new awareness diffused through him. Along with the horrible stuff he'd seen, so much amazing knowledge was in his head. It felt like he'd been training to attack the Anunnaki for a lifetime. He knew how to beat them, was certain he could succeed. Confidence flourished in the presence of the knowledge.

Kelly must've experienced it too. She released him and leaned back, drying her eyes with the side of her finger. Her traumatized expression transformed into a little smile.

"I think I know karate!" she said.

"And judo," Liam added.

Shane could sense his intimate knowledge of those martial arts, and at least five others. They were going to destroy the Anunnaki ships—he grew more certain of it with each passing second. Furthermore, he knew he could get his team out alive. Vindictiveness boiled in him. These bastards killed his aunt and his father. Now he had what he needed to get even. Glancing at his counterparts, he sensed they were all thinking the same thing.

"Because of residual fluctuation in your serotonin levels, you may experience an elevated mood for a couple of hours," Dr. Blain warned.

"Remember," Jones said with his drill-sergeant voice. "By destroying the recruit ships, you will bring us a massive step closer to ensuring the survival of your species, your brothers and sisters. We hope you live through this mission, but you must lay down your life if that's what the situation demands. Just because we've uploaded a bunch of information into your brains doesn't mean you are prepared for every contingency." He paused, studying them.

"Always the pessimist," Laura whispered.

"Or simply a realist," Tracy countered sternly.

"Trust your instincts in battle," Jones bellowed, glaring at the chattering girls to show he'd heard them and didn't approve of the interruption. "Do I make myself clear?"

"Sir, yes sir," everyone shouted, a level of respect in their voices that hadn't been there so many weeks ago.

They responded in Anunnaki. Shane suddenly realized they'd been speaking it since coming out of the neural upload. On top of everything else, they'd been taught to speak the enemy's universal tongue. He was pretty sure he could speak a crap-load of other languages now too. His brain overflowed with new knowledge, more than he could even begin to comprehend.

Jones' cautioning words soaked in. Shane was ready to lay down his life if that was what it took. But he wasn't ready to see Kelly die. His surge of confidence was subdued. He glanced at her, his newly implanted memories conjuring the white-hot reactor explosion that would vaporize flesh and bone. His stomach twisted into knots, and bile rose in his throat. He couldn't let it happen. He'd die for her in a heartbeat, but he didn't want her to die with him.

"Now you all should go enjoy your dinner," Lily advised. "I'm proud of what you've done here over the last month. You've proven you have what it takes to defeat the Anunnaki. You already possessed the courage, strength, endurance, and aggression. And now you have the knowledge."

"Helicopters will be ready to deliver you down to an airport at zero two hundred hours. There, you will be loaded onto military transports and flown to your respective targets," Jones growled. "Dismissed."

The kids didn't move immediately, all sitting and looking at each other with stunned expressions. They had been judged the best hope of stopping the Anunnaki, and their sentence may well be death. Shane knew he couldn't keep Kelly from going. He had to respect her desire to be there for the fight. Standing, he tried to shove aside his fear for her safety. Kelly and the others rose next to him.

"We have to stop them, Shane," she said firmly. "We have to make sure Nat has a world to grow up in." Her expression was resolute, conveying that she'd die a thousand torturous ways to save her sister.

"Don't worry." He scooped her hand into his, his heart

breaking at the thought of her enduring even a scratch. Forcing a smile, he tried to be encouraging. "We've got home-field advantage. The Anunnaki aren't going to know what hit them."

"Let's try to relax tonight," Maurice advised loudly enough for everyone to hear. He glanced at Shane in such a way that made him wonder if he picked up on his inner turmoil. His face was leaner and his waist much smaller than it was before. He looked older and more serious, though he still had that friendly glimmer in his eyes. "Let's consider this night a gift and not squander the time." He winked at Shane knowingly and offered a compassionate smile.

A wave of agreement passed through the room. Different nationalities intermingled with a familiarity and comfort he couldn't have imagined on that first sleepless night in the barracks. For some inexplicable reason, he couldn't help feeling wary. Something was off. Hoping he wasn't experiencing the instability Dr. Blain warned of, he mimicked the rest of the kids, who chatted excitedly about all they'd learned. They spilled out of the hangar as a unified group, the seven teams of seven no longer distinguishable.

Steve walked next to Anfisa. Their hands brushed, and Steve smiled timidly at her, red flooding his cheeks. He looked like a little boy blushing at his first crush. The overconfident, tough-guy persona he always brandished blasted away each time she glanced at him.

"Wow," Shane teased when Steve held the door open for him. "You're so whipped."

He expected the big guy to get embarrassed and to tell him to shut up. Instead, Steve smiled. "What can I say? Any woman who can kick my ass is a woman I gotta love."

Shane laughed. Thank goodness, Steve would be with him on the mission. Not to mention the fight in Atlanta, they'd gone to battle on the gridiron many times. He knew in the heat of it that Steve would not back down. He wished Aaron were here as well. Then they'd be unstoppable for sure.

At dinner, everyone seemed to be making an effort to follow Maurice's advice, or they were experiencing the elevated mood the doctor warned of, Shane couldn't tell which. People joked around, and laughter was frequent, though often restrained and tinged with nervousness.

In a lot of the simulated missions they endured in the neural upload, the teams were mixed so that kids from different nationalities fought together. He had this sense that he'd known many of them for years, though he really didn't know much about their lives from before they came here. Even though they'd spent a month eating, sleeping, and living together, the training had been too vigorous to allow much time for social interaction with the foreigners. They talked of the simulations like they were old times and laughed about the flag-capturing games and about sparring competitions they had against each other. Petrov even struck up an unprompted conversation with Shane, who'd been watching the others off to the side. He spoke of his home back in Russia, his little sister who was waiting for him there, and his older brother who had been killed by the limbic manipulator.

Petrov finished abruptly by saying, "You will have to excuse me." He walked toward the drink dispenser, grabbing a napkin on his way and dabbing his eyes. It was such a rollercoaster of emotion that Shane feared they all might be experiencing some negative side effects of the upload. What if their brains fell apart during the mission?

"It doesn't seem like we just met these people four weeks ago," Kelly mused, slipping next to him.

"I know—feels like we've been here forever," Maurice replied distantly.

"I propose a toast," Jules announced, lifting her cup. The other kids quieted and looked at her. "To the best group of people I've ever known," she paused and smiled, "for twenty-eight whole days."

Laughter erupted across the room, and then they fell quiet when her expression turned serious.

Determined to learn as much about his teammates as possible, Shane had gotten to know her better during the training. He'd discovered she was much more sensitive than she acted. He'd seen her looking at Tracy the same way he sometimes looked at Kelly, with deep melancholy over the idea that she could be killed. He noticed it the first time during a simulation. A plasma blast had hit Tracy, and the computer pulled her out of the game. It left the burnt corpse that made the simulations all too realistic, causing nightmares for Shane. Jules had frozen, staring at Tracy's body, her face contorted with horror. She forgot they were in a firefight and, before Shane could yell at her, she got shot too.

"I feel like I've grown more in the short time we've spent together than I did in my entire life up to this point," she continued, a sincerity in her voice and moistness in her eyes. "I know this sounds weird, but I love you guys. I feel like you're family." She scanned their faces, and her eyes stopped on Tracy. Jules raised her cup higher.

"Here, here," Maurice said, lifting his drink.

The rest of the kids raised their drinks and said versions of cheers and good health in their languages. The earbud no longer translated them to English, not that he needed it to. He understood them all. Dr. Blain must've had that feature deactivated. Jules sat down, and everyone was silent, the emotion growing thick in the room. Feeling a little detached from them, Shane wondered if the mood-enhancing effects of the neural upload were wearing off, the reality of the hell they found themselves in creeping in like a poisonous fog.

"I propose a challenge." Steve's deep voice crushed the solemnity. "As I am sure you are all painfully aware," his eyes twinkled with mischief, "we Americans," he struck his chest with his fist, "have won most of the flag-capturing games."

"You're only ahead by one win," Liam retorted. The Aussies and Russians were tied for second place as of yesterday.

"Yes, well," Steve mumbled. "I've never been one for trivial details."

Chuckles came from a few of them.

"I don't want to say that we are the best." He cleared his throat. "Not yet anyway. You folks should have one more chance to prove my arrogant ass wrong.

"And so my challenge, ladies and gentle-blokes." Steve mocked an Australian accent as he looked at Liam. "The first team to destroy their ship's reactor won't have to clean the bathroom ever again."

"Nothing personal," Jake said, crinkling his nose. "But

after we destroy the reactor, I don't ever want to share a bathroom with any of you again."

"Yeah," Laura replied, laughing. "Some of y'all are nasty."

The teens broke into laughter, teasing each other about their personal habits and all agreeing that Petrov took way to long to do his hair. Even the ever-stoic Chinese and Finns were in on it. The big Russian took it in stride, using his palms to check his do and telling them not to be jealous.

This round of joking went on for a few more minutes and then quiet swept through the cafeteria, the artificial bliss dissipating and anxiety over what was to come taking a firmer hold on them.

CHAPTER
TWENTY—THREE

"I'm going to get some rest," Shane said, hoping Kelly would slip away with him.

"Sounds like a good idea." She turned and walked out of the cafeteria with him in tow.

The sun had just set, and he could barely see across the base due to the encroaching night. He wanted to forget what they'd be off to do in just a few hours and enjoy being close to her, but the darker things he'd been exposed to replayed in his head.

Kelly clasped his hand and crossed her other arm over his, hugging his arm as they walked. She took a deep breath and then sighed.

"I love summer nights," she said.

"Me too," he replied, a tremor in his voice.

They'd be playing their first games of the season if things were normal. He'd been training so hard over the summer. This was the year he was going to make varsity. He loved playing football in September. The nights were still warm, but not too hot, and everyone was charged with excitement over the season to come.

"Funny how many things I took for granted." She trailed off.

"I doubt we'll ever do that again," he said, his mind struggling to find a way to guarantee her safety. "You know, they've trained backups to take our positions if someone fails or if…" He stopped himself. The words had come out before he had a chance to think. Now, he wished he could take them back.

"Or what?" She stopped walking and looked up at him.

"Or, if someone decided they didn't want to go along."

"That's great," she said, letting go of his hand. "What are you trying to say, Shane?"

"Nothing," he stammered. He knew he shouldn't be saying this to her, but he couldn't keep it inside. "I was just thinking, maybe you should stay behind… so you can look after Nat."

She crossed her arms. Even in the dim light, he could see the expression of disappointment on her face.

"Look," she said with quiet anger. "These aliens chose each of us for a specific reason. Whether it makes sense to me or anyone else, they believe I should be here. I don't have a choice but to go—to assure Nat's safety."

"Yeah, but look how all the teams are groups of kids who were already together." His mouth kept running, beyond his control. "What's the likelihood that the best of the best happened to already be acquainted? Maybe they just snatched up groups of survivors, figuring they could train anyone with half a brain. Maybe they just told us we're special to build our confidence."

"Really?"

"I'm just saying—"

"You're saying a load," she snapped, cutting him off. "But you're being selfish. You don't want me to go because you're scared I might get hurt."

"Well, yeah," he blurted, certain this wasn't going to end well.

"Ridiculous," she shouted, raising her hands. "I should have never..." She stepped closer to him. "I'm going."

"Come on, Kelly," he pleaded.

"I need to spend time with Nat." She spun away, starting across the tarmac.

"I'm sorry," he called after her desperately, sounding like a total dumbass.

How freaking stupid was he? He knew she'd blow up at him if he tried to get her to stay, but he had to open his mouth. Now she hated him. They only had a few hours before they'd have to go, and he'd just ruined what could be their last quiet moments together.

He stood in the dark and watched her walk away, his mind searching for something to do or say to make her come back. After she entered the building where the younger kids stayed, he stared at the door for a long while, willing her to come out so he could beg for her forgiveness.

The crickets and other night creatures' music seemed to grow louder with each passing minute, making him feel even more alone. It became painfully evident an apology would have to happen later, once she'd cooled off. His head drooping, he made his way to the barracks. He was being foolish, letting himself get distracted at such a critical time. It endangered both of them. He resolved to try to make it up to her when the opportunity presented itself. He had to stop being selfish— the mission required his full focus now.

Forcing his attention to all the new stuff banging around in his skull, Shane slowly made his way to the barracks. He took a shower, brushed his teeth, and crawled into his rack. Lying on his back, he stared at the bunk above, picturing different codes he'd learned. So much of the mission depended on these codes, some would open doors, and others would destroy the reactor. It was a crap-load of information, and he didn't understand half of it. What if something important slipped from his mind before he could use it?

The lights went out. He knew he needed sleep, but he was unable to slow his racing mind. He reckoned it was around midnight when Kelly joined him on his narrow bed. She didn't say anything about their earlier fight, and he didn't have the balls or energy to bring it up, though he wanted to tell her again that he was sorry. The fight was stupid, and it was all his fault. Pressing his back against the partition to give her space, he held her tight against him, breathing her in. This might be the last chance he'd ever have to hold her. He didn't feel the surge of passion he experienced on other nights when he held her. He was too wrapped up in concern for her safety to be excited, though he vowed to never mention those fears to her again.

Kelly pressed into him in a way that said she accepted his unspoken apology, her body fitting like they were designed to be a single unit. Soon after she nestled, her breathing grew heavy from sleep. Contrasting with frightful thoughts of the near future, her stimulating closeness guaranteed he wouldn't join her in getting some shut-eye, but it didn't bother him. He didn't want to miss a second of this precious time with her and did everything he could to keep from thinking of all the bad things that might happen in the near future.

"Time to go," Jones announced with a gentler voice than usual. He only turned on half the lights.

Kelly stirred and rolled out of his bunk. He yawned, breaking free of the turmoil entangling his mind for the last two hours. Across the aisle, Jules rolled out of Tracy's bunk. Steve's rack was empty. Shane groggily slipped on the plain white T-shirt and blue jeans provided, intended to make them blend with the other kids who would be harvested by the Anunnaki. Steve came up the aisle with a sheepish grin on his face.

"Look who's the big stud," Tracy said, smiling mischievously. "Spend the night with Anfisa, did we?"

"Shut up," Steve replied, playfully pushing her.

These friends were the closest thing he had left to a family, and he was glad they'd found some comfort during the night.

"Let's go," Jones shouted louder than before.

Shane rushed to the bathroom, taking a leak and brushing his teeth as fast as he could. When he came out, Jones ushered him through the front door of the barracks and onto the tarmac. A sliver of moon hung low in the clear night sky, casting its faint glow on a line of black helicopters. Perhaps it was just because he was exhausted, but he was surprised by how relaxed he felt, like a man who'd accepted his death sentence and was at peace with himself.

The rest of the kids trickled out and met up with their teams. When everyone in his squad was together, Shane led them to the first chopper, and they boarded. The engine whined and the rotors smacked the air loudly, drowning any attempt at conversation.

Shane leaned back in his seat, holding Kelly's hand. He closed his eyes, reliving simulations of the attack on the Anunnaki once again. His brain ached from being awake all night, but he was determined to stay focused. He'd sleep after these murderous invaders were blown to shit—forever if he failed.

The helicopter ride took a little over an hour, and they landed near some hangars at a large airport, which Shane figured was in Tennessee. Military aircraft, large jets painted gray and bearing American flags on their tails, waited on the dimly lit tarmac.

It was still dark out when Shane and his friends climbed onto the big aircraft. Directed by Lily, the Russians and the Australians followed them.

"I'll be flying this plane to your landing site in Egypt. Dr. Blain will be our co-pilot," Jones said, standing near the door to the cockpit. "If any of you have questions, feel free to come forward and talk to us. There's food and drinks in these coolers—eat as much as you can. Once we land, you may not have time for a meal."

Jones entered the cockpit and, moments later, the jet's

engines screamed to life. Hoping his headache would fade, Shane reclined his seat and closed his eyes. If it didn't, he was going to need Dr. Blain to work her magic on him before they landed. They were fortunate to have the doctor going with them—he had a bad feeling they'd need her services.

A nightmare of seeing Kelly shot through her belly by a plasma rifle jarred him awake. His mouth was parched, and his neck hurt. An image of her face as she died, her eyes puddled with tears of pain and fear, was seared in his mind. He lifted his head off Kelly's shoulder, and she sighed. He smiled at her to try and hide the grief he felt from the horrible dream. How long had she been propping him, too kind to move and disrupt his sleep?

"I've got to get up for a minute," she said softly. "You want something to drink?"

"Yes, please," he replied, his voice scratchy.

He blinked his eyes several times to moisten them, watching Kelly head to the front of the plane where the coolers were. She retrieved a sandwich and a bottle of water, bringing them to Shane, then she continued to the back of the plane, presumably to the bathroom.

"Ah," Steve said, twisting around and looking over the headrest of the seat in front of him. "The sleeping beauty is awake. Must've gotten kissed."

"Funny," Shane replied, yawning and rubbing his eyes.

"And with that rank breath," Steve goaded. "The girl must be totally in love with you. I'd personally rather kiss a dead skunk's butthole than have you sleeping on my shoulder."

"Bite me," Shane said.

Licking his teeth, he realized Steve might be right. He must've been sleeping with his mouth gaping open the entire time. Drinking some water and taking a bite of the sandwich, he hoped to make an improvement before Kelly returned.

"Here dude," Steve said, reaching around and handing him a tube of toothpaste. "You've got to be more prepared. You'll have to use your finger—I ain't sharing my toothbrush."

Shane chuckled, and then leaned forward so he could see in the seat next to Steve. Anfisa was asleep there, slumped low with her leg across his.

"Oh, look who's the little lovebird?" Shane whispered, taking his revenge. "You're so whipped; you even thought to bring a toothbrush and toothpaste so you can be all fresh for her."

"Maybe you should take a tip or two from the master," Steve replied.

Chuckling, Shane put a squirt of the toothpaste on his finger, balanced the tube on Steve's big head, and unlocked his seatbelt. He walked to the back of the plane, rubbing the toothpaste on his teeth. Half of the passengers were asleep. The others looked up at him as he passed. Their expressions were glum, but some of them smiled. Were they flying toward victory or their deaths? At best, it was likely a mix of both. Either way, they were brothers and sisters on this adventure, closer than he imagined strangers had ever become in such a short period of time.

At the bathrooms, a door opened, and Kelly stepped out. Shane paused, his foamy finger in his mouth. She laughed, and he gave her a toothpaste smile. Holding the door open for him, she smacked his bottom as he entered.

"What?" he asked, turning to look at her.

"Oops," she flirted, then turned and walked forward in the plane.

A surge of lust making him dizzy, he watched her go, suddenly feeling like the luckiest man in the world. Her jeans and black tank top showed off her figure, which had always been fit before but now looked even better, displaying the benefit of all the hard exercise they'd endured. Thank goodness she was over the stupid stuff he'd said last night. If only they had more time together. For a few days of normalcy—time to take her to the movies or to hang out with her at the lake. For that, he'd give his throwing arm.

"Do you reckon we would have come together if it weren't for the end of the world?" he whispered after he'd returned from the bathroom and was settling down next to Kelly.

"Yes, actually. We would've." She smiled sweetly at him, flooding his heart with warmth. "Don't think, Shane Tucker, I haven't noticed you giving me the googly eyes for the last, oh I don't know, forever," she whispered, like she knew he didn't want Steve to hear. Kissing his cheek, she squeezed his thigh and sent a warm jolt through him.

"Then why didn't we ever hook up?" he asked, their faces only a few inches apart.

"Because you never asked," she whispered, leaning closer. "Why? Was there some other girl?"

"No way. Well, at least not all the time," he teased.

She slapped his chest and leaned back, feigning jealousy.

"I just didn't have the balls to ask you," he admitted. "Figured you wouldn't give me the time of day."

She leaned in and pressed her lips to his. He hated that the wonderful feeling of being this close to her might never have happened, hated that something so awesome was a result of something so horrible. She lingered in the kiss, her eyes half closed. It was the best moment of his life, and yet, it broke his heart because he feared for her. The confusing mix of emotion made heat surge in him. He wanted to be far away with her, to hold her in his arms, to be alone with her. But that was impossible. His inner fire morphed into motivation. They'd destroy the Anunnaki, and they'd survive. They had to so he could have more time with her, to stare at her and touch her, to learn everything about her.

CHAPTER
TWENTY—FOUR

"We'll be making a landing attempt at Cairo International Airport in one hour," Jones announced over the aircraft's PA system.

"A landing attempt?" Steve sat up in his seat, Anfisa stretching next to him. "What in Pete's hell does he mean by that?"

"At least it sounds better than making a crash landing," Tracy observed.

She was sitting across the aisle, sharing a blanket with Jules. She caught Shane looking her way and smiled. He was happy his friends had this last bit of time to rest, even if the flight wasn't overly comfortable. With all the things that had happened to them in the last month and what lay head, the respite seemed like the calm in the eye of a category-five hurricane.

His focus fell on a stack of green crates with "U.S. Army" stenciled on them strapped in to the left of the cockpit door. Judging by the length and thickness of the rectangular boxes,

Shane expected they were filled with weapons. But he knew they couldn't be the plasma rifles. They'd be issued those once they were in the Anunnaki ship. These had to be guns to fight off kids who might attack on the way to the pyramids.

He thought of the battles they fought before, of the faces of boys and girls he'd shot when they were in Atlanta. The slack expression of death and sudden look of innocence they all shared were ever present in his thoughts. Right or wrong, he'd taken their lives. He couldn't stomach the idea of killing again.

"We should all eat," Laura said, standing up. "Who knows when we'll have another chance?"

Her black hair was pulled into a tight braid, and her face seemed leaner, the same as everyone else. Lily had given them their choice of clothing, and Laura had gotten ahold of a makeup kit. Wearing all black, with dark eyeliner and lipstick that accentuated her pale skin, she looked like some kind of commando vampire, thirsty for blood.

Although she'd performed beautifully in the simulations, she was the only person on his team who wasn't battle-tested. He'd have to keep an eye on her, but he had a feeling she'd do fine. She walked to the front of the plane, hanging onto the backrest of the seats to stabilize herself as the aircraft bounced toward its destination. It tilted down at a slight angle, indicating they were descending to Cairo. With that nurturing manner that didn't seem to fit her Goth appearance, Laura passed out bottles of water and sandwiches to everyone who didn't already have some.

The passengers were quiet, eating their food and likely

reflecting on the hell that lay ahead. Adrenaline stole Shane's appetite, but he forced down two sandwiches while thinking about Rebecca and the others who must've made the meal. It was one more reminder—the fate of the entire world depended on the people on this plane. Thank goodness they made simple ham and cheese. Anything fancier and he wouldn't have been able to touch it.

"Fasten your seatbelts," Jones announced. "The airport runway is obstructed by abandoned aircraft. We've found a narrow strip where we can land, but it's going to be rough."

Seatbelts clicked, and murmurs passed through the plane. Shane took a gulp of his water, trying to keep his food down. He felt a bit of motion sickness coming on. Mixed with the excitement, it tore at his insides.

A loud mechanical whir startled him, and Shane glanced at Kelly.

"It's normal," she replied softly.

He'd never flown before, and he was embarrassed and a bit shocked that the descent made him nervous, especially after all he'd been through.

Out of the window, he could see the sun rising in the east, lighting the tan desert landscape below. The city of Cairo was visible. Much of it looked poor and ancient. Some of the buildings were black, scarred by fire. Bent columns of smoke rose from others. Off in the distance, geometrical splotches of green represented the farmlands that surrounded the city and were used to feed its inhabitants. Although inhospitable desert surrounded the rural area, it looked far more inviting to him than the city below. He guessed the rest of the kids from Leeville would agree.

"Looks rough down there," Steve observed, sounding glum but not overly agitated by the fact that they'd soon be on those streets. He made a good linebacker, calm and powerful. Shane just had to point him in the right direction and say go, and Steve would crush anything in his path.

Always the quarterback, Shane's mind started coming up with every possible nightmarish scenario they might run into in Cairo. It might be better to allow his friends to be jaded and more relaxed—the result of all the hard training and the neural upload—but Shane intended to obsess over each second of the mission. He'd make sure he was ready to lead his team through whatever this city, and Giza beyond, could throw at them.

The plane made a slow, sweeping turn around the airport, listing right so Shane had a clear view of where Jones intended to land. Aircraft were scattered randomly across the tarmac, blocking runways, mangled from colliding with others, and buried in the side of the terminal, which was mostly burned. They had been away from the death and destruction for only a short while, yet it felt like a lifetime ago when he and his friends were stepping over the corpses back home. He could see random bodies sprawled on the tarmac, dreading getting down closer to them. They'd be rotten by now.

"Everyone, hang on," Jones ordered, his voice calm and fitting for the old pro at crashing that he was.

The plane flew away from the airport and came back around with a hard bank. Shane's stomach wasn't happy about it at all. He gritted his teeth, his seatbelt the only thing preventing him from falling on top of Kelly in the turn.

They leveled off, and the nose of the aircraft tilted up. Shane could see the city drawing closer as they descended. Then hangars and wrecked planes flashed by his window. The landing gear hit the runway hard and with a loud yelp from the tires, the shock of the impact jarring his teeth. Jones immediately got on the brakes, the engines screaming as he reversed thrust.

Shane pressed his legs into the seat in front of him to keep from falling forward. Kelly hugged his arm, which he'd streched in front of her. Even over the roar, the sound of screeching tires permeated the cargo bay. The plane shook, rattled, and twisted back and forth. He held his breath, waiting to be slammed out of his seat when they collided with another aircraft stranded on the runway.

As suddenly as the violence of the landing started, it stopped. Jones brought the plane to a halt, and the engines whined down. Shane was stunned. There was no way they'd made it to the ground in one piece. The other passengers shared the shaken expression he expected he wore, then Petrov let out a whoot, and they all started clapping.

"I'd say that's about all the proof anyone needs," Maurice proclaimed, unbuckling his seatbelt and standing. "Luck is with us," he hesitated, "because there ain't no way we'd be alive if it wasn't."

Nervous chuckles passed through the others. Shane guessed the preacher's son was about to make a religious comment, but he'd pulled back at the last second because some of the others tended to get uncomfortable when he had in the past.

"Okay people," Jones said, stepping through the cockpit door. "We need to get you equipped and on your way ASAP."

Jones removed the lids of the crates, revealing a variety of guns, as Shane suspected. Dr. Blain opened the side doors of the military aircraft and was swinging guns mounted to the fuselage out of the openings.

"These are AK-47s," he said, lifting a distressed rifle with a wooden stalk and grip on it. "They are very reliable and somewhat common in these areas, so they won't raise suspicion."

"I'll take one of those," Steve said, relieving Jones of the gun with gleaming eyes. "And one of these." He retrieved a short-barreled shotgun with a pistol grip out of the crate. "And, oh yeah, what's that?"

"It's a grenade launcher," Tracy said, sticking an elbow out to prevent him from setting the shotgun down. "And it's mine."

She squeezed between Steve and the crate, taking advantage of both his hands being full. After grabbing the gun, which had an oversized barrel to fire its thick projectiles, she scooped up a chain of the short, fat, bullet-shaped grenades.

"Each of you should take a vest. Be careful—the pockets have hand-thrown grenades in them," Jones said.

Talking in his drill-sergeant voice, he reviewed nuances about each of the weapons; what to do if they misfired or jammed, the delay time on the grenades, and their effective kill range. His sweeping gazes studied the teens as he spoke, perhaps assessing if they were ready. Otherwise, the lecture seemed like a waste of time. Shane already knew everything about the weapons from the neural upload.

He was the last to pick out a gun, and he wasn't the least bit enthusiastic about having one in his hands again. His experience with the M-16s in Atlanta made him go for the AK. He'd seen the Russian-made weapons in the movies, but never in real life. The guns were old, or at least made to look old— their barrels spotted with rust and the wooden parts missing most of the original varnish. He supposed so that they'd blend better on the streets of Cairo.

"Never mind the patina—she's the finest weapon ever made," Petrov announced, petting the stalk of his AK affectionately. "You'll find she is reliable no matter what the conditions. Russian ingenuity at its finest."

"Thank you, Mikhail Kalashnikov," Anfisa added, kissing her AK.

"So hot." Steve watched her with lascivious eyes.

Shane could only offer a polite smile. He couldn't wait until all this was over. He'd never touch another gun again if he had his choice. He put on a black mesh vest with four pockets running on either side of the zipper, each one holding a grenade. Then he took the backpack Jones gave him, filling it with extra clips for his gun and the dried food Jones handed out. Touching the bullets caused bile to rise in his throat, the images of the kids he'd killed resurfacing in his mind.

"Your teams will take different routes through the city," Jones instructed, handing out maps. "It may draw too much attention if you travel together."

The doctor gave them paper cups filled with vitamins that

she said would give them energy and keep them alert even if they couldn't eat or sleep for several days. Having grown accustomed to swallowing the massive tablets, the kids ingested her prescription without hesitation.

"Once the Anunnaki vessels land, it's critical you act like the other kids around you. It must appear you are under the control of the enemy. And do not attempt to take your weapons into the ship. Cast them aside when you see the others do it. You need to attract the least attention to yourselves as possible."

"Where will you be?" Tracy asked.

"We'll be hiding nearby. Once you destroy the reactors, we will fly in helicopters with reinforcements."

"If we destroy the reactors," Laura murmured.

"No time for that," Tracy scolded.

Laura glared at her. Tracy didn't acknowledge it, focused on strapping on her new toys. They'd been getting along better since their fight in the barracks, but there was still constant tension between them.

The last thing Shane donned was a green belt with two canteens hanging from it. He felt weighed down by all the gear, but he didn't dare leave any behind. Jones opened the rear hatch, a ramp that was wide enough to drive a car on. Gunshots sounded in the distance, and Shane's hand reflexively went to the strap of his rifle.

"The teams will leave at fifteen-minute intervals. Move quickly and quietly through the city. Get to the pyramids as fast as possible. The first team out is the Australians," Jones said. "Liam and Jake, you're going with the Americans. Jules and Kelly, you'll be on the Australian team."

"Wait," Shane stammered. "What? I don't think so!"

"Your affections could affect your judgment at a critical moment," Jones replied curtly. "If your attention is on protecting her, it cannot be on the mission."

"We've done some pretty crazy shit together already," Shane replied, trying to keep his anger in check. "We shut down that stupid weapon in Atlanta, didn't we?"

"I'm not disputing your abilities." Jones sighed, a rare glimmer of empathy in his eyes. "Shane, you were born a leader. Think about it. Step out of yourself for a minute. Shouldn't you be separated from Kelly for this mission?"

He searched for an argument to counter, something to prove that Kelly and he should stay together. Deep down inside, Shane knew Jones' logic was sound, and he would do the same if their roles were reversed.

"We're different," he said, refusing to give in. "We work too well together to be separated."

He looked at Tracy, expecting she'd join in the argument to prevent having Jules taken from her. But the tough girl with a blond crew cut, who he'd grown to respect more than just about anyone, wore a pained expression showing she reluctantly agreed with Jones. Jules looked offended, but she didn't turn away when Tracy walked over to her and talked in a hushed voice.

"He's right, Shane," Kelly said, barely speaking louder than a whisper. "I know you'll do whatever it takes to protect me. We have to be on different teams if this is going to work."

"No, Kelly." Sweat beaded on Shane's forehead. He

couldn't stand the idea of her being in danger when he wasn't near to help.

"You know he's right," she repeated. "This mission has to succeed. I don't want to be a distraction for you, and you can't be one for me. We have to do it for Nat and everyone else."

Shane looked into her sapphire eyes, tears glistening in them. There was no way he'd change her mind, and he knew his reasons for wanting to were selfish. His vest and weapon suddenly seemed a hundred pounds heavier. He pulled her into his arms and kissed her, struggling to keep the tears out of his eyes.

"Promise me you'll look after Nat and the other kids if I don't make it," she whispered.

"You'll make it," he replied, his voice cracking.

"Just promise me, damn it."

"Okay," he said, defeated. "I promise."

She smiled, melting his heart. He'd die a thousand torturous ways to keep her safe. His brain raced, desperate to find a reason for her to stay on the plane, some way of stopping her from going on the mission. She didn't give him another chance to object, turning away and stepping toward the back of the airplane with Jules and the Australians. He caught one last glimpse of her face just after she walked onto the runway. The kind smile she'd shown him was gone, replaced by the steely expression of a warrior—cold, hard, and ready to kill if that was what it took to get the job done.

Chapter
Twenty—Five

"Don't worry, mate," Liam said quietly, putting a comforting hand on Shane's shoulder. "My boys will keep them safe."

"Thanks, Liam," Shane muttered.

Tracy stood on the ramp next to him, a glum expression on her face. Her lip twitched like she struggled to keep from calling out to Jules. Shane's eyes locked onto Kelly, his sour guts twisting into knots. The hot desert wind shifted and blew the smell of rotting flesh and fire into his face. He blinked his eyes and stopped breathing through his nose. The Australians—Jules and Kelly with them—slipped between the hangars and out of sight. Shane looked at Tracy.

"We'll see them soon," he said, his voice weak.

She returned his gaze, her eyes damp. He didn't imagine Tracy had ever really cried, and to him, the wetness in her eyes now was essentially her version of bawling. He was beginning to think the foul odor and smoke probably caused her eyes to water when Tracy stepped closer to him. She looked up at his face, and then she hugged him. He was shocked, not having expected her to ever show such sensitivity. For a second, he just stood there, her arms around his torso. Then he remembered his manners and hugged her back.

When she released him and stepped away, she looked down and straightened her gear. Then she flashed an embarrassed glance at him before studying her watch and clearing her throat.

"Looks like we have ten minutes," she observed gruffly. "Hurry up and wait."

"Yeah," Shane replied. He wanted to give her a playful punch in the shoulder, something to show he was cool with her display of emotion. Expecting it might make her more uncomfortable, he held back.

"Let's have a look at our map," Steve suggested, making an obvious effort to distract them.

Needing the diversion, Shane unfolded the map on a table that extended off the curved fuselage of the aircraft. Maurice, Laura, Steve, Tracy, Liam, and Jake crowded around. Steve's strategy worked, at least for Tracy. She immersed herself in analyzing their route, pointing out areas where she thought they'd need to be extra vigilant. Pretending to look at the map, he glanced around at their faces. They each had their strengths and weaknesses, Shane included. Were they good enough to win this deadly game? At this point, it didn't matter. This was his team, and he had to believe in them now as much as they'd believed in him all along.

Each squad was assigned a different way through the city. His attention was drawn to the blue line, the path Kelly and the Aussie team were on. Biting the inside of his cheek, he focused on the red line that belonged to his squad. He hated to admit it, but she *was* a distraction. Apparently, she was not only the greatest source of his strength, but she was also his weakness. Even now, he was having trouble keeping his attention on the task at hand.

"Okay, team one, you're up next," Jones growled. He sat near the side door just forward of the wings, manning the mini-gun that swung off the fuselage and through the opening.

Dr. Blain sat opposite him, the same weapon pointed out of the door on her side. She looked more nervous than Jones, who was focused and calm like this was business as usual. Shane reckoned she'd never been in combat. Glancing toward him, her lips rose into a smile. The maternal glimmer that made him inexplicably uncomfortable ignited in her eyes. He smiled back and then turned away.

"Let's do this," Steve said, sounding ready to charge out of the locker room and onto the football field.

They gathered their stuff, and Shane was the first at the door. Far off in the distance, he could hear the pop of a gun. Otherwise, all was quiet.

He glanced back at the captain, wanting to say thanks. As gruff and unfriendly as Jones always tried to act, Shane knew he cared. Although he didn't like or trust him during those first days of training, he'd come to respect the rebel like he respected Coach Rice, the man he wished his own father had been more like. He looked at Tracy and Maurice, hoping they'd say something meaningful. Their faces expressed the same sentiments, but all kept quiet.

"Good luck," Jones said, nodding at them in a way that showed he acknowledged their gratefulness. There was a hint of sadness in his eyes.

"Thanks," Shane replied, wondering how many times the captain had trained soldiers and then sent them off to die.

"I'm shooting that thing when we get back," Tracy said, pointing at the mini-gun.

Jones chuckled, a coarse sound he seemed unaccustomed to making. He gazed through the sights of his weapon out of the open door.

"Stick to the mission, and you'll do fine." Looking at them again, he touched his head. "Your uploads gave you everything you need to know to succeed. But you were born with what will defeat the enemy," he added, pointing at his heart.

After nodding to the captain one last time, Shane swung the AK off his shoulder. He held it ready and walked down the ramp off the air-conditioned plane. The dry heat of Egypt stung his nose and eyes. It felt like he'd stuck his face in an oven. He glanced left and right, searching for threats.

At the bottom of the steps, he waited for the rest of his team. Tracy pulled her weapon off her shoulder and held it ready, and the rest did the same.

"Let's go," Shane said, walking briskly across the tarmac.

"Everyone, keep your eyes peeled," Tracy added. "We don't want to be surprised."

"Oh," Laura said abhorrently, retreating behind him. "That is so gross."

A corpse lay ahead, an airport worker in a blue jumpsuit. There was no way to know what killed him. The sun and heat had sucked all the water out of his body. The skin of his face was sunk in and cracked, tightening over the bone underneath. His shrunken eyeballs looked too small in their sockets, and the concrete around him was stained where his rotting fluids had seeped out and baked in the hot sun. Black and green flies buzzed around the partially mummified adult.

Shane suppressed a gag and looked away, guiding the group well clear.

"We best get friendly with it," Liam said grimly, though his accent made everything sound more chipper than it should. "We're going to see lots of dead blokes in this city."

It was evident the Australian boy had seen his share of bodies back in his hometown. His unruffled reaction brought to light the one thing they all had in common. They'd seen their parents die horrible deaths, and they had been forced to leave their bodies behind to rot. Giza was their chance for revenge.

Zigzagging across the tarmac, Shane tried to keep some distance between them and the corpses. The breeze died as they approached the terminals, and the smell grew thicker. The buildings must be filled with the dead, adults who'd turned on each other when the limbic manipulator was active. Shane stopped breathing through his nose, unable to bear it any longer.

They found an area where an aircraft had plowed through a section of the chain-link fence surrounding the airport and walked out onto the road leading into the city.

"It's a heck of a lot quieter than I remember," Jake mused.

"You've been here before?" Laura asked, seeming to crave

the distraction of conversation.

"Yeah, when I was ten," he said, a nervous tremor in his voice. He walked between Shane and her. "We came and saw the pyramids on holiday."

"That's information you might've shared earlier," Tracy pointed out. She sounded calm, like she'd done this a thousand times.

"Well, I don't remember much."

"What do you remember?" Steve asked. His eyes scanned the environment around them, and he held his gun in front of him, his grip appearing light on the stalk and ready to bring it up so he could aim and shoot in an instant.

Along with Tracy and Maurice, he looked like a seasoned soldier. Shane realized his eyes were automatically searching for threats as well. The experience in Atlanta and the training he'd received had turned him into a fighting machine. From a distance, he imagined they must look like a veteran Special Forces unit slipping into the city.

He glanced at Laura, Jake, and Liam. They looked anxious and out of their element compared to the others. They had the same training, but they were not yet christened to the real horror of combat. Shane both envied their innocence and feared it could be a liability. Knots tightened in his gut, realizing that Kelly was now on a team where five of the seven were inexperienced.

"Not much," Jake continued, running his fingers through his dark hair. "I remember it being hot."

He was leaner than the rest of the Aussies and a little shorter than Shane was. In addition to playing rugby, he ran cross-country and had a kid brother waiting for him back in Australia. The athletic boy had captured the flag for his team several times. Shane didn't know much else about him, but he knew the kid's strength and endurance would be an asset in the fight ahead.

"Yeah," Laura said, pulling her vest off her chest as if to get more airflow between it and her skin. "I can see how that would leave an impression on you."

"And I remember the traffic being a bugger," Jake said. "We only stayed for a couple of days. The pyramids were awesome."

"Anything else?" Tracy was all business.

"Sorry mates—that's all I remember."

The airport behind them, a mix of the modern and ancient buildings of Cairo loomed ahead. Random gunshots grew louder as they approached, and he hoped Kelly's team wasn't under fire.

The streets were congested with cars and trucks, some abandoned with their doors hanging open like the driver had fled in a hurry, and others with their drivers and passengers dead inside. The animals had done a number on the adults of Cairo, but there were also lots of bullet holes in the cars they passed.

"Oh man," Maurice said, putting his hand over his face.

"Don't breathe through your nose," Shane advised.

"And try not to look at them." Laura's face had a greenish hue.

It was harder to follow her advice. The dead were everywhere. Bodies hung out of windows, littered the sidewalks, and lay twisted and broken on the steps of buildings, like they'd fallen from above. There was a constant humming sound, the flies busy feeding and sowing maggots. It made him feel even sicker to think Leeville looked like this right now, though on a much smaller scale. It was easy to be disgusted at the bodies, and not recognize them for what they were. These were people—people who deserved a better end than this.

"Where are the survivors?" Steve asked, panning his gun left and right so its barrel followed his gaze. "I expected we'd be getting harassed by now."

"Clearly the smell drove them out," Tracy replied, her shirt pulled up over her nose and mouth.

Shane imagined this place hadn't been vacant since it was created. Cairo was so much older than any city he'd ever visited in the States. He sensed ghosts of the past, roaming the empty streets and welcoming the souls of the rotting corpses who'd so recently joined them.

It felt like Cairo itself was dead. He wondered what the future would be if they defeated the Anunnaki. Would the old cities be reoccupied, or would they start over with new cities? How different would they be on the other side of this apocalypse? Maybe, like the prior visits by the Anunnaki to ancient Earth, in a few thousand years, people would believe the stories of this war were just myths. People might once again believe they were alone in the universe.

These thoughts weighed heavy on him as he hurried down the street, passing towering glass office buildings, shopping areas, and temples that looked like they'd been around since the dawn of time. He noticed Maurice glance up at an old church with reverence, but Shane couldn't take any interest. He just wanted to get beyond the dead to a place where he could get fresh air.

Swarms of flies grew so thick that they had to copy Tracy and wear their shirts over their noses and mouths to keep them out. This city belonged to them now, along with squawking buzzards, sulking dogs, and feral cats. A movement ahead caught his attention. He swore he saw the legs of a body disappear, dragged inside an open door. He held his fist up and squatted, signaling his team to stop.

"Go away!" a boy's voice yelled in Arabic. "They're mine. Go find your own." Shane understood him and wondered how many other languages the rebels had uploaded into his brain.

"Sounds like one of the crazies Jones warned us about," Steve whispered. He was next to Shane, their guns pointed at the building where the voice came from.

"Leave them alone," the voice said angrily. "They aren't for you."

"We just want to pass," Shane called back in the boy's native tongue. "We won't touch anyone."

He sensed the longer they stayed here, the more agitated the boy would become. Darting to the next car, he crouched behind it, directly in front of the building. The rest of his team took turns crossing the exposed space between vehicles.

Slowly raising his head, he looked into the dark doorway, but he couldn't see anything.

A gun went off behind him, and the metal of the car's

fender complained with a loud ping as a bullet ripped through it. Shane dropped to his belly, rolling so he could bring his gun's barrel to the other side of the street. There was an ancient, five-story stucco building with most of its widows busted out. He didn't see any movement inside.

"Damn it," Steve cursed, sweeping his gun back and forth. "Where did that come from?"

"They're mine," the Egyptian boy on the right side of the street yelled angrily, firing a burst of rounds from his hiding place. The plaster erupted off the side of the building four stories up, where Shane guessed the first shooter took cover.

"We don't have time for this," Tracy growled.

She propped on one knee and took aim at the building. The grenade launcher made a whomp sound. A second later, a fireball erupted through the open window, presumably from where the first shot was fired. Pivoting toward the other side of the street, she fired a grenade through the door where the legs had disappeared.

Shane covered his head until the plaster stopped raining down, his ears ringing from the explosions.

"Holy crap, Tracy," Laura said. "You didn't even know if this one was going to try and hurt us." She rose to her feet, looking into the dusty shell of the building on the other side of the car.

Amongst the rubble was a fresh corpse, still smoking from the blast. The charred boy was lying face down, like he'd tried to leap out of the open window just as the grenade went off.

"Sorry, but we don't have the luxury to wait until they kill one of us," she replied coldly, her eyes looking at the buildings around them for another threat. "If they point a gun in my direction, they're going to die."

She sounded heartless, though he knew she was right.

"Let's move," Shane ordered, worried the noise might attract more of these poor kids whose brains had come unhinged.

They hurried along, guns aimed in every direction. The temperature had to be well over a hundred. Sweat gushed from him, and he felt like he'd go mad if he didn't get away from the dead soon. Ahead was a meat truck with greasy stalactites hanging beneath the back doors. The unrefrigerated box must've turned into an oven under the desert sun, broiling the cargo into a rotten stew. He didn't dare take a whiff, but he could guess how bad it smelled by the way flies were particularly concentrated around it.

Swatting his way through the buzzing insects, he froze in front of the truck. His eyes locked on a red Honda Civic. The hood and roof were splattered with blotches of blackish mud. A step closer revealed these were the dried, bloody footprints of dogs.

Vomit rose in his throat, and the sun's heat seemed to double in intensity. He came to the driver's window, his boots crunching in broken glass on the ground below it.

"Mrs. Morris," he groaned, putting his hand on the roof of the car to keep from collapsing. There she sat, wearing her Leeville High Football Team T-shirt. Her face was missing, replaced by a writhing mess of maggoty flesh.

"You alright, mate?" Liam asked. It sounded like he was

speaking to him from the top of a well.

He tore his eyes away from Aaron's mom and looked at the Aussie. Liam's nose and mouth were covered by his shirt, but his brow was furrowed with concern. A glance back at the car told him he was losing it. The small sedan was red, but he didn't recognize the brand. It was not a Honda. The dehydrated carcass of an old lady lay across the center console.

"I'm fine," he replied. "Just a little hot."

He smacked at the flies and lifted his shirt back up over his face, turning away before Liam could study him long enough to figure out he might be coming unhinged.

It could just be a side effect of the neural upload, but he also worried that somehow, his slave gene might have been activated and he was going crazy like the two Tracy had killed. He remembered how he felt when the limbic manipulator made him want to murder Tracy and Steve. He'd been so certain it was the right thing to do. A chill ran down his spine.

He pushed the thoughts aside, forcing his attention on the buildings they passed. Nothing could stop him from doing what had to be done. He wouldn't be distracted. He had to lead his team.

"On the left," Steve whispered, and they all dropped and pointed their weapons in that direction.

A skinny kid who looked to be about fourteen walked through the intersection a block away. He wasn't carrying a weapon, and his oversized red tank top hung loosely, showing his ribs. He disappeared between the buildings. Shane pitied the boy, who was headed toward the pyramids where the Anunnaki would land, marching toward his doom.

"Guess that means we're going the right way," Liam observed with a despondent voice.

After another mile, the street sloped upward and away from the buildings, joining with a bridge. A breeze pushed the stench and flies away, and a wide river with calm, green water flowed by below.

"The Nile," Jake muttered distantly.

"Once we cross this bridge," Tracy had the map open, "Giza is to the south."

She folded it and shoved it back into her vest. They crept up the bridge, scanning the area. Ravens screeched in the palms lining the river, and Laura dropped into a crouched position and aimed her gun at the sky. Her eyes looked wild, filled with terror.

Shane put his hand on her shoulder, and she jerked her gun toward him.

"It's okay," he promised, pushing the barrel out of his face. "They won't attack you again."

She scanned the sky once more, and her attention came back to him. Sighing nervously, she stood. Panic loosened its hold on her expression, replaced by a sheepish grin.

"The others must've already come this way," Tracy said, pointing at a wrapper from a granola bar, the same kind they were all given.

"Who in the devil could eat at a time like this?" Liam crinkled his nose.

"Probably Jules," Maurice answered. "Nothing will stop that girl from eating."

"And that's the bloody oath if it is hers," the Aussie replied, shaking his head with disbelief. "I'd be chundering after one bite."

He doubted Maurice's confidence in her appetite—Jules wouldn't have eaten if someone on her team had been killed. The little green wrapper told him Kelly was all right. Tracy picked it up, shoved it in her pocket, and then continued climbing the bridge.

They stayed low, close to the concrete guardrail as they crossed over the Nile. At the peak, they could see the pyramids rising in the south.

"Take cover," Tracy whispered, pointing at the city below.

Shane ducked behind a car and took aim at a river of kids flowing through an intersection two blocks away. Some of them carried guns over their shoulders in a casual way, like they weren't concerned about being attacked. They looked like teenagers, none younger than twelve or older than seventeen. They were all the enemy wanted for now—the second wave would collect the younger children.

"What's that guy doing?" Shane pointed at the street just below the bridge.

A kid in a black shirt was ducking behind the cars, slipping closer to the parade. He had a pistol in his hand and seemed intent upon using it to take out a few of them.

"Looks like he wants to die," Liam replied.

When the suicide gunman was less than a half block away, he stood up between the cars and leveled his weapon at the crowd. He yelled and fired the pistol three times, unimpressive bangs when compared to the earlier boom of Tracy's grenades. A girl at the edge of the mob dropped. Shane would have expected panic and screaming if this was a sober crowd, but the slave gene obviously had these teens possessed. Without appearing startled, they pivoted and charged toward the shooter. He turned and ran, firing over his shoulder without aiming. Just before the mob was upon him, Shane saw the boy laughing in a way that only insanity could inspire.

They beat him down quickly and without emotion, as casual as if they were taking out the trash. Once the gunman lay motionless on the ground, they turned and rejoined the river of kids like nothing happened. As disturbing as the scene was, it promised these kids weren't a threat to his team. Their behavior seemed entirely defensive, and they probably wouldn't attack unless someone provoked them. It was the ones walking around by themselves he had to worry about.

"I ain't keen on mingling with those folks," Steve whispered, an urgency in his tone like he wanted to get going.

"The map has us taking the first side street, so we won't have to," Tracy replied.

"Let's move," Shane whispered, advancing down to the next car.

With his friends following behind him, he hopscotched his way to the bottom of the bridge into Giza. As he was slipping between cars, one of the kids in the mob seemed to look directly at him. Shane stopped and crouched down, worried that if he continued forward, the kid might think he was charging in like the last lunatic. Either the boy didn't notice him, or he didn't view him as a threat. He said something to the guy in front of him, who also looked over, but they walked by and out of sight.

Taking a left at the bottom of the bridge, he sighed with relief once his team was between the buildings and out of sight of the mob. He'd made it this far without killing anyone, and he hoped the first life he had to take today would be that of an Anunnaki. The isolated crazies and the others who calmly made their way to the pyramids were not in control of themselves. The idea of shooting them filled him with dread, though he knew he couldn't hesitate if the situation demanded it.

The sun drifted lower, and the city grew darker. Avoiding rotting bodies, he darted along in the shadows. The cooling air reenergized him, and a breeze whisked away some of the flies and stench. He looked up and down each street they crossed to make sure they weren't running into another ambush, but all was quiet.

"Three blocks to go," Tracy whispered after they crossed an intersection that brought them closer to the hypnotized throng than before.

"Listen," Shane said, raising his hand to stop them.

A rhythmic chanting came from the direction in which they headed. It was deep and mournful, with drums setting the cadence. The music was mesmerizing, and Shane imagined it coerced the kids marching to the pyramids into an even deeper trance. He continued cautiously, the chanting sending chills down his back. It seemed primal and sinister, like it might precede some terrible ritual.

Two blocks later, a girl screamed, her desperate plea rising above the feverish music. He raised his rifle to his shoulder, rushing toward the sound. She screamed again, a torturous note that turned his blood to ice.

Then she was abruptly silenced.

CHAPTER
TWENTY—SIX

Kelly stepped off the plane, feeling like a chunk of her heart had been ripped out when she turned away from Shane. It hurt to see the fear of being separated from her in his eyes, felt like she was striking him with a mortal blow. But she knew Jones was right. Shane had been acting weird lately, and with what he'd said to her last night, trying to get her to bug out of the mission, she was worried he'd lose it in the fight if she got injured.

"Everyone, keep your weapons ready," Ethan said, more nervous than she'd ever heard him sound before.

She didn't need to be told—she'd had her finger on the trigger since they got off the plane. As they approached the city, she looked at the buildings ahead, worried about an attack from above. She wished they had a better idea of what they might have to deal with. The rebels had warned them that some of the kids would go nuts when their slave gene was activated, and her imagination had been left to decide exactly what that meant.

It filled her with guilt that she was a bit relieved to be away from Shane. He treated her like she was the center of his universe, which would be awesome in a normal situation. But even more so after her family was killed, Nat was the center of hers. She felt like she was cheating Shane because she couldn't give her entire self over to him like he did to her. She had to worry about her little sister's safety and was ready to sacrifice everything if that was what it took to guarantee it. Sometimes, Shane didn't seem to understand that.

The gun felt familiar and comforting in her hands. It was a secret that she'd been shooting them her whole life. She loved going out with her dad, but she pretended to be squeamish about hunting around her friends since she'd been a little girl. It was like there were two sides to her. One who was the cheerleading captain, dainty and as polished as she could be. The other was more comfortable in the woods, wearing camouflaged coveralls and face paint as she stalked a deer at five in the morning. It was amazing that she'd been able to keep her more rugged side a secret, especially in a town the size of Leeville. But her family had always respected her wishes not to mention it to anyone, and they owned over eight hundred acres, so she only hunted on private land. In the fight in the gym and then in Atlanta, Shane and the others had looked shocked to see she was such a dead shot. Even then, she didn't give away her secret, letting them think she was just a natural.

She felt it was okay to kill an animal as long as you planned to eat it. But killing a person was a terrible thing. In taking human lives, she'd given herself wounds that would never heal. Her religious upbringing made her fear an eternity in hell for what she'd done. Although tortured by the memories of killing and afraid for her soul, she didn't have regrets. She'd kill a thousand times over if it meant keeping her little sister safe, and she would gladly surrender to the worst fates imaginable.

She glanced at Jules, who was walking beside her with her eyes scanning the buildings they approached. The tall, wiry girl looked calm, ready to deal with whatever came at them. But there was a shade of sadness in her eyes that had sprung up after Jones made them switch teams.

"You know they're better off without us," Kelly said. She wanted to ease Jules discomfort and talking about her issues was a ready distraction from her own.

"Yeah, but..." Jules looked at her with a frustrated expression, and then returned her attention to monitoring their surroundings.

"What?" It was obvious that Jules was torn up over something, though she'd never been one to complain.

"I know I'm being stupid, but it's just..." Jules paused, her brow furrowing. "Shane was so upset that you two were being separated."

"And you're mad because Tracy didn't say anything," Kelly said, realizing what was eating at the tall girl.

"Ridiculous, I know," she replied, sounding embarrassed. She glanced at Kelly, looking to see if she agreed.

"I've known Tracy since kindergarten," Kelly said.

"Oh, the smell," Ethan said, cutting her off.

Kelly didn't dare take a whiff. She'd been breathing through her mouth since the airplane hatch opened. They pulled their shirts over their faces to keep the flies out, and she scanned the broken windows of a row of restaurants at the edge of the city. All was quiet. On the floors of the establishments' shadowy interiors, she could see dark lumps here and there. It was the last patrons, having drank and dined just before all hell broke loose. The memory of the final meal she spent with her family tried to suck her under, making her eyes moist with tears. She gritted her teeth and returned to the conversation with Jules.

"Tracy sort of loses all emotion and becomes robotic in certain situations," Kelly continued, a tremor in her voice.

"I've noticed," Jules replied, some of the tension in her voice gone. She seemed cooler about approaching the city than anyone else. "She's not exactly the touchy-feely type."

Jules had grown up in Atlanta, so she was more accustomed to the urban environment. Kelly and the Australians were from small towns. Even if everything was normal and Cairo was alive and bustling, they'd be less comfortable here than her.

"She knew it was right to be separated from you, so she didn't waste time by arguing." Kelly glanced at Jules and could see the talk seemed to ease her discontentment. It lifted her spirits too; she'd always liked helping others. Her mom used to say she liked dealing with their problems more than her own. "Having known her for so long, I can tell you that she was devastated she had to be separated from you."

Jules laughed. "That was devastated?"

"That's Tracy."

They both chuckled.

Joey, the tall, skinny Australian who was way stronger than he looked, glanced at them with appall. He seemed amazed that they could laugh with adults rotting in the streets around them and under the constant threat of being shot at by crazies.

The Australians had never been in a situation like this. They didn't yet realize how important it was to hang on to the things in life that mattered. The reasons they were here were what would get them through this. Sadly, they'd learn soon enough. She glanced at the stalky, dark-skinned kid who reminded her of Maurice without the piety. Ethan seemed fully capable of leading, but if he choked during the heat of it, she knew it would be up to her and Jules to take over.

"This is our turn," Ethan announced, stopping them at the end of the relatively narrow street. It emptied into a wide, four-lane boulevard. A grassy island with palm trees separated lanes, which were congested with wrecked and abandoned vehicles.

"Where are the bodies?" Jules asked warily, raising her gun to her shoulder.

Kelly lifted her rifle and searched the wide streets with the barrel pointing wherever she looked. The hairs rose on the back of her neck. She couldn't find a single corpse, where there should be hundreds.

"I got a bad feeling about this place," Joey said.

"Bloody hell!" Ben, the shortest of the Aussie boys, had a horrified expression on his face, his green eyes so wide they looked like they might pop out of his head. "Over there, where the street bends."

She swung her rifle in the direction he pointed.

"Are those bodies?" Ethan asked with a hoarse voice, though they all could see that they were.

Several hundred yards away, at a turn in the street where the sidewalks narrowed and the charred buildings drew closer, the road was blocked by what appeared to be a giant curtain. Hanging on a cable that ran across the lanes and the grassy divider, it hung from the two buildings' roofs to the ground and spanned the width of the boulevard. The yarn for this enormous curtain was the rotting bodies of the adults. Connected at their wrists and ankles such that each corpse formed an X, they created a pattern not unlike a chain-link fence.

"Who would do such a thing?" Ben's voice was pitched.

Kelly broke free of her catatonia, swallowed the bile that had risen in the back of her throat, and looked at the others. Their faces were slack and starved for blood, their wide eyes glued to the human curtain.

"We don't want to stick around and find out," she said. "The map has us going in the opposite direction."

"Thank heaven," Jules said.

"She's right," Ethan seconded, swatting flies away from his face. He sounded shaken, but the calm that usually dominated his personality seemed to regain control. "Now we've seen it all people. Nothing will shock us. Let's go."

Kelly wasn't so sure they'd seen it all. The curtain of corpses was frightening, but it was the demented kids who'd constructed it that scared her even more.

CHAPTER
TWENTY—SEVEN

"Damn it." Steve held his gun ready and jogged ahead of Shane toward the end of the street. It ended at the desert, and Shane expected to see the pyramids beyond.

"Stop," Tracy ordered.

Steve obeyed, looking back at them with a frantic expression.

"Somebody is getting hurt out there," he objected. "We can't just stand by and do nothing."

"We have to." Shane lowered the barrel of his weapon. His stomach knotted with concern for what had happened to the girl, but a lot more would suffer if they interfered. "We have to keep our focus," he said to himself as much as to Steve. If it were Kelly who screamed, would he be able to stay on task and not try to save her?

"When we get out there," Tracy added, looking at both of them, "we might see a whole lot of stuff that is going to piss us off. But we have to be strong. We have to go along with whatever happens until we can get on the ship and complete our mission."

She was right, of course, and condescending as usual. Luckily, they'd all learned to ignore it, knowing Tracy was one who could be relied upon to have a clear head in the face of any challenge.

"Let's check it out," Shane said, speaking loud enough to be heard over the fervent chanting. He stepped around Steve, who seemed to be trying to regroup after hearing what sounded like a murder, and slipped toward the end of the street.

The last buildings on the edge of the city were the nicest hotels, probably reserved for those with enough money to have a clear view of the pyramids. Shane kept close to the white stucco wall, creeping forward until he could look around the corner.

The streets of Giza spilled out onto the pyramid complex, three columns of possessed kids marching into the necropolis. The late afternoon sun lit two sides of the pyramids and cast the others in shadows. It was a majestic sight, one that would have awed him under normal circumstances. But now, all he could do was focus on the growing mob that they needed to intermingle with, searching for a reason why the girl had screamed.

"That looks like ours," he said to Tracy, who'd stepped next to him.

"Yep, the biggest one," she replied, pointing at the massive pyramid standing nearest to the city. "Jules and Kelly are somewhere over by that one." She moved her finger to the third pyramid, the furthest one away.

Knowing it was impossible for him to see Kelly from this

distance, Shane couldn't help but strain his eyes, searching for her blonde hair. Then he stopped himself. He had to quit getting distracted. It was why Jones separated them in the first place.

"We'd better leave our weapons here," he said, looking back at the mob.

"No freaking way I'm going into that mess without a gun," Steve countered.

"If we take these in there," Tracy said, patting her grenade launcher, "all those kids are going to turn on us. Look at them." She pointed at the closest column of teens, who were tossing their weapons onto piles just outside the city.

Steve looked in the direction she indicated with squinted eyes.

"Damn it if you ain't right," he grumbled, unzipping his vest.

"We'll stash them here," Laura said, pointing at a dumpster. "If we need them, we'll know where they are."

With all the dead littering the city, the inside of the trashcan seemed the cleanest place. Everyone put their guns and vests into the dumpster. Steve was last, acting like his hand was glued to his weapon. He slung it into the metal container and held onto it for a moment, looking out toward the desert, his face contorted with frustration.

"It's going to be fine," Shane promised, putting a hand on his big shoulder.

"Somehow, I don't believe you," Steve grumbled.

"We'd better get out there," Laura warned, looking up.

Shane followed her gaze. Three black squares with gold

edges floated high in the sky.

"The Anunnaki," he said. Cold terror washed over him, although he wasn't surprised to see them.

"What else could they be?" Tracy asked.

The chanting grew louder, alleviating all doubt.

"Let's go," Shane ordered, stepping out of the cover of the buildings.

He took slow, deliberate breaths to calm himself and trudged toward the pyramid. Having been through this before in simulations, he and his friends adopted blank faces like the possessed kids. Those poor victims had made pilgrimages from who knew where, driven by an instinct activated by the enemy. Shane came to the back of the crowd, the kids chanting so loud his ears rang. He picked up their feverous song and weaved his way in, closer to the pyramid with his team spread out on either side of him.

A boy stood on the side of the shadowed eastern face of the ancient structure, his bare chest wet and his face black like it was covered in charcoal. He raised his hands, and the chanting stopped.

"They come," he boomed, pointing at the sky. "Bring another gift to appease them."

The crowd chanted again, even more wildly than before. Four thick boys, also shirtless and soaked, climbed off the lowest blocks of the pyramid and weaved through the crowd.

A closer look at the side of the pyramid where the skinny boy stood revealed the square blocks were red beneath him. Then Shane saw the bodies, piled up on the lowest level. The wet on the boys' chest and on the stone was blood. He nearly gagged at the realization. How could these kids do something so horrible? Were the Anunnaki making them do this, like an appetizer for the cleansing war to come?

Shane looked up at the sky. The three, gold-rimmed squares were closer now, the concave region that would mate with the pyramids so dark that it seemed to suck the life out of him. He remembered the video Lily had showed them, shuddering at the thought that a blast could come out of that dark underbelly, which would easily kill them all.

When Shane glanced back at the chanting kids in front of him, he saw the four thick boys, blood drenching their arms and chests. By some terrible perversion of luck, they pushed through the crowd directly toward his team.

"They're coming our way," Tracy said into his ear at the same instant. "What do we do?"

"Try to move left," he replied between clenched teeth. "Don't make it obvious."

She slipped behind him, chanting and waving her hands in the air like she was overwhelmed by the ceremony. Shane mimicked the possessed teens as best he could, following Tracy. Liam and Steve came after him, then Jake and Maurice. When the blood-covered boys were fifteen feet away, they pointed at Laura and shouted. The kids around her turned, encircling her and cutting her off from the rest of the team.

"No!" Maurice yelled.

"Stop him, or he'll give us all away," Tracy said.

They rushed to where Laura was encircled. Shane's heart raced, dread making him ill as he saw her lifted into the air. She kicked and screamed, but she couldn't break free. Maurice pushed through the throng, trying to rescue her. After Laura was swept toward the pyramid, the chanting kids turned and beat him to the ground. Steve and Shane got to him at the same time, dragging him away from the angry section of the mob while shouting and pretending to hit him. Once the attention returned to the pyramid, Steve helped him to his feet.

"We have to let her go," Shane said in Maurice's ear. Hearing his own words, he wanted to vomit. "They'll kill us all if we try to save her, and then we won't have a chance to stop them." He pointed at the sky.

"I know, but..." Maurice moaned. His shoulders drooped, and Shane knew he understood.

Sadness crushed Shane as he watched the shy Goth girl he'd become close friends with get carried above the heads of the crowd toward the base of the pyramid. His mind searched for a way to save her. He glanced at Tracy, who gave him a look that warned he couldn't put the rest of his team at risk and jeopardize the entire mission.

The four thick boys lifted her up on the blocks toward the executioner. Fighting and screaming, she managed to break free. She turned on the nearest boy, using a sidekick right out of a martial arts movie to launch him off the first row of blocks that made up the sides of the pyramid. His heart leapt—the possibility that she'd be able to fight them off igniting a spark of hope. But there was no relenting. The other boys tackled her, joined by several spectators who'd climbed up to help them. He watched in horror as Laura was dragged higher and held in front of the skinny boy, who danced around wildly with a long knife in his hand. The blade still glistened from the last innocent teenager he'd slaughtered.

The spacecraft came low, its black, hollowed-out bottom just above the apex of the ancient structure. The crazed leader of the ceremony raised the knife. Two of the thick boys pulled Laura's arms and legs in opposite directions, holding her down though she bucked violently in their grasp. The executioner looked up at the ship, and Shane could see his mouth moving, but the loud hissing of the spacecraft drowned out all other noise.

Shane pushed forward through the crowd, unable to stand by and watch her die. But it was too late—the boy thrust the knife down at Laura.

"*No!*"

As the word formed on Shane's lips, three narrow beams of light projected from the bottom of the spacecraft. One hit the boy with the knife just before it penetrated Laura, and the others struck the two who held her. All three boys were vaporized, and the knife dropped and rolled off Laura's chest. She leapt to her feet, crawling down the blocks at the base of the pyramid with panic clear on her face. Had he not known better, Shane might have believed these invaders were here to save the people, rescuing Laura just before she was sacrificed. The whole horrible scene was downright biblical to him. He wondered how much of these kids' behavior was already being manipulated by the Anunnaki. They may have caused the barbaric ceremony just to kill the evil priest as if coming to the rescue. The possessed onlookers' jaws dropped in awe, and they went pale like they'd witnessed the hand of God reaching down to punish the wrongdoers.

Not being particularly gentle with the glazed-eyed freaks who were still chanting for blood, Shane bulldozed his way through the crowd. He helped Laura off the pyramid's foundation. Her arm had a cut where the knife must've fallen, but other than that, she looked okay. The mesmerized crowds' attention was off her now, focused on the vessel hovering overhead.

The hissing of the ship's engine made it impossible to talk, and the wind it created ripped at his clothes. He squinted up at the gold-and-black behemoth. A horn sounded, like the air horn on a big rig, yet a hundred times louder. It was an obvious warning, telling everyone to get out of the way. He grabbed Laura's forearm and pulled her through the throng, heading toward his team.

The hissing grew louder, and wind gushed away from the pyramid. Dust and sand pelted him, and his T-shirt blew up onto his shoulders. Shielding his eyes with his free hand, he plowed a path for Laura, knocking kids to the ground who didn't step aside. The vessel grew significantly larger, coming closer to the ground. A third of the ancient pyramid disappeared in the dark abyss of the underside of the ship. The gold perimeter of the vessel's bottom was as wide as a city block. If the kids didn't get out of the way, it would crush them.

"Run," Shane yelled as soon as he saw his friends.

The noise and the wind kicked up by the landing craft drowned out his voice, but they got the picture. They turned and sprinted a hundred yards, Steve, Shane, and Liam at the front of the squad, clearing a path. Some of the kids turned and ran with them, but others stood their ground, chanting and swaying back and forth, their wide eyes fixed on the ship. The wind blew harder and hotter. There was a loud humph, then a blast hit him, knocking him to the sand and sending him tumbling away from the pyramid. He was blown at least another hundred yards before the ship impacted the ground, sending a shockwave through the Earth that would've knocked him down if he weren't already on his face.

The wind dissipated, the ship's engines whining to a gentle hiss. Lifting his head and shaking the dirt and sand from his hair, Shane stayed low and took a count of his friends. They were sprawled around him, their disoriented faces plastered with dust. Six of them. He hadn't lost one yet. Laura still looked shaken, but she appeared to have subdued her panic. She flashed an appreciative smile at him that didn't feel deserved. He hadn't saved her. If it weren't for the spaceship vaporizing her capturers, she'd be dead.

He crawled to his feet and surveyed the surroundings. His heart thumped in his ears such that he could barely hear the coughs of the dust-choked kids around him. The cloud kicked up by the Anunnaki vessel obscured everything, and he didn't know if he was facing Giza or the ship. A warm breeze whisked the dust away, and though it wouldn't have done him any good, he suddenly wished he'd held on to the AK and his grenades.

CHAPTER TWENTY—EIGHT

Trotting away from the curtain of bodies, Kelly, Jules, and the Aussies turned onto the wide boulevard. It was a direct route that would get them to the pyramids before anyone else.

The Pyramid of Menkaure was their destination, the furthest from Giza in the Necropolis. They were assigned the fastest route through Cairo, so all the teams would get to their targets at about the same time. She hadn't minded the idea of it when she looked at the map, but she didn't like how exposed they were now. The wide street they ran down offered little cover, and it felt like they'd be easy to spot from several blocks away.

She feared the people who'd made the gruesome curtain were camped out in buildings nearby. If they'd done that to the dead, what might they do if they found someone alive?

"This is way worse than Atlanta," Jules said, trotting along next to her.

"Hopefully, these psychos won't be as organized as Shamus' gang was," Kelly said, clinging to a thread of optimism.

While the daily runs during training had been torture much of the time, she was grateful for the peak physical condition they were in. They moved along at a decent pace, and she started to feel better once they were a couple of blocks away.

"Whoop, whoop," came a call from the left side of the street.

"Down," Kelly said, dropping behind a burnt-out SUV. She searched the shadows at the base of the buildings, looking for the source of the noise.

"I got movement on the right," Ethan whispered.

Kelly glanced to the side of the street to which their backs were exposed, adrenaline flooding her veins and clearing her mind. At least ten kids crept out of a fast food restaurant that had all its windows busted out.

"What are they wearing on their faces?" Jules asked, a tremor in her voice.

"No way," Ben whispered. "Those sickos are wearing skin masks."

"I think I'm gonna chunder," Joey said, but he held his rifle at the ready.

The crazies approached the edge of the sidewalk and hovered cautiously, studying them as if to assess whether they were accomplices or victims. Kelly's heart thumped in her ears so hard it hurt. More crazies were coming out on the other side of the street, also wearing the peeled off and dried faces of adults as masks. Their eyes were hidden in the shadowy eyeholes. The mouths of the mask were distorted, open in ghastly expressions from the drying process, and revealing the chins and necks of their wearers.

Closest to Kelly, a skinny girl who was wearing a bearded face from what must've been a fairly large man, reached slowly to the back of her belt and produced a chef's knife. Its blade was soiled, caked with blood and dirt. The sun glinted off the girl's otherwise unseen eyes, and Kelly sensed that she was smiling beneath the rotting beard face.

"We need to run," Kelly said in a calm and quiet voice.

"Agreed," Jules whispered.

"Go!" Ethan shouted.

They pivoted and ran down the street at full speed, dodging wrecked cars. The crazies cheered and gave chase. Nothing in the simulations prepared them for this. Though terror had a firm grip on her, her experience and training helped Kelly keep her head. She looked back and could see that the scrawny teenagers, whose brains had come unhinged from the slave gene, were in nowhere near the physical condition that her team was. Already, there was a football field between them.

Though he was the shortest, Ben was able to out sprint any of them. He was leading the group, running with his gun held across his chest.

Kelly thought she saw something move between cars she passed. Quickly dismissing it as her imagination, she dodged left and followed Jules around a large panel truck.

"Up ahead," Ben yelled, stopping them and taking aim with his AK.

Fifty yards down the boulevard, a small group of skin-masked teens popped up from behind cars. One had a rifle, and the others had makeshift spears and bats. The shouts of the crazies pursuing them grew louder. They were corralling Kelly and her team, closing them in on both sides.

"We can't stop," Ethan said.

He raised his gun and fired a shot over the disturbed kids. As Kelly expected, they didn't scatter. More kids wearing skin masks stood up from behind cars, like they'd been hiding and waiting in ambush.

"Okay, this won't do," Joey said frantically.

He fired a shot, and the boy holding the rifle dropped dead. His counterparts shrieked, seeming as if they'd lost the ability for speech. Their brains were completely scrambled. These poor teenagers had devolved into something less than human but far worse than any animal. Kelly charged forward with her team, the sight of her rifle aimed on only those who blocked their way. They were terrifying, but she also knew it wasn't their fault they were acting this way. One of the kids closed in on her, a knife in his hand. She hesitated, her finger on the trigger.

"Move out of the way!" she yelled at the boy in Anunnaki and then Arabic.

Ignoring her, the crazy and his friends came at Kelly, Jules, and the Aussies. They raised their crude weapons, coated with the gore of countless other kills they'd made. Reluctant to take their destroyed lives to the last moment, Kelly's finger eased back and the AK made a loud pop. The skin-masked boy was thrown onto the hood of the car behind him, and the powder burns around the bullet's entry wound testified to how close he was before she'd fired. Hoping to be merciful, she'd shot him through the center of his heart, giving the poor boy death before he rolled off the car to the ground.

The discharge of her weapon seemed to act as a signal to the rest of the team. The bloodthirsty shrieks of the crazies were drowned out by the sound of gunfire. A mob materialized in front of them, and they were forced to stop. Ethan lobbed a grenade, blasting a path forward.

"Keep going!" he shouted, sounding calmer than he had before the fight started.

Once she overcame the struggle of making that first shot, and realized there was no option but to fight their way out, Kelly settled into the battle. They'd fought so much in training that she felt more focused once the bullets started flying. She hated that they were taking lives, but at the same time, there was a sense of control, something she didn't feel when they were on the retreat.

"Behind us," Jules said.

Flipping her gun over to that direction, Kelly fired into the fifty charging crazies. She fished out a grenade, pulled the ring with the pinky finger of her gun hand, and tossed it into the mob. Then followed it with well-placed shots into those closest to her team.

The explosion launched bodies into the air. One fell at her feet, his mask separated from him in the blast. He was dead, his chest and neck bloody from shrapnel but his face undamaged. The Egyptian boy's slack expression made him look so innocent that it filled her with sorrow. This was just a kid—someone's brother and someone's child.

Seeing their counterparts killed did not deter the unhinged teens. They rushed in to take the others' places, determined to sink their nasty weapons into Kelly and her friends. Feeling like this had to be a strange and horrible nightmare, she fired her weapon again and again, keeping the insane kids back. Their disgusting masks and animal screams weren't enough to completely dehumanize them. Kelly was painfully aware that each shot she fired killed another innocent. She blamed the Anunnaki, and her lust for revenge swelled even more.

"We gotta get out of here," she said, determined to take as few lives as possible. She also worried about their limited supply of ammunition, fearing there were more crazies closing in than they had bullets with which to stop them.

"This way," Ethan yelled, pointing toward a side street. It was dark and narrow, and she hadn't noticed it before.

Relieved to see an exit, Kelly took up the rear, running backwards alongside Jules. The team crossed the boulevard in pairs, able to hold off the mob pressing in on either side. Ethan led the way into a narrow street just as the crazies came close enough to use their spears.

One made a thrust at Kelly, and she whipped her AK sideways to deflect the spear, then swung the barrel around and put a bullet in the kid's chest. Running backwards and dumping rounds into the crazies, they moved deeper into the alley. The buildings on either side forced the skin-faces tighter together, preventing them from surrounding Kelly and her team.

"We got more on the other side," Ethan yelled from behind her.

"Aw, come on," Kelly groaned, glancing over her shoulder.

Kids were charging in, most of them armed with guns. A fresh wave of fear came over Kelly. They were trapped, and she only had one grenade left. The whole team was going to die in this alley, and the mission would be over before it really began. Failing meant the Anunnaki would be one step closer to getting Nat. She couldn't let that happen. Fishing the last grenade out of her vest pocket, she pulled the pin.

"Kelly!" Jules shouted.

She lobbed the grenade into the skin-faces and at the same time saw a makeshift spear flying through the air. Time seemed to freeze, at least long enough for her to make out the details of the crude missile. It was composed of the wooden handle of a broom or a rake, and had a large kitchen knife lashed on at its tip. In that frozen moment, she could see dried blood and little chunks of flesh on the blade and the wooden shaft.

Diving and twisting her body to avoid the spear, she couldn't move fast enough. Its gory blade slid deep into her shoulder above her left breast. She felt the tip pierce through her, burying itself in the underside of her shoulder blade. She was more horrified at the idea that she'd be taken out of the mission—that she'd no longer be able to fight for Nat's safety—than at the notion of being killed by the disgusting weapon. As she crashed to the ground, the handle of the impaled spear smacked a car's hood and she yelped in pain.

CHAPTER TWENTY—NINE

The golden spaceship materialized through the dust, resting over the Great Pyramid of Khufu and looking way too big to ever take to the sky. It was similar to the one Shane had seen in the simulation, but much larger. Also unique to the command ship was a spire rising from its peak, reaching higher than any skyscraper. The reflective exterior of the ship glowed brighter than the last light of the setting sun. Although he couldn't help being frightened, he was in awe of the vessel. It represented technology beyond his wildest dreams, and a species as old as time.

He glanced at the kids who'd been chanting until the gust created by the ship knocked them down and blew them out of the way. They were changed, appearing to be under a deeper level of hypnosis. Some rose to their knees and bowed, while others stood staring at the vessel with slack expressions. Aside from coughing, no one uttered a sound.

"We'd better mimic them," Shane whispered, a tremor in his voice. "We have to get inside that ship." As realistic as the simulations had been, he was more confident before seeing the actual vessel towering in front of him.

He adopted the expression of the entranced kids around them, slumped shoulders, a loose jaw, and eyes wide open. The sky grew darker, the last of the sunlight fading. The three massive pyramidal ships emitted a soft, yellow glow, illuminating the necropolis. He wondered how Kelly was doing with the Australian team at their pyramid, resisting the urge to break off from this crowd and run to try to find her. Something told him she was safe, at least for now.

There was a loud whoosh, like a seal being broken. An opening the width of the side nearest them formed on the bottom edge of the ship, rising from the ground.

The hull flowed upward, revealing the stark, white interior that looked like it belonged to an ancient Greek or Roman palace. In the center, the wide escalator rose up to the city somewhere high above. This ship was so much bigger than the ones they'd trained in. Its city must be like the capital of this armada and in proportion with the vessel's size. No doubt, its coliseum would put the others to shame. Faces peered down off the balconies and over the railings, hundreds of Anunnaki looking out at the kids. Shane imagined those same faces sitting in their flying stadium, laughing and cheering as they looked down upon the slaves, who they forced to fight to the death. His anger boiled.

Most of them wore white clothing and some even had on togas like the statues adorning their courtyards. Such an odd garb for these advanced space travelers, though it did fit the interior design of their ships. It struck him that the marble inner pyramid of the vessel could be equated with Mount Olympus, and he reckoned these bastards must think of themselves as gods. The alien spectators pointed and chattered with each other, appearing excited about the human livestock gathered on the sand below.

Soldiers in red armor holding plasma rifles across their chest lined the lowest terrace of the inner pyramid and spilled out on either side of the opening, contrasting sharply with the white and gold. Most of these soldiers had no emblems on their armor, indicating they were lower ranking Anunnaki. Shane spotted a couple of the elite Shock Troops, which Jones had warned them to avoid. With only his jeans, T-shirt, and no gun, he felt vulnerable and weak. Glancing at his team, he tried to convey this was the most delicate part of their mission. They couldn't be discovered, at least not until they got hold of some weapons.

A distinguished looking Anunnaki man with silver hair rode the wide escalator down from higher parts of the ship, stopping thirty feet above the crowd. Shane could see his face looked much younger than his hairstyle let on. Most of the spectators appeared to be of similar age as Lily and Jones, around thirty years old. Of course, he knew the rebels had crashed on earth well over twice that many years before. Just how old they were, he had never really speculated. For all he knew, they might be hundreds of years old. Older. The spaceman's gold cape caught the desert wind and floated out beside him. Otherwise, he was clad in white pants and a long-sleeved, white shirt.

"Kneel," he boomed.

The kids who weren't on their knees dropped, their eyes cast down as if they suddenly feared looking upon these supposed gods who would turn them to stone. Although it disgusted him to do it, Shane copied them.

"Rise."

A shuffle of commotion erupted across the crowd, everyone coming to their feet. And then total silence pervaded.

"Kneel," the alien ordered once again.

It was a test. If someone didn't do what they were told, the slave gene must not be working in that teenager. Then the Anunnaki soldiers would dispose of them. Thousands of kids dropped to their knees once again.

"Rise."

Everyone snapped to their feet and stood motionless, staring up at their Anunnaki master. There was applause and cheering from the spectators on the ship. Shane's hands started to close into fists. These aliens had no respect for humans, were looking down on them like they were property and not people. He was to be the one to teach them some manners, and he couldn't wait to get started. Forcing himself to relax, he took a deep breath. He'd have to keep his anger in check for a while longer.

"Enter," the alien said, pointing at the ramp that led into the recruit processing chambers deeper in the vessel.

The slaves crowded forward. While maintaining a stupefied expression, Shane pushed through them. His people had to get on with the first recruits. All the teams needed to make it to the reactors at a similar time, and his had the biggest ship. If the others destroyed theirs first, the Anunnaki might stop taking in recruits.

Shifting his eyes, he saw Steve and Tracy weaving their way forward on either side of him. He couldn't risk looking back to make sure the rest followed. His mind, so freshly stuffed with useful information, was analyzing every aspect of the scene around him, assessing threats and preparing responses. It seemed like an automated process, running in the background of his thoughts, his neural upload and the training doing its job. Though he was afraid and worried about Kelly and his teammates, he also felt confident and lethal. After making it to the ramp that ascended into the ship, he fell into one of the many lines forming there.

Unlike the stiff alien soldiers, who held their guns across their chest and motionlessly studied the slaves through the tented glass of their V-shaped visors, the "citizens" who watched from the safety of the higher balconies made a lot of noise. It sounded like they were having a party, perhaps celebrating the apparent conquest of the human race. In the periphery of his vision, he could see some of the white-clad spectators leaning over the rail, pointing at the passing slaves. Were they picking out the ones they wanted to buy? Planning fights for their coliseum? The scene made him want to crush them even more. These smiling aliens were responsible for the horrific deaths of his aunt and father. Although the thought of violence and of killing turned his stomach, he wanted to make them pay for what they'd done and stop them from the terrible things they planned to do.

The silver-haired orator stood above on the idle escalator, and Shane sensed he scrutinized every slave passing beneath. He couldn't wait to be out of his gaze, fearing something would give him or his team away. When he was directly below, it felt like the Anunnaki's attention fixed onto him. He had to make an effort to keep the expression of relief off his face when he passed into the gray holding chamber and out of the alien's view.

Shane exhaled, realizing he'd barely breathed since mounting the ramp. He had to be more relaxed. Along with thousands of other teenagers, he crowded into the large room like cattle at the processing plant. His line walked halfway across the metallic floor and stopped, standing stiff and tall, soldiers at attention. By the change in their posture and the hardening of their expressions, he guessed the aliens were already programming them and began acting accordingly.

His peripheral vision soaked up everything around him. Running through the woods and dodging the others in flag-capturing games had sharpened it. He had a sudden fantasy of what it would be like to play football with his senses all tuned up like this. Plus, he was more physically fit than he'd ever been in his life. Hopefully, once this all was over, he'd have a chance to find out.

Up near the ceiling, black spheres floated, studying the teens. The inhabitants of the ship were gathered around monitors, watching video recorded by cameras inside the spheres, and congratulating themselves for the fruitful crop. Or perhaps they were looking for the ones like Shane and his friends, those people who were not under their control. He made sure his eyes stayed straight forward, worried about the multitude of things that could give them away.

His back ached from standing so stiffly, and he found limited relief when his line moved forward every couple of minutes, making its way across the room. To his sides, he could see Steve and Tracy in lines of their own. There was nothing to do but have faith that the rest of his team was just behind them.

He pitied the controlled kids. They were oblivious to the danger that lay ahead, clueless to the fact that their free will was stripped away and soon they'd be made to fight each other, to kill each other as a way to weed out the weaker ones. Shane hoped he wouldn't be forced to take any of their lives. It was bad enough to kill criminals out of self-defense, but these kids didn't have a choice. And he guessed many of them were regular teens who were trying to survive and recover from losing their parents when their slave genes took over.

It took half an hour for him to cross the chamber, the constant scrutiny from the cameras floating above keeping him on edge. Although he doubted any of them could win an Oscar, his team's ability to mimic the enslaved teens was apparently good enough. Soon, they stood at arched openings leading into the next phase of the processing plant. Shane knew this was where they would be given their armor and weapon. He also knew they'd be eyeing the recruits even closer in this chamber than at any other stage.

CHAPTER THIRTY

Kelly moaned, gritting her teeth and breathing deeply to recover from the shock of being hit. Carefully wrapping her right hand around the sticky, wooden handle of the spear, she gave it a tug and screamed at the shockwave of pain.

The tip of the dirty kitchen knife was lodged firmly in bone. She was lying on her back, with the spear handle leaning against the hood of a car. While she was in an enormous amount of pain, she'd been hurt so much during training that she was able to keep her head. Bile filled the back of her throat. She swallowed hard to keep from vomiting, terrified at the agony the convulsions would cause her. She had to get it together and remove the spear from her shoulder.

The Aussies and Jules where standing above her, fighting off skin-faces. They were trapped in the alley and far outnumbered. She feared the skin-faces would soon overrun them. They'd finish her off, and she wouldn't have a chance for revenge against the Anunnaki, wouldn't be able to save Nat. A barrage of gunfire echoed between the buildings, and Kelly expected her friends to drop dead.

Not a single one joined her on the ground. They held their weapons pointed toward the skin-faces who'd chased them into the alley, seeming unconcerned about those who'd entered from the other side.

Unable to endure being out of the fight for a moment longer, Kelly huffed for air and built her courage. She wrapped her hand tightly around the spear handle, screamed, and jerked with all her strength. Dislodging from bone, the knife came free. The spear bounced on the ground near her head. Her scream faded to a tormented groan, and she rolled to a fetal position.

As the pain dulled, she perceived the alley had fallen quiet.

"Kelly?" Jules squatted beside her, putting a gentle hand on her back.

"I'm okay," she said weakly.

"If that's okay, then you're the baddest of the bad asses," Jules replied. "Let me help."

"No, it's not as bad as it looks." As much as she tried to sound normal, her voice didn't hide the discomfort she endured.

She wasn't ready to be helped. This injury couldn't stop her from completing the mission. Pushing off the bloody spot where she'd fallen, she slowly rose to her feet. She blinked away the spots in her eyes and reached for the memory of a conversation she'd had with her mom years ago. Her mom revealed to her that girls were much tougher than guys, warning it was a fact that guys hated being reminded of. There was nothing else overly special about the moment, but it was one of those cherished memories that had gotten her through hard times on more than one occasion. She clung to the memory, gleaning strength from it.

Her clearing vision revealed a crowd of armed kids behind the Aussies. They didn't have on masks and looked normal except for they all grinned blissfully and in an almost stupefied way. Apparently, they were with it enough to fight off the skin-faces, who were all run off or sprawled across the hoods of cars, riddled with bullet holes.

"Come with us, brothers and sisters," a boy near the front said in Arabic. "We go to meet with angels." He looked at Kelly, sincerity in his eyes. "You will be healed there."

These kids were clearly under the influence of the Anunnaki, on a pilgrimage to the necropolis to surrender to the aliens. When they'd landed in Cairo, Kelly was concerned about encountering these possessed teenagers. After the run in with the skin-faces, she couldn't be happier to see them.

The boy and the rest of the dazed kids didn't wait for an answer. They turned away and walked back down the alley, joining a river of kids flowing down the next street.

"Someone should take you back to Dr. Blain," Jules said, her eyes filled with concern as she stared at the three-inch gash in Kelly's shoulder.

There wasn't much blood, the wound so jagged it clotted quickly. It was a miracle it didn't hit her heart or lung. She took it as a sign she was meant to keep going. The spear lay on the ground at her feet, its tip disgusting. Without some medicine soon, she was going to get a nasty infection. The

Aussies stood around her, all attention focused on her wound.

"No," she said through clenched teeth. "We have to get to the pyramids and complete the mission."

Ethan's eyes met hers. "She's right. And the boy is right. She'll be treated there."

The Anunnaki would repair any injuries and cure any diseases the slaves had during the harvesting process. Kelly just had to stay strong until they made it to the ship. Hopefully, whatever germs and nastiness she'd been infected with wouldn't take her down before she got there.

"Let's go," she said firmly.

Grimacing, she picked up her gun with her good side. Resting the barrel over her shoulder, she held it by the pistol grip with her finger near the trigger. Jules' eyes were filled with concern. She was definitely the yin to Tracy's yang. The latter wouldn't have given her a second glance, though she'd learned it wasn't because she didn't care. Tracy just seemed so afraid of appearing soft and got all tense when the situation demanded even a measure of compassion.

On first impression, Jules looked and acted even tougher than Tracy. Over time, she'd learned that this tall and lean girl with piercing green eyes was a total sweetheart. Her concern was a hindrance right now, Jules needed to focus on the mission and not on her. Not giving her a chance to object, Kelly stepped around her and headed to the other end of the alley. The parade of kids passed on the street beyond.

She didn't look back to make sure anyone else followed, afraid someone would try and talk her out of continuing. Although each step hurt, sending jolts of pain radiating away from her injury, she was determined not to let it show. Her dad had taught her how wounded animals would hide their pain until the very end, so they wouldn't appear vulnerable to predators. If they could do it, so could she. She wouldn't acknowledge the wound, would make it to the ship and do what had to be done to save her sister.

"They look awfully happy," Ben whispered ominously.

"If we're mingling with them, we need to look the same," Ethan warned.

At the end of the alley, Kelly paused. The street was packed from sidewalk to sidewalk with a parade of teenagers coming from the east. She took a deep breath, bracing herself to step in and be whisked away by these kids. They hadn't planned to intermingle with the enslaved teens until they were close to the pyramid, but this seemed like the fastest and safest way to get there now.

Dismissing the fear that somehow joining with them would cause her to lose her free will, she stepped into an opening in the ranks. She sweated from the agony each step caused her and fell in behind a boy wearing a strange, brim-less hat and a white dress that looked like a long-sleeved shirt stretching all the way to the ground.

Jules stepped in on her left side and Ethan on her right, the rest of the Aussies behind them. The blissful teenagers seemed glad to move aside and make room. Though they were surrounded by hundreds of kids, none of them talked. They kept their eyes forward, smiling and marching toward a horrible destiny.

How long had they been delayed by the attack of the

skin-faces? She worried too much time was lost. She made an effort to go faster, stepping around the boy in front of her, but the little burst of speed taxed her to the point that she almost had to stop, and the pain left her dizzy.

"You guys need to push ahead and leave me here," she said, panting.

"I don't see any reason for leaving you," Jules countered, sounding agitated. "We're headed in the right direction now, and we'll be there in no time."

"We're already behind, Jules," she said firmly. "You guys need to make up some lost time." She glanced at her, trying to convey that she wasn't asking. "I'm gonna be useless once we get there anyway. At least until they heal me."

Jules didn't look at her, seeming like she'd decided she wasn't leaving her and there was nothing Kelly could say to change her mind. Anger flashed in her. All that mattered was completing the mission, and Jules was suddenly turning into a mother hen.

She looked over at Ethan. When he returned her gaze, she was relieved to see him nod.

"She's right," he said, just loud enough for the others to hear. "We've got to press forward." Looking at her, he spoke with a quieter voice. "You think you can handle recruiting the enslaved kids after we blast the reactor?"

"Of course," she replied as confidently as she could. She didn't want to give him any reason not to leave her behind.

He nodded again. "Alright, good luck." To everyone else, he said, "Let's go, people."

Ethan slipped between two of the possessed teens ahead

of them. They parted, not appearing the least bit bothered about being passed. The other Aussies followed. Jules was the last one, hanging back.

"Go, Jules," Kelly demanded. "I'll be fine. They need you. Everyone needs you."

Her lower lip protruded slightly, and her brow furrowed. She kept her head straight a moment longer, pretending to ignore her. Kelly didn't stop staring, conveying that she wouldn't back down. Jules finally glanced over and frowned.

"Damn you," she growled.

"I'll see you soon enough," Kelly said in a softer voice. "Once this is all over."

Jules eyes looked damp. She didn't seem to think she'd see her again. Kelly smiled at her and then turned her head forward, assuming the increasingly dazed expression of those walking around them.

Her tall, crew-cut-wearing friend let out a shaky and extended sigh. Jules pressed forward, pushing between the kids to catch up with the Aussies. Within a few seconds, she was gone. Darkness seemed to close in, though there wasn't a cloud in the sky. Kelly felt terribly alone, surrounded by hundreds of teens who were slowly losing themselves, their minds being erased by the Anunnaki.

CHAPTER
THIRTY—ONE

The kid in front of Shane stepped through the door, and he followed, trying to keep his eyes forward. Adrenaline coursed through his veins, making it hard to stand still in the line.

His heart thumped so hard he feared one of the aliens standing next to the bright lights on either side would notice the arteries pulsing in his neck. Or they might see the drop of sweat making its way over his temple and pull him aside to find out what kept him from acting blissfully stupefied like the rest of the teens. Somehow, he was allowed to continue into the chamber past each inspection point.

He listened as he stepped forward, afraid he'd hear one of his friends get discovered. This room was darker with only the lines of kids illuminated by spotlights. Anunnaki stood in the shadows between the lines. Seeing them gave him a measure of relief. They wore white lab coats that looked straight out of one of his dad's girlfriend's fashion magazines, not armor. It meant the enemy believed he and his team were just as enslaved as the rest.

"Shed your clothing," a soft, female voice ordered in Anunnaki.

The kids in front of him obediently stripped and tossed their clothes into round chutes that whisked them away. Then they promptly returned to the position of attention, displaying no modesty at being nude.

He couldn't afford a moment for embarrassment. When it was his turn to drop his pants, he did it quickly, mimicking the boy ahead of him. Then he focused on the boy's curly, brown hair and tried to keep his mind clear, afraid his blushing would be the thing to give him away. The lights blinded him, and he couldn't see the faces of the Anunnaki on either side, but he could feel them looking at him. A history lesson about the South before the Civil War came to mind. This must've been how the African slaves who stood on the auction block felt.

Ahead of the curly-haired boy, he saw an Anunnaki soldier step up to the line and tug someone aside. For a moment, she was in Shane's line of sight, a tall, olive-skinned girl with long, black hair that reflected the bright light. The soldier guided her off to the side and into the shadows.

They were either picking out the kids who didn't look fully hypnotized or choosing slaves for other purposes besides soldiering. He knew this was another hurdle they'd have to cross, but it still took him by surprise when he saw her taken away.

Stay calm and breathe.

Shane took another step. Trying to get a picture of his surroundings with his peripheral vision was making his eyes burn. Giving up, he focused on the brown curls ahead. He could feel their eyes on him. They whispered to each other and made approving sounds. The curls moved forward, and he followed. After fifteen paces through the blinding lights, he passed into a darker area.

His eyes adjusted, and his courage swelled. If he could make it past such close inspection, surely he was home free. There wasn't an opportunity for him to try to look back and see if his friends made it.

Green wedges of light came from both sides. They were scanning him. The curly-haired boy raised his arms, and Shane threw his up without hesitation. There was a loud hiss. Flashes of red sprang from the floor and shot down from the ceiling. Through his visor, he could see the back of curly's red armor, the black stripe of the slave soldier running between his shoulder blades.

Armor covered every part of his body from his head to his feet. Stifling a sigh, he was relieved to be masked and hidden from the view of the enemy. Most of the simulations he remembered from the neural upload were conducted from this point on, so he felt like he was practically home free for an instant. But then he began to worry that the suit would be monitoring his vitals and other data closely—it might be reporting to his new masters' computers. They could be watching him even more closely than before.

A sudden burst of cool air puffed from the interior lining of the armor, like it sensed his sweating and was trying to cool him down. The suit and its onboard computer were capable of so much; they'd seen only half of what it could do in the simulations. Slowing his breathing, he tried to act as mesmerized as he had before. He followed the armored slave ahead of him as he moved toward the next chamber.

He worried about his friends. Some of them had to be in his line behind him, and he never heard the commotion that would come from their discovery. But at least two teammates were in other lines, which had now been separated into individual tubes. They had to make it to the chamber where the slaves would receive their final neural upload, and then they'd be reunited.

The female voice that told them to strip before played softly from speakers near his ears. It relayed a story of people coming from the stars to influence man and explained it was the Anunnaki who brought humans out of the Stone Age. She claimed they'd fought off other alien species that tried to take the planet in the past, and said they were here to help humans defeat a new enemy. As if activating the slave gene wasn't enough, the enemy was brainwashing their new recruits. If Shane didn't know they planned to pit humans against each other for sport and then use the winners as slave mercenaries in wars throughout the galaxy, he might've believed they were here to help.

The next chamber would be where he and his friends could slip away into the passageway that would lead to the reactor. A soldier standing near the entrance gave him a rifle, but the charge gauge for it in his helmet read zero. Arriving at the large chamber, he met with hundreds of red-clad humans standing in ranks. They tilted their heads back, their rifles across their chests. They were receiving the neural upload that would teach them how to use their new armor and weapons and give them their mission plans.

Once the upload was complete, the slave soldiers relaxed. They removed their helmets and started talking, examining their weapons and armor.

They seemed free, mingling with each other, joking and laughing like they'd been together for years. But they were speaking Anunnaki. This was scarier than an army of glazed-eyed automatons. Via their neural upload, these teens had the education of a Navy Seal, and they were wearing the high-tech smart armor of a super soldier from the future. But what made them most formidable was that they would all be fully committed to fighting for the Anunnaki.

Taking off his helmet, he overheard the kid in front of him talking excitedly about the mission ahead, grateful for the opportunity to avenge his parents. These were the perfect slaves. The Anunnaki actually made these kids believe in what they were fighting for, convincing them that they were under attack by another group of aliens.

His team gathered together, and he glanced around and saw no Anunnaki watching their corner of the hangar.

"You got this?" he whispered to Tracy, nodding toward the chattering new recruits.

She nodded and gave him a thumbs-up.

He hoped the communications between them weren't being monitored. It seemed unlikely—there were too many people in this room to listen to every conversation. Once they placed the Shock Troop decals on, it would sever the suits from the ship's computer, and they wouldn't have to worry about being overheard.

He turned and walked toward the small access hatch that should be in the back left corner of the room. It was hidden between two metal beams that rose from the floor at an angle, part of the skeletal structure of the pyramid-shaped vessel. He tried to be casual, though he was holding his breath the entire way. The beams provided cover, and he sighed with relief once he stepped between them and saw the service hatch. Except for Tracy, the rest of his team slipped over to join him, Steve and Laura first.

"Holy crap," Steve whispered. "I can't believe this ship is for real."

"Believe it," Shane snapped. "Stay focused."

Shane rested his fingers on the control panel to the right side of the hatch, his stomach doing somersaults because he worried some of the codes had slipped from his mind. Trying not to think about it, he entered the first sequence that came to him. All the information he needed was supposed to be in his brain, though he feared it was a jumble and would prove useless when he called upon it. His fingers danced across the screen, regurgitating information from his mind in an almost involuntary process. Nothing happened. He narrowed his eyes, trying to focus on letting the information flow from him.

Failing a second time, Shane glanced back at his friends, sick with concern. What if the enemy had somehow found out they were coming and changed all the access codes?

"Let me," Laura whispered, gently pushing him aside and putting her hand over the controls. Her fingers danced confidently over the alien symbols, and the door made a whishing sound as it leapt aside.

"Thank God for you, Laura," Maurice said. "I don't think my mind retained any of that stuff."

Shane made a sound of agreement, relief flooding his veins. Laura had always been the best at operating the Anunnaki computers in the simulations. He'd been thinking all along that he'd have to be the one to input the sequences into the reactor controls to destroy it, and had been stressing so much that he made himself forget the hatch access codes. He should have recognized this was probably Laura's purpose, the reason she'd been selected to be on his team in the first place.

Beyond was a narrow, gray corridor, lit by a string of lights running along the ceiling. Shane imagined it wasn't too different from what might be seen on a modern naval warship. Other than the control panels at the hatches, the overall appearance of the behemoth spacecraft was not as high tech-looking as he would've expected an alien vessel to be. The Anunnaki seemed to have gone out of their way to make the ship seem almost antique in some ways.

"The maintenance corridor," Liam observed excitedly.

Hope surged through him. They'd made it this far, and Kelly's team probably had too. He started to believe in the rebels' impossible plan.

They climbed through the opening, and he looked out into the crowded chamber before closing it. He hated leaving Tracy all alone with the slave soldiers, but she was the best person for the job.

The hatch snuffed all sound coming from the holding

chamber. They stood motionless. Cocked heads inspected the fresh silence, and wide eyes blinked in disbelief. The corridor sloped upward, curving deeper into the spacecraft. Not wasting any time, Shane took his armored glove off and retrieved the two small circles of material hidden between his cheek and upper gum.

"Put them on," he ordered. They wouldn't be invisible to the ship's computer until they had the Shock Troop symbol unraveled across their armor.

He stuck one on his chest, and it spread like living paint across the glossy, red surface, forming the emblem of the Shock Troop as promised and covering the black slave stripe. He handed the other to Steve, who placed it on his back. Then Shane returned the favor. Once they were all disguised, there was another pause, like they expected something dramatic to happen.

Overcome with relief that they were essentially invisible now, Shane chuckled at the tension.

"It's okay, people," he said quietly, looking in each of their eyes. "We're kicking butt. We just have to keep doing what we're doing, and we got this."

"Yeah," Steve seconded enthusiastically. "It's on!"

The others sighed and appeared to relax as well, their growing confidence showing on their faces.

Shane put his glove and helmet back on, heading up the corridor with his friends in tow. They were over the halfway point—the hardest part might be behind them. They just had to play the Shock Troop card if they encountered the enemy along the way.

A couple of hundred yards up, Shane came upon a hatch on the right.

"We should find charged weapons in here," he said, butterflies returning to his stomach as Laura placed her hand on the control pad. Each of these hatches had different access codes, and he wasn't sure he remembered any of them. What if Laura didn't retain them all either? This mission could go to hell in a hurry if they couldn't open hatches.

Yet again, the first sequence that she tried worked. The opening revealed a small, empty chamber with glass sloping away from the floor, like the window of an air traffic control tower. There were three chairs and a computer terminal in front of the glass. Shane stepped into the room and looked out of the window. Below, he could see the Great Pyramid. Long poles reached away from the ship, down to rest on the massive stones. The dim light reflected off streams flowing up through the cracks in the ancient pyramid's stones. They were all different colors—white, gold, silver, yellow, black, and transparent like water. They flowed through the pyramid and into the mouths of the poles, which were apparently pipes.

"Like a giant tick," Jake said distantly. "Sucking Earth dry."

Chapter
Thirty—Two

"No use in staying here and watching the show," Steve said, nodding toward the hatch. His red armor added so much bulk to his already-big frame. Holding the plasma rifle, he looked more formidable than ever. "This ain't what we're looking for."

"He's right." Shane opened the cabinet with rifles in it, the reason they'd stopped in this chamber. "Swap your weapon with one of these."

He retrieved a plasma rifle from the rack and replaced it with his empty one. As soon as he took hold of the new gun, a horizontal bar showed up on the charge gauge in his helmet.

"These babies are live," Liam said after taking his weapon. "Now it's time to get even."

Holding the fully charged plasma gun in his hands brought to mind images of the holes it could sear through flesh and bone, the lives it could take. It was the deadliest weapon he'd ever held and, inevitably, he'd have to kill with it. He swallowed the metallic taste in his mouth and watched his team swap out their rifles. After glancing both ways to be sure it was clear, he slipped out of the chamber. He signaled for them to follow and continued climbing into the ship.

Looking down at the weapon as he walked, he came to terms with what had to be done. He desperately wanted revenge, but he couldn't stand the idea of killing again. One moment of hesitation at the wrong time, and it would be his friends who'd be getting killed. A question struck him that made him feel even sicker. Was he more worried about taking the lives of those who'd destroyed his, or afraid he might enjoy it?

"Heads up," Steve whispered.

Two Anunnaki, wearing the white jumpsuits of engineers, came down the passageway toward them. As he'd been taught in the simulations, Shane immediately adopted an air of confidence, pulling his shoulders back and walking as tall as he could. His friends fell in a line behind him so they could pass the aliens. Sweat beaded on his brow, and the armor blasted him with a puff of cool air. His breathing seemed to roar inside the helmet, though he tried to stay calm and have faith in his disguise. He marched toward the engineers, hoping they'd ignore his team.

When they drew close, the Anunnaki's eyes widened. They stepped to the side and stopped, putting their right fists over their hearts and bowing their heads as Shane and his friends passed.

The disguise worked brilliantly. Cool relief flooding through him, Shane dared a glanced over his shoulder and saw the engineers hurrying down the passageway, like they didn't want to be under the scrutiny of the soldiers for any longer than necessary.

"That was easy," Laura whispered.

"Yeah, but it's gonna get a whole lot harder," Shane warned, not wanting anyone to get cocky.

Another hatch appeared on the right.

"This should be the one," Shane whispered, holding his breath and stepping aside so Laura could enter the access code.

The door leapt open, revealing a long passageway. It was narrower than the one they'd been climbing, with metal ribs spaced every twenty feet and the ceiling curving overhead.

"This looks like it," Liam said eagerly, pushing his way past Shane into the passageway.

"Reminds me of the tunnel under Atlanta where I whooped that ass," Steve teased, nudging him. When the pressure was on, he never failed to interject a dose of humor.

"Yeah, those were some good times," he replied with a tense chuckle. "But I'm pretty sure I was the one doing the whooping." Although Shane wasn't keen on remembering the nightmare they'd been through in Atlanta at this time, he did respect what Steve was trying to do.

Glancing up and down the main corridor, Shane ushered his friends into the passageway. He worried their chances of being discovered doubled with each passing second and was amazed they'd come this far without problems. The hatch closed, and they headed toward the engineering compartment.

"I wonder how the other teams are doing?" Laura said, her voice pitched with anxiety.

"I'm sure they're fine," Shane replied promptly, unable to keep the concern out of his voice. "We just have to hope they're on schedule."

Thinking of the timing issue once again, he suddenly felt like the plan was too ridiculous to work. It seemed impossible for seven teams spread across the globe to hit seven targets at about the same time with no communication between them. There was no choice but to have faith. They passed the point of no return as soon as they mounted the ramp leading into this wretched ship.

The access tunnel rose upward. In spite of the armor assisting their movement, they were huffing by the time they came to the next hatch. They were all in peak physical condition, but he reckoned the stress caused them to breathe too shallow. This hatch carried the strange warning symbol he remembered, indicating it was a blast door into the reactor chamber. He exhaled some tension and rallied his courage.

"This is it," he said, looking at his friends. "Once we get inside, we have to go straight to the reactor control panel. Laura, you stay with me. You guys distract any engineers near it. Don't act aggressive. They may not suspect us until it's too late."

"Quarterback sneak," Steve mused.

"Exactly."

"Hey," Laura said, laughing nervously. He couldn't see her face, but it sounded like she was trembling. "I am not a ball."

In the wake of a chuckle, he thought of Tracy. She'd fought alongside him in every conflict since the world went to shit. She was always cool in these situations and wolverine-vicious when it came to a fight. But she was also a born leader, which was what it would take to get the teens organized once they were released from Anunnaki control. Whether he liked it or not, she was right where she needed to be.

"Put it here," Shane said, sticking his gloved hand out, palm down.

Steve put his hand on top, and the rest followed.

"We are one," he said, channeling Coach Rice. "The individual can be crushed, but the team is indestructible."

"Go team," Steve added, a growl in his voice.

They broke, and Shane nodded for Laura to input the code into the screen next to the door. The thick hatch slid into the wall, and a low roar poured through the opening.

"Let's do this," Jake said with forced enthusiasm.

They stepped through the hatch into the massive chamber. It was shaped like a pill standing on its end, a cylinder with a curved top and bottom. The reactor core, a column of bright white light, stood before him. It operated at near-full capacity, providing power for the control of the slave soldiers and for the resource extraction processes happening through the Great Pyramid under the ship. The excess of power would send the core well beyond Earth's atmosphere before it exploded. Shane looked left and found the main control panel. About thirty engineers were scattered around the reactor compartment. It was less than he had to deal with in any of the simulations.

His confidence soared—this might be way easier than expected. He made a beeline for the control panel, Laura beside him. The engineers were preoccupied with their jobs, and no one seemed to notice the Shock Troops marching into their space. Stepping onto the elevated platform, he drew the attention of the engineer working at the control panel. Looking over his shoulder, his eyes grew wide at Shane's approach. He leapt to his feet, put his fist over his chest, and bowed his head.

The alien would sound the alarm if they tried to touch the control panel. There was no other choice. Before the engineer could stand upright, he drove the butt of his plasma rifle down on his skull. A splatter of blood defacing the back of his white jumpsuit, the engineer was flattened onto the floor. Shane hadn't intended to kill unless there was no other choice, but the adrenaline and the amplified strength the suit gave him caused him to strike too hard.

Stepping over the body, he knew he'd better get used to taking lives again. He was about to help execute everyone in this chamber.

Laura sat down at the controls and pulled off her gloves. She rested her hands over the backlit surface, and they immediately started dancing across the screen. Long and complex sequences of codes flowed through her fingers like she'd done this a thousand times.

Shane knew the gist of what she was doing but had lost some of the details provided in the neural upload. If she failed, he had to hope someone else on his team retained everything. Sweat ran down his face into his eyes, and he realized he was panting like he was running a marathon. He took a deep breath of the cool air the suit blew in his face and tried to relax. This was going to work. He'd get everyone out alive.

Glancing up, he saw the other engineers approaching, confused looks on their faces.

"Just finished the first stage," Laura said, confidence growing in her voice.

Five metallic clanks came in quick succession from the domed ceiling high overhead. It was the upper hatch, through which the explosion would be directed. Above the reactor chamber, a thick ring around the coliseum floor was rising to the peak of the golden pyramid. It would form a barrel designed to project the blast out and not destroy the rest of the ship. Shane had an intimate knowledge of what was going to happen to the reactor. What he couldn't predict was how fast the Anunnaki would react. Warning lights flashed, and an alarm sounded.

The shouting engineers rushed toward the reactor control station, waving their hands. Laura looked up from her work.

"We got them," Shane shouted. "Stay focused!"

He stood next to her, Steve on the other side. The lightning thwack of a plasma rifle firing made him look over at Jake. Two engineers with charred holes in their bodies collapsed to the floor.

He expected to feel sorry for them and get angry with the Aussie for shooting too soon, but he felt a surge of rage and sensed the same anger growing in his friends. Liam fired the next shot, and the engineers fled.

"Second stage completed—two more series to input," Laura reported. Her hands flew over the control screen even faster.

The ship Kelly, Jules, and the Australians attacked was smaller. They should've made it to the reactor controls by now. Perhaps they'd already destroyed it and were joining the fight for control of the ship.

"Better hurry up," Steve shouted to Laura. "This just got real!"

Anunnaki soldiers spilled into the reactor compartment, genuine Shock Troops leading them.

"I finished stage three, we're almost there!"

Brilliant pulses from a plasma rifle passed between his shoulder and Laura's elbow, melting through the guardrail on the other side of the control panel. He cringed, expecting the next shot to sear through his skull. He turned his rifle on the soldier who'd fired at him and dropped him to the floor.

A yelp came from his left, and one of his friends fell at Shane's feet. Firing on the charging enemy, he couldn't look down to see who it was.

"Liam!" Jake shouted, answering the question.

"Damn it," Shane snarled, taking aim at the closest Shock Troop. He and Liam had become good friends over the last month, and it tore him up that the cheerful Australian now lay dead at his feet. He couldn't lose anyone else. They had to finish so he could get his team out of here. Anunnaki soldiers kept spilling into the compartment, and they were closing in.

Glancing over his shoulder while firing, he saw Laura was working as fast as humanly possible. But it didn't seem fast enough. He was afraid to accept it, but it was starting to look like there was no way they'd make it out alive, whether they destroyed the reactor or not. He suddenly felt cold in spite of his nervous sweats, and then a debilitating realization coursed through him. They were all meant to die from the beginning. The rebels had hinted at the fact enough times, but he'd always believed they'd find a way to make it. It wasn't his imminent death that grieved him. It was Kelly's. Keeping her safe had been his singular motivation since all this started. He'd failed her. Damn the rebels. He wouldn't have backed out if he knew this was a suicide mission, but he would've done everything in his power to keep her from going, regardless of whether it made her hate him or not.

Laura screamed. Shane spun right and fired a shot at an Anunnaki soldier who'd slipped around the reactor core so close it had to be cooking him. Killed by the blast, the alien fell off the platform into the column of light. His body was burned so fast it looked like a shadow for an instant, and then it was gone.

Shane turned to Laura. She was moaning in agony, and everything below her left elbow was gone. The plasma shot was so hot that it cauterized the wound, so she wasn't bleeding.

"Get up, let someone else take over," he yelled urgently, reaching to help her.

"No," she groaned, sounding like she might pass out. "I'm almost done."

The armor's first aid system must have delivered a dose of some heavy-duty painkillers. The stub of her arm hung beside her, and she kept her head faced forward, her visor focused on the controls. Her remaining hand continued its dance across the screen, though not quite as fast as before.

Any doubt he had about the reason the rebels chose her vanished, though he feared she might succumb to her injuries before she finished. He had to leave her to it. It would take too long to relay where she was to one of the others, and he wasn't sure any of them could do what she was doing anyway.

"Done," she shouted.

"Let's go!"

Keeping his gun leveled at the enemy and firing, he put his other hand around her good arm to help her stand. Laura shrugged him off and grabbed her weapon.

"Where?" Maurice yelled desperately.

A blast of white light hit him in the chest. It melted through his armor and flesh, and came out of the other side without shifting his body off its balance. He stood motionless for a second, a hole the size of a baseball through him and his gun still aimed at his assassin. Already too dead to pull the trigger, the gentle preacher's son collapsed to the floor.

"Maurice!" Steve shouted.

Overcome with a flash of anger, Shane swung his weapon toward the soldier who'd shot his friend and fired. Steve reached down and grabbed Maurice's limp arm, dragging him back with them. Worried he'd get shot, he almost yelled for his friend to leave the body. But what if Maurice wasn't quite dead? Dr. Blain could patch up just about anything, could bring the gentle kid back from the edge if he still clung to life. He suddenly felt guilty for leaving Liam behind at the reactor controls, but the enemy was between them and the Aussie now.

The Anunnaki charged with a ferocity that made him

think they might believe he and his friends were part of the rebellion they had so viciously crushed. Shane pulled the trigger down and held it, plasma bursts erupting from his rifle so close together they looked like one solid beam. There was no place for cover, no place for them to hide from his enraged reprisal. Ten of the enemy dropped to the floor, smoking holes through their bodies. Twenty more stepped in to replace them. The charge indicator for his weapon was dropping fast. The reactor core glowed brighter, and his visor became shaded to keep it from blinding him. Even if the enemy didn't kill the rest of the team, the reactor explosion soon would.

Laura was in trouble. The red helmet covered her face and its mechanical muscles made it possible to fight to her last breath, but she stumbled, and he guessed she was barely hanging on. He had to do something. Continuing to fire his weapon, he stole a glance around the chamber. The enemy was almost surrounding them, blocking all exits he remembered using during the simulations. A line of small, round hatches on the bulkhead to their right was all they could get to.

"The escape pods," he yelled.

"They won't work…" Jake replied, pausing to fire a shot, "…on the planet's surface." His voice was ripe with anger and grief.

He was right. The pods were designed for escaping from a ship flying in a planet's atmosphere or in space. They could be killed if they used them, but death was certain if they didn't try.

"No choice!" Shane yelled firmly, determined to get

someone out alive.

Slipping his free arm around her waist, he steadied Laura, and they backed toward the hatches. Even though she had to be in a world of hurt, her aim was impeccable. Every shot met with alien flesh before finding a home in the thick walls encasing the reactor.

"You took everything from me!" she screamed with agony in Anunnaki and shot the two who were closest to her through their chests.

She resisted him, as if wanting to pull out of his grasp and charge the enemy instead of escaping. Knowing she might be losing it, he tugged at her to encourage her along. She relented, seeming too weak to struggle free. Continuing with him toward the bulkhead, she fired her weapon with lethal results the entire way.

The alarm warned the end was near, the rhythm of its threatening notes becoming faster. Some Anunnaki soldiers retreated, shouting frantically as they pushed their way through the hatches that led out of the chamber. A few of the Shock Troops persisted, advancing on Shane and his friends.

The team made it to the escape pods, and Shane grabbed a handle on the first one he came to and jerked it down. The five-foot in diameter hatch opened, and he pushed Laura through it.

"Get in!" he yelled to the rest.

Steve took another shot, killing one of the three Anunnaki left. Then he hoisted Maurice's limp body up and into the escape pod. The second Anunnaki gave up and raced toward the closing hatch where his comrades had fled. Shane took a couple of wild shots at the last Anunnaki, who ran toward him like she'd decided there was a better chance of survival joining his team in the escape pod. Or she was determined to go with them just so she could kill them all. There was no way she'd make it—she was too far away. Spinning around, he dove into the pod after Jake.

"Here we go," Steve shouted, sitting up at the controls.

The controls to the hatch had been hit by a plasma blast, and it couldn't be closed. He braced himself for the pod's launch, wrapping his arms around a seat near the back.

At the exact moment the pod detached from the reactor chamber and accelerated toward the surface of the ship, a blinding light poured from the reactor's core. It lifted the last Shock Troop, slamming her through the open hatch and over Shane's head. A white-hot fireball filled the passenger compartment, and even through the protection of his armor, he could feel the heat of the explosion. It threatened to cook him like a lobster in its shell.

The pod shot out of the ship into the air, and the fire was sucked out of the rear hatch. Shane's eyes were glued to the fireball erupting through the golden pyramid's hull after them, afraid it would catch the tiny craft and burn them all to a crisp.

After rising up away from the ship for a long instant, the pod tumbled. His body slammed against the floor, ceiling, and walls, the craft trying to buck him out. In one of his airborne moments, he saw two of the passengers slide past him in flashes of red. The centripetal force flung them out of the open rear hatch, and then smashed him down onto the metal floor.

CHAPTER
THIRTY—THREE

Kelly slowly opened her eyes, focusing on a metallic gray ceiling. She lay on her back on something cold and hard. A metal table perhaps. That deeply rooted instinct, the voice all animals shared that warned them a predator was nearby, told her to keep still and quiet.

A youthful man in white clothing stepped into view. His face was soft, like he couldn't grow a beard, yet he looked to be at least thirty years old. His brown eyes focused on her shoulder. The memories of everything that happened in Cairo returned to her in a flood, but she was stunned and confused over how she'd gotten here.

Keeping her eyes pointed at the ceiling, she perceived a blue light passing over her wound, the pain vanishing. Acid flooded her stomach, and it felt like her heart turned into a block of ice in her chest.

She was in the Anunnaki ship! The fog cleared from her mind, and she remembered entering the vessel with the possessed teens. She'd been so delirious from her injury that she could hardly believe she'd made it so far. But then what happened? She must've passed out, and they brought her here.

Her instincts were correct—laying still was the right thing to do. Hoping she hadn't done anything to give herself away, she congratulated herself for making it into the vessel. With any luck, the rest of her team was already in the reactor compartment.

Unable to look around, she wondered if she was alone with the Anunnaki doctor. She couldn't hear anything, but there could be rows of operating tables on either side of her, Anunnaki quietly working beside each one.

Her bloody tank top stuck to her chest, tugging uncomfortably on her skin as it dried. At least he hadn't needed to cut her shirt away to treat her. She'd be forced to strip out of her clothes in front of the aliens soon enough. Meanwhile, she had to resist the urge to reach up and tug the material away from her body, no matter how irritating it became.

The doctor standing over her was the first of the enemy she'd encountered. While she'd feared the Anunnaki since meeting the rebels, she'd also fantasized about taking revenge. She suppressed a desire to attack him. If they were alone, she was certain she could kill him. The neural upload had furnished her with hundreds of ways to take lives with her bare hands. It would happen so fast that he'd barely have a moment to be surprised.

Unfortunately, until the reactor was shut down, she had to pretend to be one of the possessed teens. He finished treating her, and the table tilted upright. A footrest at the bottom kept her from sliding off.

Once she was in the vertical position, she discovered she wasn't alone with the doctor. A line of teenagers with slack expressions slept walked by in front of her. Nervous that the alien who'd just treated her was watching, she stepped forward and turned left into the line. She kept her eyes glued on the kid ahead of her, following the other human slave patients. In the periphery of her vision, she saw injured teenagers enter from the other side and step onto the tilting examination tables after the treated ones stepped off.

The line turned out of the brightly lit healing factory and took Kelly down a darker passageway. It opened into a large holding chamber filled with possessed teens, probably the one in which she'd passed out earlier.

Kelly fell in the ranks behind the patient ahead of her, waiting for the power failure that would set these slaves free. She prepared what she'd say to the teens to get them to attack the Anunnaki. It wouldn't take much. Pointing out the aliens as the ones who'd killed their parents ought to get quite a few of them fired up in a hurry. With any luck, too much time hadn't been lost while she was unconscious, and she'd get her armor before the reactor was shut down.

An alarm sounded and lights started flashing overhead. Excitement surged in her veins, and her mind grew clear and focused, as it did when she was attacked by the skin-faces. Kelly kept her eyes forward and her face slack, knowing she had to appear possessed until after the power was cut.

Surveying the closest soldier in her peripheral vision, she planned her attack. The Anunnaki were weaker than humans were. In spite of the armor, her target appeared smaller than she did. Kelly was confident she could take the soldier's weapon. Then she'd turn and fire on the Anunnaki on either side of her. She would show no mercy. The aliens were responsible for the death of her family and of so many other families on Earth and across the galaxy. How many innocents had they slaughtered? How many teens of different species had they turned into slaves? She let the anger grow in her, ready to fuel her aggression when the time came for attack.

Hopefully, one of the teens would come out of it fast and, without much effort, she could convince them to pick up a rifle and join the fight. She'd never liked how so much of the mission seemed left up to chance, but she came to terms with the odds being against them early in the brutal training.

"Man battle stations," a female voice said through the intercom at a pause in the alarm. "Emergency lift off."

What was going on? The ship trembled, and she guessed it was breaking away from its pyramid docking station. Panic gripped her, though she managed to keep the dazed expression on her face. The Aussies must've failed—the ship was flying away. She studied the kids around her. They were still in a deep trance, no chance she'd recruit them to fight. She couldn't let the ship take off—she had to attack. But she was unarmed and the Anunnaki soldiers had full power to their suits. Probably given some command through the speakers in their helmets, they lifted their rifles to their shoulders and took aim at the slaves.

Was the rest of her team dead? Had they been captured? Nothing in her training prepared her for this. Kelly focused on her breathing to maintain a calm demeanor. It was nearly impossible for her to keep still and not do something, but she'd be blasted if she made a move. The ship trembled a final time and became stable. She sensed it was airborne. It was carrying her away from the Earth, away from Nat.

Her eyes grew moist with frustration, but she accepted there was nothing she could do right now. She'd have to bide her time and hope the rest of her team had not been discovered.

"The other ships were attacked and disabled," a quiet voice to her left said.

In the periphery of her vision, she saw an Anunnaki Shock Troop soldier had stepped out of a narrow passageway and was speaking to another soldier who stood guard by the wall of the chamber.

"Rebels?" the soldier being spoken to asked incredulously. "How is that possible?"

"We're going to run neural and biological scans on every recruit," the Shock Trooper continued, ignoring his subordinate's question. "Keep your people on high alert. Assume there are enemy insurgents on this ship."

"Yes, sir."

Kelly's blood ran cold. She and her team were trained to pass the general inspection that all the slave recruits endured, but they couldn't hide that they weren't under the influence of the slave gene if the Anunnaki subjected them to a closer examination. Terror and panic washed over her, but she kept her head. She would do her best to stay undercover. She sure as hell wasn't going to give herself away by freaking out and attacking the enemy too soon, though that was what every cell in her body wanted to do at the moment.

CHAPTER
THIRTY—FOUR

Without the flow of energy from the ship's reactor, the armor lost most of its strength-enhancing capabilities. When Shane bashed against the other side of the tumbling craft, his arm landed behind him, and he felt it snap, pain exploding through his shoulder.

A millisecond later, he was levitating in the center of the pod, looking up at the moon through the open hatch and expecting to die. He was aware the instant the craft hit the ground. It stopped moving in less than the blink of an eye, and he slammed down onto the control panel, into darkness.

Waking with a stunning headache, he opened his eyes to a blurry warning flashing inside his helmet on the narrow display just above his visor.

Vital signs unstable. First aid system malfunctioning, it read. *Seek medical attention.*

Pain enveloped his right shoulder, but other than that and a concussion, he didn't feel like anything was wrong. He tried to get up, to see if anyone else was still in the pod, but his legs didn't respond to his command.

With his one good arm, he groped his body from the chest down, finding his hips at a sharp and unnatural angle to his torso. He'd broken his back.

"No," he groaned, panting frantically.

Please remain calm and seek medical attention, the narrow screen above his visor read, apparently able to sense his panic.

"Great advice!" Shane broke into hysterical laughter, tore his helmet off, and hurled it across the dark pod. He immediately regretted throwing the helmet, hoping he hadn't hit anyone.

Methodically breathing in and out, he focused on subduing the panic, regaining a semblance of control. Dr. Blain could fix this, if he could stay alive long enough to get to her.

Funny how he felt uncomfortable in her presence. He'd come up with all kinds of sinister reasons why he didn't like her, but in the end, maybe she just reminded him of his mom—always there to patch him up when he scraped his knee. Maybe he needed her to help fill that void, but he was too scared to admit it. He sure wished she were doting over him now.

Tears forming in his eyes, Shane kept still and tried to get his bearings. He felt a surge of warmth in his veins. The suit had administered a dose of pain medicine. Recovering his senses, he replayed the events that had brought him to this point in his mind. Liam was dead, vaporized when the reactor exploded. He felt guilty for it—they shouldn't have left him behind. What if he was unconscious but clinging to life? In the heat of battle, they'd given up on him too quickly. Thank God Steve had grabbed Maurice, though he was probably dead too. All but one had made it into the pod. Two had been tossed out in flight, though the armor might have still been energized when they hit the ground. He hoped one of the ejected passengers was the Anunnaki Shock Troop soldier. Most of his team could be alive. Unless they'd all fallen out when he couldn't see, one or two of them were still in the pod.

He could hear sounds of battle off in the distance. Jones and the rebel-trained army of teenagers must've rolled in to help with the fight. All the reactors must've been destroyed. He hoped Kelly and her team had fared better than his. At least Tracy was probably still alive, leading the freed teens against the supremacist a-holes who inhabited the ship.

It was too dark in the pod to see if anyone lay unconscious around him. Shane strained his ears to pick up a sign of life. He remembered seeing Maurice shot through the chest, and a flood of grief puddled his eyes. He'd lost so many people. According to the annoying message that had been displayed in his helmet, he'd likely be joining them soon.

A pained groan came from the darkness off to his left.

"Is somebody there?"

He strained to listened, hopeful it was one of his friends. The darkness surrendered a shaky exhale and a moan. It sounded like a girl, and she was hurt bad.

"Laura?" He peered in the direction of the sounds. "That you?"

Before she could answer, a loud screech pierced the air,

metal scraping on stone. Shane closed his eyes and crossed his arm over his face for protection. He expected some part of the craft would collapse on him, delivering the final blow that would bring the end. The pod rocked back and forth gently, seeming like it was teetering on the edge of an abyss. It found a resting place, and for the moment, the inky darkness grew still and silent once again.

The female coughed weakly.

"Hello?" he called in English. "Laura?"

"No," the voice answered in Anunnaki and then coughed. "Not Laura."

"Are you okay?" he asked before his cloudy brain concluded she was an enemy.

"I…" She paused, a tremble in her voice. "Not so good. Funny question, I'd think you'd want me dead."

It had to be the last Anunnaki soldier, the one blasted into the pod when the reactor exploded. He wasn't sure what to say. Listening to her labored breathing for a moment, he hated that he actually wanted to help her.

"Who are you?" she queried hesitantly.

"I'm Shane."

"You're human?" Her voice grew steadier and surprised. The Anunnaki must've thought the rebels had attacked, never suspecting their harvest had turned on them. "How is this possible? Who helped you?"

He felt weak, too feeble to have a conversation, but he knew he had to take this opportunity to learn as much as he could. He also didn't want to give away too much just in case she was the one who got rescued first.

"Why do you think someone helped us?" he finally asked.

"Oh." She groaned, pain seeming to crush her. Panting for a moment, she then said to him, "You needed to know too much to do this." She huffed again. "It had to be the rebels," she added, whispering with uncertainty, like she was trying to convince herself.

He didn't reply, afraid she might catch him in a lie.

"But they couldn't have gotten here—they didn't have any long-range vessels," she said, sounding tormented by the question.

"Then I guess it's a mystery," he replied, fighting off a wave of dizziness.

She chuckled weakly and coughed. "Humor is definitely one of your species more admirable characteristics."

Shane pressed his good elbow down on the control panel, trying to lift himself once again, but he couldn't move.

"At least we beat you," he said, laying his head back and sighing wearily.

"Beat us? Why would you want to do that?"

"You were here to take over the planet," Shane played along. "You leaked technology to our stupid government that caused them to kill our parents. And that," he paused, explosions and screams echoing in the distance, "is the sweet sound of revenge."

She moaned again, and he suspected the end was near for her. With the way he felt, it probably wasn't far off for him either. He strained his ears for the sound of approaching helicopters, hoping help would be on the way soon.

"How do you know we are responsible for your parents'

death?" she asked wearily. "Who told you?"

"We figured it out," he replied cryptically.

She let out a sound of frustration, and they fell quiet.

"What's your name?" he asked, hating the silence.

"I'm Hanne," she replied. "And until you attacked us, I thought we were here to help you."

"What do you mean?" He felt weaker and cold. He must be losing blood. "Help us?"

"Yes," she replied. "We were passing near your solar system, and we picked up the signal of a very powerful weapon being activated on your planet. We came to investigate."

"Investigate?" he said incredulously. "Why activate the slave gene and start arming kids? It doesn't look like you're here just to see if we're alright."

"How can you know so much?" She coughed a wet-sounding cough. "I'm dying," she said quietly. "Why would I lie to you? I have nothing to gain."

Shane lay silent. What was her angle?

"You didn't answer my question," Shane groaned, pain flaring up in his shoulder as he shifted his weight.

"Why were the kids hypnotized?" She coughed again. "Thousands of years ago, we came to this planet and enslaved humans. We genetically modified you, infecting you with our genes to make you more advanced. We also put in a gene that makes it easy to control you."

"So we are the perfect slaves?"

Her frustration seemed to give her a burst of life. He fed on her energy, goading her to say more.

"No, you *were* the perfect slaves," she corrected, sounding irritated. "We have long since abandoned such behavior, and as a people, we are sorry for what was done in the past."

It sounded eerily similar to the story the rebels had told them.

"So why control us now?"

"We did it to help protect you. We feared your planet was under attack, so we activated the gene and armed you so you could defend yourselves. Once your assailant was identified and defeated, we planned to release you, and help you to rebuild your world."

Shane couldn't imagine what she hoped to achieve by this, but her deceit was starting to piss him off. His head spun. What was he supposed to think? Maybe she was trying to turn him on the rebels. If she died and he lived, she could be hoping to undermine her enemy through him.

"It seems impossible," she said quietly. "But how else could they know enough about our ships to do what they did? How else could they resist the slave gene?" She paused, and he heard her take a little gasp. "Anunnaki rebels helped them. It had to be."

It almost sounded like she was talking to someone else. He suddenly worried that she might be in communication with her comrades and was too delirious to realize he could hear her. It was just as likely that her mind was coming undone and she was talking to herself. He didn't answer, didn't want to say anything that might be used against the humans.

"But we crushed the rebellion so long ago," she said distantly.

A screech cut through the darkness. The pod shifted, and

he sensed they were about to fall.

"Do not trust them, Shane," Hanne said desperately.

The pod broke loose and flipped, flinging him into the opposite side of its hull. There were loud crashing sounds, and he was slammed back and forth like a pinball, banging his head again and again. It felt like the craft was bouncing down a steep hill. When it came to a rest, Shane landed on something padded.

"Hello?" he called once he caught his breath. "Are you there?"

Listening intently, he could no longer hear her labored breathing.

She must have died. The rest of his team might be dead too. What were the chances Kelly survived? Grief tore at him. It took all his strength to roll onto his side, and he welcomed the pain exploding from his shoulder. He wished he could feel pain below his waist, or anything down there for that matter. An image of Matt, lying on the asphalt with his leg sheared off, flashed through his mind. Then Aaron, his guts spilling from the gash in his abdomen. Now it was his turn, but no one was around to see him off.

He rolled from the bench onto the floor, cursing at the agony the short drop caused him. Raising his head, he realized the pod had come to a rest with its open hatch pointed at the necropolis. Half a mile away, Shane saw the command ship he'd attacked. The moonlight reflected off its white marble interior through the dark frame of the outer hull. The golden skin must've been created by energy from the reactor, because it was now gone. He could see the ship's coliseum, stark white in contrast to the barrel-turned-smokestack that had ejected the reactor's core into space.

A smaller ship, the one to which the Russians were assigned, was in a similar condition. The last vessel, the one Kelly, Jules, and the Australians were in, was lit up. No smoke came from it, and the outer skin was intact. Flashes from plasma rifles erupted around all three ships, but most of the battle was focused on Kelly's. Jones' backup army was trying to disable it, to prevent it from launching. There was a loud, grumbling sound, and a cloud of dust obscured the necropolis. Terror seized him. The golden pyramid lifted off the ground, rising into the night sky.

CHAPTER
THIRTY—FIVE

"No!" he groaned.

Pulling his uncooperative lower half behind him, he made his way to the hatch with his one good arm. He felt an explosion of strength, intending to claw across the desert to the retreating ship and drag it back to Earth so he could rescue her. Managing to get out of the pod, he depleted this jolt of energy, succumbing to his injuries. He collapsed a couple of yards away. Dizzy from the pain and the apparent loss of blood, he noticed the inside of his armor felt wet and sticky around his chest.

He wept into the sand. He'd lost her.

He was sprawled facedown. Holding on to the last of the sun's heat, the ground was warm against his cheek. It was a sharp contrast to how cold his body started to feel. Pain engulfed his abdomen, like he'd swallowed a bag of razorblades. His armor's first aid system must've stopped working. He gasped for air, coughing when he sucked dirt into his throat. A measure of strength returned, and he used it to roll onto his back.

The escaped recruit ship was still visible, a golden pyramid rising up into the dark heavens. Climbing until its shape was no longer discernable, its yellow glow and size distinguished it from the stars. It adopted a speedy flight across the night sky, entering into space and orbiting the planet with man's puny satellites.

Angry tears clouding his vision, he watched it race toward the horizon. Off in the distance, the battle with the two disabled Anunnaki ships grew quieter. He hardly cared—didn't care about anything except that Kelly was gone.

But there was no guarantee she was dead.

Staring up at the heavens, that desperate thought sparked a little flame of hope in him. He was freezing, but he was too weak to shiver. His abdomen seemed to inflate like a balloon, pressing into his lungs and forcing his breaths to grow shallow. How would he get her back? He didn't have a clue. But maybe Jones and the other rebels could help. If there was a way, regardless of how dangerous, he was going to do it.

The flame of hope diminished as the ship slid out of sight. It seemed to be tearing his soul away from his flesh, dragging it beyond the horizon and surrendering his broken body to the desert. Suddenly overwhelmed by exhaustion and heartache, he trembled, exhaling all the air from his lungs. The natural inhalation didn't follow as it should. His head spun, and his vision blurred. He focused every reserve of dwindling strength, determined to stay alive so he could save her. Try as he might, he couldn't take another breath.

Darkness closed in and stole away his pain, quieting his

panic. Deafening and blinding him, it crushed his senses and devoured his thoughts. It destroyed everything until there was only one flickering image floating in the emptiness. It was Kelly, standing close to him. Focusing on her beautiful face, he knew as long as he could see her, he was still alive. He reached out to her, trying to press his lips to hers one last time. His fingers passed through her ethereal image like she was made of smoke. He couldn't stop her from fading—didn't have the strength to hold the shadows at bay. Lethal darkness billowed through her ghostly image, and she was gone.

EPILOGUE

Shane heard garbled conversation. Tracy barked orders, her voice louder and firmer than the others were. She did it so well, like she was born to be a drill sergeant. He wasn't alert enough to understand what she was saying. Hands pressed under his sides, raising him. Pain erupted from everywhere. He opened his mouth to beg them to stop, but he couldn't get enough air into his lungs to speak. The voices were muffled, and he passed out again.

"He's coming around now," Dr. Blain observed. "Give him some space."

Shane opened his eyes, blinking them into focus on a cracked, white plaster ceiling.

"Kelly!" He sat bolt upright, and spots flashed across his vision.

"Easy there, big guy," Steve said, putting his hand on Shane's arm. "You were jacked up like nobody's business a couple of minutes ago."

"Steve," Shane said. "You're alive."

"Yeah," he replied, a sad smile on his face. "I'm fine."

"But Kelly…"

"She's not dead, Shane," Lily said ominously. She was sitting at a table nearby, one of the advanced holographic computers the doctor used in front of her.

"So we're going to rescue her." He tried to shrug Steve off so he could stand.

"Not so fast," Dr. Blain warned.

"In due time." Lily looked away from the computer. "But there's something we must do now to save her life."

"They have to shut off their earbuds," Steve said, his voice cracking.

"You can't," Shane objected, terrified. "She'll be enslaved."

"A part of her will remain conscious," Lily replied.

"We don't have a choice," Dr. Blain added, firmness in her tone that he'd never heard before. "You have to trust us."

After his interaction with the soldier in the escape pod, Shane wasn't certain who he could believe. Rescuing Kelly was everything to him, and he'd sign with the devil if that was what it took. In hindsight, much of the alien's story didn't make sense. For now, he had to side with the rebels. Even if they were the enemy, he'd use them until he guaranteed Kelly's safety.

"Will we be able to get her back?" he asked.

"There's a good chance, yes."

"A good chance?" Anger flashed in him.

"They'll suspect a tainted harvest," Jones growled, sounding impatient. He was standing on the other side of the dimly lit room, which had no windows and only one old, wooden door. It smelled dank and earthly, probably underground. The captain's worried gaze changed to angry frustration. "The Anunnaki will find them if we don't do this."

Shane looked at each of the people in the room. Both the rebels and Tracy and Steve's faces said they'd already debated over this while he was out. They'd decided it was the right thing to do. He was surprised they were even asking him, though it did give him more faith that the rebels could be trusted.

"I've made the connection," Lily said excitedly. "Everyone's earbud except Kelly's has been deactivated."

"Shane," Dr. Blain urged. "We don't have time."

"Do it," he said, afraid of losing her forever.

Lily nodded and returned her attention to the computer. Shane looked at Steve, whose brow was heavy with concern. Then he glanced at Tracy, grateful his friends were alive. She returned his gaze, her eyes expressing the same heartache he was enduring.

"We will get them back, Shane," she said, sounding so determined that it fanned the little flame of hope still burning in his heart.

"You're right," he replied, his voice growing steady. "We will."

THE END

ACKNOWLEDGEMENTS

I want to thank my wife Amanda, who reads everything I write and cheers me on through the joys and tribulations of being a writer. Thanks to Emily and Logan, my beautiful children, who constantly remind me that we are born with imagination abound, that we just have to remember to listen to our inner child and creativity will come naturally.

Thanks to the amazing Clean Teen Publishing team. From the first interaction I had with you, I knew I was dealing with a rising star in the publishing industry. Thanks Rebecca Gober, Marya Heiman, and Courtney Nuckels. And thanks to Cynthia Shepp, my editor, who found a home for orphaned commas, ironed out confusing sentences, and was always there, tirelessly helping with edits to the last detail.

Thanks to Jennifer Anne Davis, my writing partner from the beginning and my friend of many years. I am happy to follow in your footsteps and learn from your persistence and unwillingness to settle for anything short of success. And thank you Celso who had the patience to see past the crudeness of my rough drafts and offered enthusiastic encouragement. Also thanks to the beta readers at Clean Teen Publishing and Melanie Newton and the Clean Teen Publishing Street Team for reading and promoting my book—you are integral to the success of all CTP writers.

ABOUT THE AUTHOR

Born at the end of the Vietnam War and raised on a horse farm near small town north Georgia, N.W. Harris's imagination evolved under the swaying pines surrounding his family's log home. On summer days that were too hot, winter days that were too cold, and every night into the wee morning hours, he read books.

N.W. Harris published his first novel—Joshua's Tree—in 2013. It was no wonder that with his wild imagination and passion for all things word related, that N.W. Harris was named a quarter finalist in Amazon's Break Through Novel Award Contest. In early 2014, N.W. Harris joined the ranks with Clean Teen Publishing when they signed his new young adult apocalyptic adventure series—The Last Orphans.

In addition to writing, N.W. Harris has been a submarine sailor, nurse, and business owner. His studies have included biology, anthropology, and medicine at UCSB and SUNY Buffalo. He is an active member of SCBWI and lives in sunny southern California with his beautiful wife and two perfect children. He writes like he reads, constantly.

CPSIA information can be obtained at www.ICGtesting.com
Printed in the USA
LVOW07s2343240415

435949LV00002B/4/P